SCRIBES
MAUREEN FOSS

Scribes

MAUREEN FOSS

CAITLIN PRESS

Caitlin Press Inc.
8100 Alderwood Road,
Halfmoon Bay, BC V0N 1Y1
www.caitlin-press.com

Text design by Kathleen Fraser.
Cover design by Pamela Cambiazo and Vici Johnstone.
Author photo by April Roberts of A&B Photo, 100 Mile House, BC.
Printed in Canada.

Caitlin Press Inc. acknowledges financial support from the Government of Canada through the Canada Book Fund and the Canada Council for the Arts, and from the Province of British Columbia through the British Columbia Arts Council and the Book Publisher's Tax Credit.

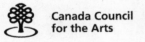 

Library and Archives Canada Cataloguing in Publication

Foss, Maureen
    Scribes / Maureen Foss.

ISBN 978-1-894759-68-7

    I. Title.

PS8561.O7724S37 2011   C813'.54   C2011-904967-8

Scribes *is dedicated to my husband, Gary Young, my family, and the all-knowing Quintessential Writers Group—Betty Keller, Rosella Leslie, Gwendolyn Southin and Dorothy Fraser.*

Contents

I	✎	9
II	✎	22
III	✎	34
IV	✎	52
V	✎	66
VI	✎	81
VII	✎	93
VIII	✎	114
IX	✎	127
X	✎	143
XI	✎	158
XII	✎	166
XIII	✎	189
XIV	✎	207
XV	✎	224

I

THE THREE OF THEM ARRIVE as one. Jemima in her old Buick, Sari in her truck and Mariah in her rusty blue beater, chugging up the quarter mile of tree-lined driveway. They pull up under the portico, switch off their engines and gather up their manuscripts. Slinging bags over their shoulders, they open their car doors and meet at the bottom of the stone stairs leading to Bunny deLore's ornate front doors. She's there to let them in. Her writing group.

They claim their chairs in Bunny's library, the same chairs they've taken every Tuesday evening for the six months since they answered Bunny's advertisement in the *Grievous Times*:

> Attention Writers: Evening group forming to support,
> encourage and gently critique your craft. All genres.

Bunny had needed a diversion other than her charities and shopping, something akin to a book club to occupy her mind in the long hours spent alone in this big house. Alone, that is, except for the ancient housekeeper, Gerda—but she couldn't be considered company. Anything but ... Gerda has been part and parcel of the deLore family since their Vancouver days when Bunny's husband, Leland, was a frail, doted-upon child with severe asthma and she had been hired as his nanny. When they moved to the town of Grievous for its clear dry air, they had moved lock, stock and Gerda von Hauffman.

Mariah Flint cracks her pages over her knee. "I've done last week's corrections to *Derek of Dunston-Greene,* such as they are, but I still disagree with Jemima that my heroine is too perfect. However ..."

Jemima's face is unreadable. There's not even a twitch of an eyebrow. From the start Mariah has vigorously opposed any suggestion for adjustment to her work, although upon later reflection at home, she does make the suggested changes.

"However, your point might be valid."

This is a first!

"Perhaps a new angle," Mariah continues. "A heroine with a small flaw. Not a club foot or anything, but maybe a double set of eyelashes or a mole on her neck."

"I'd hardly call that a flaw," Jemima contends.

Mariah hands typed pages to each of the group. "I'll just carry on then, shall I?" she says as if Jemima hasn't spoken. "Reading pages sixty-seven to seventy-four ..." and she pokes her heavy black-rimmed glasses up her nose's oily slope.

> Derek dismounted from his lathered stallion and strode to where Willow lay sprawled on the grass, her long skirt hiked over her scraped knees, her slippered foot caught in the spokes of her bicycle.

"Would she be wearing long skirts if she was riding a bicycle?" Jemima wonders aloud. "Or slippers, for that matter?"

Mariah glares from beneath her home-cropped bangs.

Jemima waves her off. "Just asking."

> The copper curls she'd spent so much time smoothing down into a knot sprang from the ribbon and cascaded over her pale face sprinkled with honey-coloured freckles.

"That could be another small flaw, Mariah," Sari Button offers. "Freckles."

"Ah," Mariah says, "now that's something I can use."

Sari smiles and ducks her head.

Derek stood over her, his riding breeches taut across his thighs, her lilac dress reflected in his black riding boots. "Are you hurt, Miss?" His voice was thick with concern. Willow pointed to her foot still in the spokes and with one hand he lifted the bicycle. She slipped her foot out and he caught it before it hit the ground. Her cry of pain showed in his eyes as troubled clouds that darken a summer's sky.

Mariah flips to the next page and the rest follow. As she reads, she becomes the characters—Willow with a voice like grade A butter and Derek's full of testosterone and worry. Her wide face softens and the cords in her neck all but disappear as she finishes what she has written. "Well?"

There's a general shuffling of paper. No one wants to go first.

"I have a problem with line three on page sixty-seven," Bunny begins hesitantly.

Mariah hollows her cheeks.

"I like Derek's lathered horse, but how does Willow skin her knees on grass?" Bunny decides to sandwich the criticism between two compliments. "Though honey-coloured freckles are a nice touch."

Mariah strikes a line through *grass* and adds a question mark as a reminder, should she later decide improvements are necessary.

Deflecting the anticipated storm, Bunny rises. "How about tea before we continue our critique of *Derek of Dunston-Greene?*" It seems more civilized to hide behind a cup of hot tea while Mariah fends off criticism with her viperous tongue. As Bunny heads to the kitchen, she asks Jemima about the lemon fluff tarts she featured in her *Grievous Times* column this week. "Do you know if that little Watkins man still sells lemon extract? I'd like to make them for when PJ comes over tomorrow." Of course, since her daughter's visit will be short if she comes at all, why bother?

"That would be Mr. Beaver," answers Jemima, trailing after Bunny. Jemima is always pleased when her food column is mentioned. "Yes, he's still the Watkins man but he can't get about on his own anymore. His wife helps him drive—he steers and she shifts." Seeing the look of puzzlement on Bunny's face, she adds, "He has arthritis."

In the too-large kitchen, Bunny arranges Peek Freans on the plate for Jemima to carry back, makes the tea and then returns to the library to partake in the further discussion of Mariah's tale of shuddering flesh and weighted sighs. Bunny thinks Mariah should really be scripting murder and mayhem. Sari is the one who should be the romantic. And Jemima—well, Jemima is suited to her cooking and gardening articles if you're not fussy about facts. Bunny has been writing fiction. She would rather be writing a book on orchids or even travel, but she knows little about orchids and hates to travel alone. Her only solo excursions are her twice-a-year visits to the Canyon Ranch Spa outside Tucson, where she weans herself from scotch and takes classes in Pilates or calligraphy. She has tried to get her daughter to come with her but to no avail. And, of course, Leland travels all over the world on business and is not interested in travelling with her for pleasure.

"When Derek sweeps Willow into the saddle and rides away home to seek a doctor," asks Jemima when they resume, "what happens to her bicycle?"

"Who cares?" Mariah demands.

"Your readers will, Mariah. They'll wonder."

"They'll be so interested in what's going on in the saddle, with him rubbing up against her as they ride over his estate, that they won't remember the bloody bicycle."

"You think sex will replace details?"

"I'll have detailed sex."

"M-m-m-m," Jemima acquiesces. Then, after a weighted pause, she adds, "I thought we were to write about things we are familiar with."

"Droll, very droll," Mariah sniffs.

Bunny offers punctuation advice and at last Mariah's session is over.

Sari Button clears her throat and apologetically hands each person a single handwritten page. "Mooney was sick with the flu all week so this is all I have done." She clears her throat again and begins in a sing-song voice.

> The slap and
> tickle of the
> brook
> as it chuckles over
> lips of bearded
> rocks ...

Bunny's eyes glaze over and she listens non-judgmentally. She's not sure she fully appreciates poetry. What can she say about something as personal as slaps and tickles and beards? Sari's offering ends on an upbeat note as all her poems do. If her writing reflects her life with James and young Mooney, it's a perfect life, Bunny thinks. Sunshine and gumdrops. But how does she cope with James still not working? Management closed the mill three months into the strike, hauling away what equipment they could with non-union drivers. The writing group had all seen James and his fellow workers on television, beating at the scab trucks with their signs before hunching their shoulders and trudging away. Now while Sari's at work, he looks after Mooney and keeps an eye out for collectibles—mostly ceramics—at garage sales. Sari doesn't say much about James, just smiles and says he's fine.

"You go next, Jemima," Bunny says. "Yours is probably more entertaining than mine."

Jemima hands out her sheets and settles back to read aloud what she has written for her column.

> Summer time means picnics, baseball games, weed-
> ing, family visits and a pickup truck full of zucchi-
> nis. What to do with them? I've used the larger of
> these lovely green vegetables to chase away visitors
> that have overstayed their welcome, as doorstops, in

baskets at the front gate with a Free sign, in casseroles, bread, cakes, muffins, soup, frittered, broiled, stuffed and baked, fried, raw and pickled. New gardeners sometimes make the mistake of planting too many hills of them and then wonder what to do with the growing bounty. A local woman who stopped by the newspaper office with a request for recipes for zucchini was asked how many she had—fourteen cardboard boxes full! She gave all fourteen boxes to the Food Bank. They are happy to get any garden excesses you may have. Call Gert at the drycleaners and she'll take your information.

And don't forget to plump up those giant pumpkins languishing in the heat. The Fall Fair is September 3rd at the Civic arena. I'll print up some hints for displaying flowers and produce closer to the time.

And speaking of zucchinis, the following recipe has been rated a 3.76 out of 5 by Joe, my husband, who is the quality control for this column. Joe was feeling cranky when he gave it 3.76 so take that into account when preparing.

Caremelized Zucchini with Fresh Mint
    2 Tablespoons good olive oil
    A pound of zucchini cut into 1/3-inch slices
    3 Tablespoons finely chopped fresh mint
    1–2 Tablespoons balsamic vinegar

Heat oil over medium-high heat and sauté zucchini until golden brown, about 2 minutes per side. Season with salt and pepper or lemon pepper.

Add mint and balsamic and serve.

"Joe was being generous when he gave it—what?—3.76. I wouldn't. have given a thank you if you served that stuff to me," Mariah grouses.

"Might be just the thing, Jemima," Bunny encourages, "but I think you'll find there's another 'a' in *caramelized*. And for line six about the baskets, how about trying something like—outside the front gate free zucchini are displayed in baskets. And maybe move that bit about the pumpkins to the end so it doesn't break up the piece about zucchinis."

"They all went, you know—the zucchinis—though people more than likely took them to feed their horses and chickens than for dinner."

"Sari, do you have anything to say about Jemima's work before we go to mine?" Bunny asks.

"It sounds homey and ∴ informative." Sari imparts a brief smile to Jemima as reassurance. "It would be nice to know more about tomatoes. My mother always had problems getting them to ripen. I don't have the space in my yard, otherwise I'd be growing some."

Jemima, busy making note of Bunny's comments, smiles gratefully. "I need to pad the column anyway so tomatoes would be good filler. Can't go wrong there. Thank you, Sari." Jemima collects her pages from the others and tucks them away in her bag.

Bunny hugs her writing to her chest. "I've started something new. No more short stories for now, unless, of course, you don't like what I've written." Her pages are paper-clipped together and she distributes them to the others. "It's going to be about a woman who finds out her husband is cheating on her and decides she's going to do something about it."

> Tiara Ballestaire hadn't had sex with her husband for eight months. She'd tried subtly by purchasing filmy nighties, bathing in sweet-smelling water, planning special meals he didn't show up for. She didn't fight with him nor chastise him in any way in case it upset him. She found she was losing herself to find him. She

and Lance had been married for twelve years. Twelve childless years, as Lance did not want children.

But now she was suspicious. He was distracted and he was buying new clothes—clothes designed for a younger man. And he sported a one-day beard on weekends like the film stars did. He also rented a red sports car, just to see how it felt, he said. She didn't get to ride in it, but *he* did on his next conference in Las Vegas. Since when did lawyers have conferences in Las Vegas? Tiara had called him there but the desk clerk informed her that "they" had checked out. Later Lance had assured her it was like using the royal "we."

He got calls and there was no one there. One Sunday when he was actually cutting the lawn himself, a blue sedan pulled to the curb and he walked over to it, crouched down on the passenger side and, after shoulder-checking the house, spoke to whoever was driving. He laughed at something the driver said, then a few minutes later stood and patted the top of the car as it drove away. Tiara, at her desk upstairs, could not see who was driving nor could she read the plates at that distance. When casually asked about it later Lance said it was a lost tourist and could she please make him a gin and tonic.

"He's whoring around on her," Mariah barks. "What a bastard."

Bunny looks startled at the interruption. It takes her a moment to find her place again and continue reading.

She saw the same blue car again the following Sunday but on the opposite side of the boulevard. Shortly thereafter, Lance abruptly left the house saying he had work to do at the office and wouldn't be home until late. She called his office but there was no answer.

Sometimes he smelled different, as though he'd

used another soap to shower with.

Finally one November night he came in and went straight upstairs to change. When he returned, she asked if he wanted his dinner. He declined, saying he was too tired to eat. He thought he'd just go to bed.

It came out without her even thinking about it— "Are you having an affair?" Her words had hung in the air and he scattered them with a wave of his impatient hand.

"Here I work twelve-, thirteen-, fourteen-hour days and you have the audacity to ask me if I'm having an affair?"

"Well, are you?" She was still seated by the fire, the cat in her lap.

"I won't even dignify that question with an answer." And with that, he turned on his heel and went upstairs—into the guest bedroom. That is all the excuse he needs to move out of her bed. He stood accused and to Tiara he was found guilty.

She dropped by his office in December to see when the staff Christmas party was being held. When she asked the receptionist for Lance, the girl buzzed his office and out came a small, slightly chunky woman in a tailored black suit with more cleavage showing than a staid lawyers' office should allow. In her cleavage was a lovely teardrop-shaped diamond pendant. "I'm Candice Lily, Mr. Ballestaire's legal assistant. He's in a meeting right now. Can I be of assistance?"

"I was hoping my husband could take time out for lunch."

"Your husband," Miss Lily said archly. "I think not. He's very busy today."

"Do tell him his wife dropped in, won't you, Miss … uh …"

"Lily."

"Ah yes, like the deadly camas." Tiara gracefully
did an about-turn and left the premises.

"Aren't men just pricks," Mariah snorts. "I can just see him doing
that to Tiara, and doing it without a conscience." She stubs a finger
at the second page of the manuscript. "You have some issues with
verb tenses."

"Where?" asks Bunny.

"The line that came after the 'guest bedroom' bit. It should read
'That was all the excuse he needed.'"

"Right, I see it now." Bunny circles the offending words.
"Anything else?"

Mariah is still hot about the subject. "How come she's letting him
get away with it?"

"Well, she's not, Mariah. You'll see in future work that she's going
to do something drastic."

"Good for her!" Sari says, with more enthusiasm than usual. "I
hope it has something to do with a dull knife or a pair of scissors."

AT THE CLOSE OF THE evening, Bunny watches the group's cars dip and
jounce toward the end of the driveway, the dust they raise powdering
the lower branches of the scarlet oaks that border it. For Bunny, the
moments after the women leave are like a power failure. Now the
house is too quiet, too dim, no matter how many lights are on.

She gathers the china, her cup the only one with a lipstick imprint
on the side, and garburates the cigarette floating nose-down in the
dregs of Mariah's tea. Bunny will wash the dishes herself because,
if Gerda spots them in the morning, she'll start banging cupboard
doors to show her disapproval. Gerda thinks this writing group is a
bad influence on Bunny. Instead of fooling around with these women,
Gerda is fond of saying, Bunny should be trailing after her husband,
Leland, on his business trips, ironing his shorts and starching his
Hong Kong–made Egyptian cotton shirts while he closes mega-deals
for Mega-Oil Inc. and pacifies rebellious oil workers in far-flung lands.

But first, before the dishes, Bunny will have a little scotch on the rocks. And when she finishes washing the dishes, she pours another scotch and lets it mellow next to the sink. Midway through drying the last cup she is interrupted by the ringing phone. She throws the tea towel over her shoulder and drains her drink before answering. The throaty voice of Leland's secretary, Miss Spring-Dunning, inquires about Bunny's health and the weather back in Canada (both fine), then asks her to please hold while she puts Mr. deLore on. *More likely, while she pushes Mr. deLore off!* "One moment, Miss Spring-Dunning," Bunny says, "while I see to a bit of business first." She pours her third scotch. One good thing about Leland—well, two really—is his exceptional taste in scotch and the money to buy it by the case. The bottle in Bunny's manicured hand is a rather good 1964 single malt—Black Bowmore Islay from the Western Islands. She adds a splash of tap water, which would cause Leland to draw a quick intake of breath were he home to see the affront. "Miss Spring-Dunning? I'm available to speak with my husband now." Her tone is crisp, quite the opposite to Leland's.

"Darling, how are you?" His voice is like warm chocolate over ice cream. Soft and fluid at first but during the course of the call it will harden to a shell you could crack with the back of a spoon. "Did I catch you at a bad time?"

"No, Leland. I was just washing up after the girls."

"Ah, yes, your little writing session. Still meeting then, are we?"

Bunny sips carefully from her glass so as not to disturb the ice cubes. Leland will be listening for such telltale signals. "How are you doing, Leland?"

"Never better, my dear. Miss Spring-Dunning brought it to my attention that our anniversary was yesterday. I felt so badly about missing it that I had her order a little something that will be couriered to you."

"How kind."

"And Joy? How is she?" He refuses to call their grown daughter PJ as Bunny does. He feels Pride-and-Joy is no name for a businesswoman. "I've left messages on her machine."

"That's very touching, Leland. PJ's doing well. Climbing that corporate ladder rung by bloody rung. Vice-president in charge of something-or-other. She says she's coming out here tomorrow, but we'll see. She talks a good story. Like father, like daughter."

"Don't start," he says, clipping his words. He doesn't like to be reminded of his failings, particularly those that call into question his devotion as a spouse. After all, he is quick to remind her, she does have the house, her ample monthly stipend, her little writing group. And he comes home whenever possible, which seems to be less and less in the last half-dozen years.

The line is very clear tonight. No hums or buzzing during the moment's silence that follows their exchange. Outside the house, beyond the orchard, the coyotes yip, seeking contact with one another.

"Your mother called, Leland. She says she can no longer stand on the leg affected by the gout." There's no reply. "Hello? Are you still there? I said your mother's failing, Leland."

"Mother has been failing for a long time," he returns. "I think she enjoys the attention."

"Whose attention? Certainly not yours."

"I'll fire off some flowers. Roses or something. This line seems to be going. I'll have to sign off."

"Where are you? Is there a number ...?"

A series of clicks and the line is dead.

"Hello?" Bunny drops the receiver, wishing he were still on the end to experience the percussion. One more scotch and so to bed.

⌀

THE LARGE NEON NUMBERS ON the clock read 2:13 but Bunny's waking idea won't wait until morning. Moonlight streaming through the lace curtains helps her find the slippers next to the bed. She is so fired up that she doesn't bother with her robe. Upon reaching the landing, she flips on the great chandelier—five and a half feet of dusty crystal dangling above the staircase.

In Leland's study, sitting at his turn-of-the-century Stickley desk that also houses her computer, Bunny searches for the phonebook in the only drawer that isn't locked. On the front of the phonebook is the information sticker she slapped on it when it came with the phone bill: CALL RETURN Press *69. An automated voice informs her that the last incoming call came from 604-555-1232. The message repeats as she writes it down. 604? *What's Leland doing with a B.C area code? He's supposed to be in Indonesia!* It takes her two tries before she calms enough to hit the proper numbers. A phone purrs and a cheery voice greets her. "Pacific Pleasures, good morning. How may I help you?"

"My husband called from there earlier. Is this a hotel?" The voice assures Bunny it is. "Do you have a Leland deLore staying there?"

"I'm sorry," says the receptionist, lowering her voice. Bunny knows she's not at all sorry. "That information is not available. But if you give me his room number, I can connect you."

"Does that mean he *is* there?"

"I'm sorry," she repeats. "I cannot divulge that information."

"Madam!" says Bunny heatedly. "This is an emergency."

"If you will please leave your name and number," she singsongs, "I'll have Mr. Perkins, our night manager, call you at his earliest convenience."

Pointless. Bloody pointless. After slamming down the receiver (twice in one night!), Bunny wonders how many other callers have growled in that woman's ear? Getting back to sleep now will be a challenge. Perhaps a scotch and milk.

II

EARLY THE NEXT MORNING WHEN Mariah Flint lowers her lumpy feet, toes like dahlia tubers, over the side of her bed, she feels all of her fifty-six years. She gropes for her glasses on the night table. When they're in place, she shuffles down the hallway to the bathroom, hiking her threadbare nightgown in readiness, muttering as she goes, complaining about drinking one cup and peeing three. Returning to bed, she folds her arms over her chest awaiting sleep, but in the shade-darkened room, her mind mulls over the evening spent at Bunny's.

"Stupid name for a grown woman," she utters aloud, not for the first time. She will show them! *Derek of Dunston-Greene* will be her best work to date. No more pussyfooting around the sex scenarios, no more fading to black with soaring violins and fireworks in the background. Readers want the real goods—the thrust and parry. *Just let Jemima find fault with my sex scenes. How the hell would she know if it was right or wrong anyway? Certainly not by personal experience.* She snuffles a laugh at the thought of Jemima working up a head of steam to mount her poor old Joe, but when she goes to rub her eyes, she realizes she's still wearing her glasses and replaces them on the bedside table. Thinking about the coming day wipes the smile from her face. Brief hours from now she will have to drive to the nearby town of Bayonet to pick up Flora Flint Plumtree, her seventy-three-year-old mother, because Flora is being kicked to the curb by the kindly folks at the Briar Rose Pioneers' Residence. The management says she is out of control. Noisy. Disturbing the others at odd hours. A poor loser at bingo. Foul-mouthed—though it really isn't Flora who is foul-mouthed, even though she has a few choice words in her vocabulary. It's Geezer Hollinsbee's damned African Grey.

When Geezer had to rush to Seattle to attend his sister's funeral, he persuaded Flora to bird-sit with the promise that he'd bring her back a huge bottle of cheap American gin.

Unfortunately, the bus trip down and rich food at the get-together after the cremation were too much for Geezer. His quiet demise at the party went unnoticed until his body was bumped from his chair by two young cousins doing a vigorous polka. With Geezer's ill-timed passing, Flora became the ginless foster mother of the ungrateful bird who cussed sharply at being confined to his cage in her small room. He was used to free rein in Geezer's basement suite, the door to his cage always open. The bird's angular name, Axel, was chosen by Geezer because it could be chisel-cut onto a nameplate for his cage, and for the past thirteen years Axel has used this nameplate as his dinner gong. This, along with his cursing, has made him unwelcome at the Briar Rose, and by noon Flora and the bird will be en route to the back bedroom of Mariah's two-bedroom cottage. Mariah is not prepared.

Her raisin-brown eyes snap open as she feels the hair-shirt heat prickle her chest. She throws back the blankets, kicking her legs over the mound of them. Using her nightie as a bellows, she pumps cooler air over her torso and curses the late mid-life flashes that leave her puffing and red-faced. She hauls herself upright, searching for her cigarettes on the night table. *How come Roland and Velma can't take Flora?* she asks herself—not for the first time. *She's Roland's mother, too. Sure as God made little green apples, it was Velma who said no! And just because brother Clive is a bachelor is no reason for him not to have her. We could rotate Flora's visits. Three weeks on, six weeks off.* Goosebumps pebble her skin and after inhaling another half-dozen lungfuls of smoke, she carefully pinches the glowing end from the cigarette into the ashtray, then balances the butt on the edge. She hauls the blankets over her shoulders and allows herself to topple back onto the bed. *I haven't even made up her room yet. I'm not ready. Not now—not ever!*

❧

MARIAH IS ON HANDS AND knees in the tub, head under the tap, rinsing the shampoo from her hair, when the sound of the ringing phone calls a halt. Blindly she turns off the faucets, steps out, gropes for a towel and makes a flat-footed run for it.

"Don't hang up," she orders, halfway down the hall. "I'm coming!" Her wet hands bobble the receiver but she saves the fumble. "Hello? Hello?"

"It's about time you got up," says a querulous voice on the other end. "I've been sitting next to my suitcases since breakfast and here it is ..." There's a pause and Mariah uses the time to wipe her eyes on the end of the towel. "... quarter to nine."

"Piss off! Piss off!" the parrot says.

"Shaddup."

"'Scuse me?" Mariah says.

"It's that bird of Geezer's," Flora explains. "Mouth like a longshoreman."

"Why are you calling?"

"Come and get me!"

"Tell me the bird is staying there." Mariah's towel is slipping and she grasps it with her free hand. "Flora?" Her mother has always insisted her children call her Flora in the hope that she may be mistaken for their sister rather than their mother. When forced to admit to motherhood and required to explain away the absence of Mariah's father, she takes on a stoic look and confesses that she was widowed at a very early age. That she lost her brave young husband when he fell from a tree as he was returning a baby bird to its nest, or that he was tragically lost in a mid-Atlantic storm while sailing solo around the world, or ... His death has varied in every new town. "Flora?" Mariah repeats.

"The bird is packed and waiting as well," she says unapologetically. "It's a sacred trust sort of a thing."

"Boogie woogie bugle boy, a-a-a-ark," squawks the bird.

"And I can expect you when?" Flora continues.

Never! Never! Never! "An hour."

They hang up simultaneously, each thinking she's the first to.

Mariah dials Clive's number. The phone at the other ends tolls until the fifth ring when the answering machine takes her call. She waits impatiently for the beep, then says hotly, "Clive! I know you're there. Pick up the phone." She gives him a scant ten seconds. "If you don't pick it up, I'll be sending Flora over to you on the next bus."

"Hullo?" says a sleepy voice.

"I want to talk to you."

"Uh-huh."

"Clive, I can't do it. Do you know she has a bloody bird?"

"Uh-huh."

"They've evicted her, do you understand?"

"Uh-huh."

"Clive! Goddamn it, can't she at least spend *some* time with you?"

"Who?"

She can visualize him in his silk pyjamas, spread out luxuriously in his double bed. No hot flashes, no varicose veins, nothing that wakes him up at 5 a.m. midway into a worry. What she wants to do is yell and scream and heave the phone at the wall hard enough to leave a dent, but the wheeze in her breathing is developing again.

"Who's coming, Lump?" Clive manages to say.

She must stay calm and breathe evenly. Clear her mind. "You haven't heard a damn thing I've been saying, have you?" Breathe evenly. One. Exhale. Two. Exhale. Three …

"Sure. Sure I have, it's just that I—"

"Clive, Flora is history at the Briar Rose Pioneers' Residence. You do remember she's been living there?"

"I—"

"You do remember visiting her there, don't you, Clive?" she asks acrimoniously.

"What do you want me to do, Mariah? I can't keep her. I am, after all, employed."

She shifts the receiver to her other ear. "What's that got to do with it?"

"I'm not here a lot, what with the tours and all."

"Take her with you. Leave her in Algeria." Breathe in. Out.

"You're not being practical, Lump. You know I'd love to have her, but …" He grunts as he sits up. "Let me put that another way so it doesn't sound like such a blatant lie. I'd love to help you with her but …" He pauses. "Hang on a minute. I can't function without a coffee." He drops the receiver onto the bed then pads to the kitchen. Returning to the phone, he asks, "Still there?" He hopes she isn't. "Like I was saying, if she has to live with someone, you're the best person." He slurps his first mouthful.

"Cli-i-ve," Mariah whines.

"At least until we find another place. How about I look around here? That suit you?" He is rushing the conversation now. "Look, darling, must run. I'll call you. Kiss, kiss."

Mariah feels drained but the wheeze is gone.

BUNNY AWAKENS WITH A START, then lowers her pounding head back onto the pillow. Her sinuses are blocked and her eyes hurt in the intruding light. Gerda kicks the bedroom door again, and Bunny realizes this is the noise that startled her from sleep. Carefully she sits up and edges her legs out of bed, finding only one discarded slipper where two are usually neatly placed side by each. "Oh, gawd," she protests, using her hand as an eyeshade as she glides to the door.

"Can't hold zis tray all morning, Missy," Gerda complains from the other side of the closed door. Even though she's nearly seventy years of age, Gerda has the stamina and temperament of a packhorse.

Bunny opens the door and steps aside. "Put it there," she directs, pointing toward the night table.

Gerda sweeps the table's clutter with her sharp elbow, sending a book to the floor. "It's late. Miss Joy call and say she not coming. Big important meeting. And za Mister call already from Egypt. A place viz two names like Benny somesing. Had a B, had a S."

"Egypt, is it? I think the word you're looking for is Bull Shit."

"I sink not, Missy," Gerda says, clattering the breakfast tray onto the table. She turns to face Bunny. "I sink you better clean zat mouth before za Mister call back."

Bunny tries staring Gerda down, tries looking past the wire-rimmed glasses sitting crookedly on the old woman's face, past the porcelain teeth wobbling in the lipless mouth. "You're excused, Gerda," Bunny says loftily. "Surely there's a floor to wash."

Gerda scuffs across the carpet in her flattened slippers, slamming the door on her way out. She has a long history with the deLore family. She was nanny to Leland until he no longer needed nannying, and was kept on as housekeeper at the family home until a year earlier when Bunny and Leland had their twenty-fifth wedding anniversary. Then she arrived on their doorstep as Mother deLore's present to them. When Bunny complained about Gerda's foul temper, Leland argued, "But she's practically family."

"Well, so am I," Bunny asserted, but he shrugged off her protests.

"After all," he said, wishing to dismiss the subject once and for all, "Mother never had a problem with her in all those years." Bunny became convinced that if she gave him an ultimatum, he would be hard-pressed to decide between her and Gerda. The only concession he would make was to move Gerda into her own place instead of settling her into PJ's old bedroom. Now he pays Gerda's rent on a little apartment that is within biking distance. She also has an account at the taxi stand should she not be up to cycling over to the house in the wet and cold.

"Egypt!" Bunny grumbles, her anger building as she enters her ensuite bathroom. She opens the mirrored cabinet containing the Aspirins and unplugs the cotton wadding from the bottle. Shaking out two extra-strength tablets, she throws them to the back of her throat, swallowing them without benefit of water. She replaces the cotton and puts the bottle back, but as she shuts the cabinet, she takes a moment to inspect her face in the mirror. This might not be the best time of day for self-examination, she thinks, but continues anyway, feeling the need for a small measure of punishment for all those scotches last night. Her eyes look a little bruised, but the face carries her forty-nine years well, the result of good haircuts, frequent facials and a stress-free existence. She snorts at the thought of a "stress-free existence" and turns from her reflection, admitting she still has her looks and to hell with everybody.

Leland will not in all probability ask for a divorce to marry Miss Spring-Dunning. There have been other Miss Spring-Dunnings, going as far back as their early married days in Calgary, which is why he moved her to this house in the first place while he stayed on there. It gave him the opportunity for travel with a series of personal secretaries and, of course, allowed him to keep his distance from both her and his mother. But eventually each affair collapses and he finds his way home to Grievous with some kind of bauble for her and a renewed interest in his marriage. Bunny knows how this works because she, too, was once Leland's secretary, but he was single at the time and she persisted in her demands for a wedding. She really should just take everything he owns and throw him out, but he is so sweet when he's in recovery from a failed affair.

⌘

SARI BUTTON SPENDS HER WEEKLY day off from the Belle Mode Beauty Bar working at her second job, the Grimaldi Sisters Funeral Home. She unscrews the top from a jar of hair gel and gazes past her own reflection in the mirror to appraise the body of the late Mrs. Jellis, laid out behind her on the pink-sheeted table. Death does not have to be in black and white, say the sisters Grimaldi, owners of a chain of two funeral salons. Their private motto is framed and cross-stitched in shades of cobalt blue and violet: *Put the FUN back in FUNeral.* Sari turns, rubs the gel between her palms, then runs them through the thinning hair of the deceased. She wipes her hands on a towel, places a tray of rollers next to Mrs. Jellis's ear, and begins rolling the crown hair in sausage-sized green cylinders, six in all, then four smaller black ones on each side of her head leading like a corduroy road to the tops of her waxy ears. The back does not have to be set, as the plump sateen pillow will come right up to meet the stiffly curled and permanently lacquered hair. The air is heavy and Sari sighs as though it's the first breath she's taken today. She looks for the Grimaldi sisters' small portable radio, spotting it on a shelf across the room. She turns it on, and after a long warm-up the radio broadcasts a tinny country and western hurtin' song. Sari hums along with the music as she dumps the unused rollers into a bag, replacing them on the table with the makeup tray. She likes this part best—putting life back into lifeless cheeks. She'll even tint the marble-white ears with a bit of blush, her own special touch. Sari holds the bottles of foundation up to Mrs. Jellis's skin, choosing a rose-beige. She applies it with a damp sponge, frowning in concentration as she spreads makeup on a face that last saw cosmetics on a wedding day more than half a century ago. Even then it was just a touch of colour on her lips and hard pinches to her cheeks. As Sari rinses the sponge, she catches sight of herself in the mirror above the sink. She's unhappy with what she sees. Too thin, too pale, too pinched. The blue half-moons beneath her eyes are the unwelcome result of James's prolonged unemployment and the stress of day-to-day living.

She rifles through the eyeshadow in her tray, discarding blue and grey, settling with uncertainty on a pinky-mauve for Mrs. Jellis. Coating her small sable brush with colour, she's ready to erase years, but as she rests the heel of her hand on the body's cool cheekbone, she is distracted by thoughts of home and her gaze travels to the high, gritty window set in the wall of the room. Instead of the usual blank blue sky of summer, threatening clouds are somersaulting over one another. When she walked to work earlier, it looked dismal to the east. Now as the radio calls for storm warnings after noon, static begins to replay the lightning strikes happening out of her range of vision. She sets the eyeshadow on the cadaver's pigeon chest and leaves the room, passing through the changing area and into the staff room. A card table holds a telephone and a cup labelled ten cents per call.

"Hello, James. It's just me. How's Mooney?" She carries the phone with her as she peers out the window onto the street. The wind tumbles papers and debris that will soon be hammered to the pavement by the rain. "Did ya hear anything about that job at the

shoe store?" She sets her face to receive disappointing news, a prac-
tice she has almost perfected. "But you'd be a *good* salesman, James,"
she argues. "I'd certainly buy shoes from you." She fingers her long
French braid as she listens to her husband, then her face lights up in
surprise. "What's the occasion?" After James explains, she tells him
she loves him and says goodbye, grinning as she hangs up the phone
and returns to finish her job.

Still smiling, she dusts the brush across Mrs. Jellis's finely pleated
eyelids. "My husband, James," she tells the cadaver, "says I'm to listen to the radio to hear a request he sent in. My birthday was in
February, so I wonder what it's for?" They had celebrated her twenty-
fifth birthday by taking young Mooney to the neighbouring town
of Emmett where a new Steak and Egg House was having its grand
opening. After dinner James had popped a balloon at the till and got
their dinner free. They laughed about that and said they should have
ordered the apple pie and ice cream after all.

She checks her watch. "He said we're to listen at five minutes to
twelve." Sari plans to have Mrs. Jellis all finished by then anyway—
blow-dried, combed out and ready for company. "Your Sid is coming
to visit and my James is sending me a song. Makes the day sunny
after all, doesn't it?"

But outside the trailer where they live, James is sliding the last
box of his collectibles into the back of his truck. Mooney's walker, his
rocking horse and his Jolly Jumper poke out from the assortment of
boxes and knotted garbage bags. James looks up as thunder scrapes
the hills and rattles down the brown grassy slopes. Though he hears
Mooney crying from his crib, his bottle empty, James takes the time
to drag a mould-mottled canvas tarp from beneath the trailer. He
shakes it out then flings it over the open back of the truck. He loops
the laces over the truck's tie-downs, cinching them until the tarp is
drum-head tight.

Mooney, now outraged at the lack of attention, is screaming a
high-pitched squeal that only tapers off when James enters the trailer and approaches his crib. With a blanket James wipes the teary,

drooly face, then picks up the child, straddling him on his hip and singing to him as he heads to the kitchen, "I'm being followed by a Moonshadow, Moonshadow, Moonshadow." James offers Mooney a bottle from the supply lined up on the counter, then takes him outside to the truck and fastens him into the baby seat before returning to pack the bottles and the last four disposable diapers into the diaper bag, collect the bank card to the family fortune of $89.76 and the almost-full coin jar labelled Mooney's Loonies.

A TUMBLE OF FIBROUS CLOUDS rolls across the floor of the wide valley toward Grievous Township, and down Mayne Street the short march of automatic street lights twitch orange as though readying for sunset instead of midday. In the blowing grit, dogs turn tail and scurry under porches. In the Grimaldi Sisters Funeral Home the lights flutter overhead, but Sari takes little notice as she holds the blow-dryer to the curlers rolling over Mrs. Jellis's head. She shakes the dryer when it hesitates then realizes it isn't the appliance but the power fluctuating. Through the high windows she sees lightning split the gunmetal sky, and the thunder that follows it over the Grimaldi's tin roof rattles the fluorescent lights in their holders, but it isn't until a fir tree on Roundabout Road loosens its clutch on the earth and leans into the power lines that the power goes off. The townspeople stop for the moment, faces upturned. The lights in the funeral home fade to pink dots. In the gloom Sari ducks below the level of the table. She isn't afraid, exactly, but it seems sensible somehow not to be the tallest living thing in the room. She waggles her wrist trying to reflect a little light off the gold numbers on her watch.

"Come on, come on, come on!" she urges the blackened lights when she reads the time. "Don't quit now." She crosses the room in a crouch to test the light switch then darts to the radio to spin the knob. When there's no blurt of music she lifts the radio from the shelf, turning it over to see if it runs on batteries, not that she has any if it does.

"Well, that's just great," she says, returning it none too gently to the shelf. Another thwack of thunder and she scurries to the changing room, where it's stuffy and dark, to squat on the floor, hugging her arms around her knees. She drops her face into the comforting triangle between knees and chest, her upper arms against her ears to muffle the sound of the world outside. She smells hairspray and undertones of her own baby-powder-scented deodorant. She should phone James and tell him the power is off, but then he probably knows that already and anyway she knows she shouldn't use the telephone during an electrical storm. Moments later her arms relax and she catches herself dozing off. The sensation is so pleasant that she curls onto the floor beneath the coats, her head on the toe of a rubber boot.

In Emmett, thirty miles away, the announcer at the CPMF radio station apologizes for being two minutes late with a special request for Sari from James. He says he hopes he can get both songs in before the noon news and thanks James for his five-dollar donation to the Children's Fund. "And now for Sari, here's a Willie Nelson favourite, 'She's Out of My Life,' and we'll follow that up with 'Moonshadow.'"

JAMES OFFERS MOONEY ANOTHER COOKIE from the box of Arrowroots placed between them, but with every drum roll of thunder Mooney sucks in his trembling bottom lip and turns his head against his shoulder, clamping his thumbs in his fists.

The worn truck tires hum along the steaming highway, and the shroud of clouds recedes in the side-mounted mirrors. With the flash and jangle of the storm behind them, Mooney finally releases his lip and accepts a cookie, looking it over carefully before cramming it into his wet mouth. James gives him an appreciative smile, feeling a jolt of love in his chest for his red-haired son. Mooney—Moonshadow—is promising to be very much like himself: cautious, restless and looking for something else, somewhere else. This baby, who sometimes has an old look around his eyes, gazes beyond the room, beyond the town, beyond the horizon.

James pulls his attention back to the road and as the time nears 11:55, he thinks of Sari but without the same jolt of love. It'll take time for her to puzzle out that first song, and when she does, she'll be on the run for home, but she'll only find *her* stuff. He doesn't feel unhappy about leaving her. Right now he just feels driven. Her silent suffering, the jobs circled in the newspaper, the choking feeling that sends him outside the trailer for air no matter what the hour. He feels like rolling down the truck window to howl at the wind but instead cracks it just enough to check the temperature. Too cool yet for the boy. James lowers the creased brim of his baseball cap against the brightening sky. *She'll be okay in a week or two. Maybe now she can get some sleep without the boy and me crashing around half the night.* With peanut butter and banana sandwiches bagged on the floor, sweetened iced tea in the thermos and all this highway unrolling before them, James begins whistling lightheartedly. *I'll send her a postcard at Christmas. Let her know we're doing okay.*

III

"YOO-O-O HOO-O! J-O-OSEPH," JEMIMA CALLS from the open kitchen doorway. "Lu-u-nch." She turns to the counter, snugs a knitted cosy over the Brown Betty teapot and carries it to the Arborite table in the dining room. She places the teapot to her right on a hot mat she's made from leftover yarn and intertwined rubber jar rings. She hears Joe's tires come up the ramp and hit the porch, and a moment later his wheelchair swings through the open door.

"Jeezus Murphy, why are the windows steamed up?" he asks, removing his cap and hanging it on the doorknob.

"Go wash for lunch. It's a special treat."

"Aw-w, cripes, it's not sacrificial Wednesday again?"

"You should be very happy to be sampling what's going in my column. Lots of people would die for that opportunity."

He smiles. It's not often she leaves him an opening like that. "Some die that others might live," he says. He's pleased with himself as he wheels to the bathroom to rinse the workshop grime from his hands.

Jemima, arms knotted over her generous chest, leans against the stove awaiting her husband's return. Once he's at the table she presents the lunch. "This," she says, watching him take his first bite, "is an onion sandwich on steamed brown bread. That's why the windows were fogged: the bread must be steam cooked for four hours, then baked for another thirty minutes." She rushes on, "The recipe calls for two cups sour milk, three-quarters of a cup molasses …"

Joe rolls his eyes as she recites the ingredients.

"… one cup yellow cornmeal, cup and a half of graham flour …"

"Tea," he says around a mouthful of sandwich, jabbing his stubby finger toward his cup.

"Don't talk with your mouth full, dear. One cup whole wheat flour ..."

"Um-m-m, very nice. How'd you make the onion?"

She checks the paper next to her spoon for the sandwich filling recipe. "One medium-sized green pepper ..."

He drops his head, pretending to sleep until she finishes.

"... and a tablespoon of mayonnaise." She sits back as though she's already eaten and laces her hands over her round stomach, eyeing him as he finishes his meal. Joe directs his finger again and this time she undresses the teapot, pouring hot, strong tea into Joe's plastic travel mug then into her bone china cup seated on its bone china saucer. She claims tea isn't tea without a saucer.

"What else do I have to try?"

"How was the onion sandwich?"

"Okay, I guess."

"Rate it from one to five, Joe. You know how it goes." She stares at him intently and he takes it as a threat. Aside from the onion fumes and the heartburn that will strike in thirty minutes, he charitably rates it as a four-point-seven-five and gives her a nail-blackened thumbs-up. She smiles and snatches his plate away, trotting to the kitchen to get the second course. On her return she eyes the fringed rug beneath the table where Joe's tires have caught the edge, curling it over on itself. "Joe, you're curling the rug again."

Joe backs off and reparks the wheelchair over the flattened fringe. He looks into the steaming bowl on his flowered placemat. "What the hell is it?"

"Spot pudding. A half-cup of brown sugar, a half-cup milk ..."

Joe sighs and thrusts his hand under his chin, bracing his elbow on the table to wait her out. He blows to cool the contents, then, from around the edge of the bowl, spoons pudding into his mouth. The spoon darts in and out as he is anxious to eat and be gone.

"... Then bake thirty to forty minutes at 350° until brown."

"Hm-m-m, tasty," he says, without making eye contact. "Well, Mother, you did yourself proud. I gotta go."

"One to five, Joe."

"Five. Five. I'd say she's a definite five." Joe snaps the top on his plastic mug and rams it between his thin thighs. "After I finish cleaning the lawnmower, I got to do up those dinin' room chairs for what's-her-name." He settles his cap on his head and opens the door. "Damndest thing, those chairs. Ticky-tacky."

"Mrs. Branson-Carver."

He swings around on the porch. "Huh?"

"Mrs. Branson-Carver. The chairs in the shop?"

"That's her. You'd think that some mucky-muck from the mill would make enough money to buy a decent set of chairs, wouldn't ya?"

"You figure he's still got a job with the mill shut down?"

"Yeah, those types always got a paycheque coming in. Shiny shoes with no cow shit on 'em." He freewheels from the porch, down the ramp, across the blacktop and through the door of the shop. On a good day with a tailwind, he can travel clear across the shop and end up bumping into the planer. Today in the rain his ride falls short and he stops just inside the darkened doorway. He tries the light switch just as Jemima calls from the kitchen doorway, "Power's gone off!" He sets his tea on the workbench and looks for something he can do that doesn't require electricity. Anything so he won't have to return to the house. The first wave of heartburn rises and exits in a belch. He opens the second drawer down and brings out his secret stash of Tums, the label smeared with grimy fingerprints. He pops two tablets into his mouth, crunching them like candy between his square teeth as he watches the rain streak the dusty window above the workbench.

A peaceful twenty minutes pass before his quiet contemplation is interrupted with the sight of Jemima and her folded umbrella fussing out the back door. She takes a moment to retie the plastic rain hat under her chins, then clomps down the steps in her rubber boots, opening her umbrella as she goes. Joe scoots to the dismembered chairs and grabs a piece of sandpaper, applying it to a rung as Jemima heaves open the garage door. "Dark in here," she announces as if it's breaking news.

"Yup."

"I'm going for the mail, Joe. You have any bills to go out?" She's hoping that someday he will send out invoices and actually receive full payment for work completed.

"Not today." The distant rumble of thunder makes him wonder if Jemima knows the danger of being in a storm with an umbrella and he thinks fleetingly about giving her a pocketful of nails. "Have a nice walk."

✍

WHEN MARIAH BRAKES SUDDENLY AT a red light, the back seat comes perilously close to avalanching to the floor, taking the African Grey's cage with it.

"For the love of Mike," says Flora, "do you drive like this all the time or is it just for my benefit?" She coughs and fans the air with her *Cosmo* magazine. "And put out that cigarette! It's bad for the bird, not to mention *me*."

Mariah has lit up and exhaled only once, but now she's determined she will not bend to her mother's will and clamps onto her cigarette long enough to stream out smoke that smacks the windshield and curls over the dash before she rolls down the window. Only then does she discard the lengthy butt onto the roadway. As she does so, her view in the rear mirror takes in the swaying bird, hanging by his beak from his swing, clipped wings folded, feet balled on scaly stick legs.

✍

SITTING ON THE CURVED SEAT in the bowed window of Leland's study, Bunny deLore is having cookies and scotch after spending a good part of her Tuesday afternoon feeding the next installment of her novel into her computer. Out of the corner of her eye she sees a lone figure trudging up her driveway. From this distance the person looks like a red dot, so Bunny pulls back the silk sheers to have a better look. Somewhere in the house is a pair of field glasses, but she has no idea where. She hopes it's not one of Gerda's Jehovah's Witness friends or she'll feel compelled to purchase another stack of pamphlets. "Gerda?" she calls from the study door. "Ger-da-a-a!" She checks her watch and wonders if the quiet in the house means that Gerda has left for the day. In the kitchen a plastic-wrapped plate on the counter—her dinner—tells her that Gerda has already departed on her bicycle, and Bunny calls off her search.

By the time Bunny returns to the study and again peers down the driveway, the walker is more than halfway to the house, and she is able to identify the slender figure by the red sweater hanging almost to the knees. "It's Sari!" she says, absently reaching for her scotch and not finding it. "Now what did I do with it?" Bunny retraces her steps, locating the drink where she left it on the grand piano. She wipes at the water ring on the black walnut and grimaces at the ghostly circle appearing like a life preserver on the antique wood. She scoops a crystal hedgehog from among the other useless bric-a-brac in a nearby étagère and centres it over the blemish, then knocks back her drink and marches the empty glass to the kitchen sink.

Sari, deep in thought, looks up when she hears her name called, surprised she's already at the house. She raises her arm in acknowledgment at Bunny, who is dwarfed against the frame of the massive carved entrance doors. Sari admires this woman, sleek in her well-made expensive clothes, and hopes that the day never comes when Bunny recognizes anything of hers that Sari has purchased from the thrift store.

"You're an early bird," Bunny says, coming down the stone stairs to meet her.

"Why didn't you bring the truck?"

"James has it," Sari murmurs.

"Sorry, dear, I couldn't hear you with the birds chirping."

"I said James has it, so I walked." Sari gives a fleeting smile and fidgets with her papers.

"Are you okay, Sari? You look a bit pale." But the girl looks more than just pale, and Bunny is alarmed to see how very thin her legs appear in the leggings beneath the long red sweater.

Sari sets her mouth and looks down at her feet. "I'm tired, I guess."

Bunny, feeling a rush of tenderness, throws a comforting arm around Sari's shoulders and leads her toward the house. "Come and have a little shot of brandy. That'll buck you up." She senses Sari's reluctance but chats cheerily all the way to the library. "Now you just sit down and I'll get you a drink."

Sari would like to tell her not to bother but she doesn't have the strength. Instead she drops her bag at her feet and sinks into the but-ter-soft leather chair as if it were hers to keep. She accepts the crystal snifter offered by Bunny and cradles it in her hands. This much she knows, even though she's never actually had brandy before—that you warm it in your palms and swirl it around and sniff apprecia-tively. She's seen it in movies.

"Would you like something to eat after your long walk?" Bunny hovers, anxious to please. "I haven't had dinner yet and Gerda always leaves enough for three." Sari answers with a nod, then takes a tenta-tive sip of the brandy, trying not to choke as it burns her mouth and throat. Bunny pours herself one as well and as she carries it toward the hall, she announces, "Just give me a minute to warm up the plate, okay?"

Gerda has bound the plate in four sheets of Saran, each layer at a different starting point. When the plastic is finally stripped, Bunny realizes the worst—slabs of over-cooked liver are rigid beneath their blanket of greasy onions, and the juice from the carrot and raisin salad is running over the side of the plate and dripping onto the counter. Holding the plate at arm's length, Bunny carries it to the sink and slides the food into the garbage disposal. She rinses the plate and turns on the appliance that will consume her dinner for her. Ten minutes later she has finished preparing an impromptu meal and arranges it on a tray before downing the last of her drink. She plucks a small orchid from one of the plants on the window ledge and places it on the plate.

"I hope this will suffice," she announces as she enters the library.

"Gerda left something unspeakable so I had to improvise." Bunny sets the tray on a low table and shifts it so it can be shared by the two of them. "There's cheese and olives and a nice rye bread, a bit of cold chicken and black bean salad. Sorry, but that's it." She offers Sari a plate and napkin.

Sari's head lolls against the back of the chair. Her glass is empty and her cheeks are flushed.

"Would you like another brandy?"

Sari mutely holds up her glass but Bunny thinks better of refilling it and sets it down on the liquor cabinet instead. "Let's eat first, shall we?" she says, settling into her chair to spread a linen napkin across her knees. "Like having a picnic in the park." The clock in the music room strikes the half-hour. "The rest of them will be here soon. Tuck in."

Sari follows Bunny's example and smoothes her napkin over her knees. She realizes the brandy has made her lightheaded, so she choreographs her movements as she layers a slice of bread with white cheddar and black pitted olives.

At one point Bunny gets up to turn on the stereo in the music room, masking the sounds of food being chewed and swallowed in stilted silence. "Boccherini, Minuet in A major," she explains when she returns. She tries to remember the last time she had company for dinner. Probably it was when PJ, in her designer business suit, dropped in unexpectedly to borrow some money. PJ had stiffened when her mother gave her the same impulsive hug that Sari had accepted earlier. She is always cordial but distant. Bunny lays the blame on her daughter's private school upbringing, plus Leland and his mother, who had her outnumbered.

"Thanks for dinner," says Sari, placing her empty plate on the tray. "I was hungry after all."

Bunny picks up the tray. "I'll just run this to the kitchen."

Sari moves to the window and parts the sheers. "Jemima's here and Mariah's coming up the road."

"Will you let them in?" Bunny calls back as she strides down the hallway. "I'll get the cookies and make the tea."

When the group is comfortably settled, they chat over their cups until Bunny calls a halt. "Who's going first?"

"I will," Jemima says before Mariah can open her mouth. "It falls short of being perfect—"

"Good," Mariah interrupts. "That'll give us a meaty bone to chew on." She digs in her purse for her red marking pen, relishing the editing ahead of them. A slash here, a rearranged paragraph there and— her personal favourite—a misplaced modifier. "Let's get at it."

Jemima hands each of the others a copy of her work and wishes now that she'd spent more time on it. She clears her throat.

> Spetember is almost upon us, the month of shortened days and leaves turning colour. It's not too soon to cast your eye into the garden to see what should be brought in for the winter ahead. Although summer's drowsy days are almost over there's still more good weather to come. Sternbergia will be giving us a display of crocus-like flowers just when you think there's nothing more to admire. And the dahlias, which have been nothing short of spectacular, did not fare well in last week's storm. Their tender heavy heads bowed beneath the weight of water, snapping the stalks usually too short to make a proper arrangement with which to decorate a table or what-have-you.

Jemima hears the click of Mariah's tongue and sees the quick movement of her hand circling, underlining, editing the page on her wide lap. She reads her remaining page less confidently, stumbling over words, tripping over punctuation. "I said it wasn't perfect," she finishes lamely. "There's also a recipe for spot pudding and onion sandwich on steamed brown bread but you don't need to see that."

"Right, then," begins Mariah, pushing up her glasses. "On page one, line one, September is spelled wrong, there's repetitious wording and I find some of your sentences too clipped." She launches into a spirited attack on structure, spelling, and style. Then, finally noting the look on Jemima's broad face, she tempers her comments with a brief snippet of praise. "But your description of sneezeweed and goldenrod is bang on. I would put the Latin name in italics, of course, otherwise it's fine." She sits back, satisfied that she has done all she can for someone with such limited talent. "Bunny? Sari? Anything more to add?"

Bunny steps in to take back control. "I agree your description of goldenrod is very visual. Mariah caught all the spelling and punctuation, but I wonder about 'casting your eye into the garden.' It could be taken literally." She illustrates the plucking and throwing of an eye. As Jemima makes a note to change the wording, Bunny faces Sari, who has not offered any comments so far. "Anything more to add?"

Sari shakes her head.

"Then it's your turn, dear."

Each woman receives Sari's single piece of paper, handwritten in a cramped black script. Sari leans over her knees and begins reading in a monotone.

> Yawning gape of crushing jaws
> the fetid breath,
> My spiral down the rotting throat of despair
> to the rumbling gut of
> disconsolation.
> Mired and half-eaten
> I embrace my final hours.

In the silence that follows, Sari continues to look down, not wanting to see the expressions on their faces.

"Jesus Christ, where did that come from?" asks an unbelieving Mariah.

"Sari?" Bunny leaves her chair to kneel beside the young woman. "What's the matter?"

Sitting back and crossing her arms over her chest, Sari says in her little-girl voice, "Nothing's wrong. Why?"

Bunny covers Sari's knee with her hand. "You seem down, dear. And that poem … it's just not you."

Sari brushes aside Bunny's mothering hand and stands, spilling her papers. "How the hell do you know if it's me or not?" she demands. She flings her arms, the long sleeves of her thrift-store sweater flopping over her hands. "Maybe this is the real me. Blackhearted and bitchy! Mariah doesn't have a monopoly on that!"

Bunny, wide-eyed, still crouches next to the chair Sari has abandoned. Behind her Jemima is gauging Mariah's reaction and she sees the telltale mottled veil, like sweet pea netting, rising from the V-neck of her shirt. This only happens when she drinks red wine or when she's working up a head of steam.

"I will not be insulted by the likes of you," Mariah says tightly, her posture now rigidly upright in the chair.

In the clumsy silence that follows Sari's arms fall heavily to her sides and her chin sinks to her chest.

"Maybe it's the brandy speaking," Bunny says, rising from the floor. "I'll make some fresh hot tea, shall I?" She removes the tray from the table and leaves the room.

Mariah's mottling has crept across her cheeks and her white-knuckled fingers crush Sari's poem into a ball. She exhales loudly and begins gathering her papers to shove into the side pocket of her baggy purse. Jemima launches a pleading look at Sari, who is now shrinking back into the leather armchair.

"I certainly know when I'm not wanted," Mariah splutters, working her broad bottom toward the front of her chair, readying for liftoff. "You don't have to hit me on the head with a turnip."

"Sari?" says Jemima, trying to catch her eye.

After a shuddering sigh, Sari quietly apologizes.

"What's that?" Mariah demands. "Can't hear you, girl."

Lifting her hair from her face, Sari repeats, "Sorry, Mariah. I'm just tired."

Mariah is disappointed she can't make a grand exit, trailing righteous indignation like a scarf. She looks toward the door and back at Sari who has drawn her legs up to clasp them. "Well," she begins, "being tired at your age ..." She searches for words to end the sentence and decides to let it hang. She's still standing when Bunny returns with the tea tray.

"I brought a special teapot for this round," she says with forced cheerfulness, conscious of the pinched looks and constricting silence. "Leland sent it for our anniversary." The sound of the tray being set on the table rings sharply. "He's in Egypt, you know, but I think the teapot came from a company in San Diego." She hears herself babbling and tries to slow the rush of words. She fusses at removing the tea cosy. "Miss Spring-Dunning probably did the shopping as I can't see Leland actually placing an order at a china shop." As she lifts the teapot, "It's a Small World (After All)" plays in a music box tinkle and repeats and repeats as she goes from cup to cup.

"Will you tell that thing to shut the fuck up?" Mariah snaps.

Bunny holds the offending teapot at arm's length, her face stricken. "I don't know how to turn it off!"

Jemima suggests dropping it on the floor, but instead Bunny replaces it on the tray. The music stops abruptly when it's set down, but the ghost of it hovers. Sari fans it away with a wave of her hand. The four of them find their cups to be of great interest and they make appreciative noises about "lovely china, good tea, nice and hot."

"Now where were we?" Bunny interjects. "Oh, yes, Sari's poem." She wants to say Sari's lovely poem but it isn't. It's dark and horrible. "Anyone?"

With no one to critique the poem, it is set aside. When she wrote it, Sari hadn't really cared whether they would like it or not. Now that it's out in the open, she feels exposed, a snail out of its shell or a turtle on its back. She hears only part of Bunny's introduction of her own work, thinking instead of the whereabouts of James and Mooney.

"I confess I didn't get much done," Bunny says as she hands out copies of her work. "You'll remember that Tiara Ballestaire has found out her husband is cheating on her again with another of his secretaries." She clears her throat.

When Tiara goes through Lance's suit pockets, she finds receipts, gum wrappers, bits of paper with names she doesn't recognize. This has become routine since she found the jewellery slip that named Miss Lily as recipient of a gold chain with a teardrop-shaped diamond pendant attached to it. Miss Lily from his office. The one Leland called too cool and distant to be a receptionist, but whom he hired as a secretary.

The festering wound that was her self-esteem has bloodied her vision of her marriage. This was not his first encounter with these loose women, but she really couldn't see what his appeal was. He was short, hairy and had no sense of humour. So it had to be his power and money these women were attracted to. Come to think of it, that's what had done it for her when *she* was his secretary. He had purchased a golden elephant pin for her coat and then a tennis bracelet once the affair had become more serious. Those were heady times. He had divorced his wife—or rather, she had divorced him.

But something would have to be done about this current affair. Tiara was tired of the deception and playing his games.

The next time the bank statements came in the mail, always in his name, she steamed the envelope open and was surprised to see the amount of the balance. She was given the fairly generous sum of three thousand per month to run the house, pay the bills and still have a little left over for nails, hair and other essentials, but she hadn't realized just how much was actually there gathering interest. Lance had reached his dream of being a millionaire before he was forty. Tiara couldn't remember what her own dream had been.

Beneath Lance's name on the account was hers.

She had always known it was a joint account, but he had told her this was for income tax purposes only and not to go fooling around writing cheques and messing up the numbers. If she needed more, she had only to ask. The money, of course, was half hers as it stood, but it could all be hers if Lance met with an unfortunate accident.

"How does one find a hit man?" Tiara wondered aloud. "Do I advertise? Hang about in pool rooms?" She flipped open the Yellow Pages and looked up firearms dealers. So many to choose from, she thinks, scanning the names and trying the numbers listed. Most of them hung up on her or threatened to call the police. She then remembered the detective agency she'd hired to follow her husband. They had been successful beyond measure. Her call to Jake Digby met with a lengthy hesitation, and she stepped into the abyss. "This is so confidential, Mr. Digby, you won't believe it," she says. "You know that I am married to a very influential man so I don't want my name associated with anything illegal."

"Mrs. Ballestaire, hiring a hit man *is* illegal."

"Please, just casually drop a name and let me handle it," Tiara begs.

"Give me your number. Maybe Mr. Smith will call. Can't guarantee it."

Tiara hung up the phone and felt the thudding of her heart. It could be done but could she live with the remorse? Well, she thought, she'd damn well try.

Bunny looks up from her reading to gauge the others' reactions.

"Do you realize that on line seven you've called the husband Leland instead of Lance?" asks Jemima.

"No!" Bunny flushes. "I couldn't have."

"Freudian slip?" Mariah asks beneath raised eyebrows. She chuckles at Bunny's distress.

With her hand to her chest Bunny calms herself and laughs it off. "My oversight. And there's probably a lot more. Good eye, Jemima."

"Do you really think you'd have a hope in hell of getting a hit man that easily?"

"For the sake of this story, Mariah, I made it possible. I can't dwell on her problems in getting the guy. I simply want her to get on with it."

Sari puts up her hand. "You've mixed your tenses, Bunny. Some of it is in the past tense, some in the present," she says. "And I think I'd want her getting mad after reading the bank statement. She's got to have more reason to want her husband dead besides him having another woman."

"She's right," Jemima affirms. "She's got to be irate and sort of go off half-cocked."

"That's what she should be doing to what's-his-name ... Lance," Mariah says. "Make him half-cocked—not just kill the bastard."

Jemima chuckles behind her hand as Bunny collects her papers.

"All through with Bunny then?" Mariah says, reaching to the floor where her papers are stacked into four piles. "Only got four pages of *Derek of Dunston-Greene* done with my mother carping over my shoulder every minute."

"Your mother?" they reply in unison.

Mariah glowers. "You think I don't have a mother?"

"She's living with you?" Jemima asks.

"Why not?" Mariah demands defensively.

Bunny, resuming her role as hostess, says, "You must bring her by, Mariah. Maybe she'd like to sit with a cup of tea and listen to the readings."

"Are you out of your goddamn mind?" A lumpy mist sprays the manuscript in Mariah's tanned-leather hands. Like a camel, she has a tendency to spit when annoyed. "There's not a snowball's chance in hell." That concludes the discussion and Mariah snaps papers to each member of the group.

Bunny thinks she will invite Mariah's mother anyway. Maybe not for the group's readings but it would be nice perhaps to have tea with the dear old soul. Get her out of the house and away from her irascible daughter.

"The last we saw Derek and Willow," Mariah prompts, "they were riding together over the estate toward the mansion."

> Derek's steed picked his way carefully up the gravel path through the centuries-old pines of Dunston-Greene Manor as if he were aware of the precious cargo atop his silvery back. Although feeling faint from the throbbing in her ankle, Willow grasped the hard knot of saddle horn and hung on.

At a loud guffaw from Jemima, Mariah peers owlishly through the lenses balanced on her nose. Her mouth pinches like a drawstring bag. "What's the problem?"

Jemima waves her off. "Sorry, Mariah, but it conjured up a picture that just struck me as funny."

"Well, I fail to see the humour."

Bunny looks across to Jemima with a half-smile that could go either way, depending.

"I just pictured Willow," Jemima says, smirking, "desperately holding onto this knob she *thought* was the saddle horn."

In spite of herself Sari grins behind her hand. Bunny clicks her tongue in mock disapproval after stealing a look at Mariah.

"Are you through laughing at my expense?" Mariah waits dramatically for the tittering to stop before she holds up her manuscript and continues.

> Derek smelled the lavender in her sun-warmed hair and held her closer. He could see the top of the chapel on the grounds, which meant they would see the mansion from around the next bend. "How is your foot after the long ride?"

> Willow looked up at his ruggedly handsome face
> and replied, "Hurts like a bitch!"

"That's not what my copy reads," says Jemima, leaning over to examine Sari's paper. "What does yours say?"

"I was just seeing if you're paying attention," Mariah says with a rare show of good humour. She continues.

> Willow looked up at his ruggedly handsome face and replied, "I don't think I'll be able to walk on it. It's looking quite puffy." She held it out for Derek to observe and the action threw her off balance.
> "Whoa, little lady," he cautioned. "Stay up here with me. We're almost there." He halted the horse to point out the manor through the trees, then spurred the horse on to clear the woods so she could see the whole of the mansion grandly settled into the surrounding countryside.

As her story unfolds, Derek and Willow dismount and Willow is carried into the house past the butler and housemaid to rest, swathed in a cashmere throw, on the chaise longue. Derek trots off to inform his mother, Lady Dunston-Greene, that they have company.

"After listening to the work produced here tonight," says Jemima, "I think I'd like to write more than just my regular piece for the paper. I feel I'm being left behind, literarily speaking." She waits for a contradiction but none is forthcoming. "I could try ... well, not romance, because Mariah covers that, and Bunny, you've got mystery and adventure, and Sari, you're the poet. What does that leave?"

"Travel," Bunny suggests.

"Horror," says Sari.

"Dog stories," Mariah offers flippantly, "with happy endings."

"Well, I'll think on it for next time. Good writing, girls."

Minutes later they gather their belongings and head for the door, but Sari hangs back, reluctant to leave.

"Are you riding with Jemima, Sari?" Bunny asks. "Or is James coming to pick you up?"

Sari fiddles with the cuffs of her sweater and looks toward the open door. "I guess I'd better ride with Jemima," she says, but makes no move to catch her. "Or … could I …?"

"Could you what, dear? Do you want me to drive you?"

Sari avoids Bunny's eyes, and when she hears the cars start, she clutches her purse to her chest and runs into the night.

"Strange," Bunny says, closing and bolting the door before going to the bow window to watch the tail lights wink down the long driveway.

∽

JAMES SETTLES YOUNG MOONEY INTO the wooden playpen he has crammed into the motel room's empty coat closet. The baby is fretful and feverish, his new teeth cutting through swollen red gums. In less than thirty minutes James is to be at work at the twenty-four-hour Shell service station across the highway.

"Damn it, Mooney, lie down and go to sleep." James' patience is coming to an end. He slams the closet door on the child and finishes getting into his pants and the Shell shirt with *Ralph* monogrammed on the pocket. It still holds the acrid smell of its previous owner despite being washed in the sink.

The job pays $9 an hour. He works the graveyard shift from 10 p.m. to 6 a.m. but considers himself fortunate that he can run across the road and check on Mooney whenever things slow down. He also gets day-old donuts for a dime apiece at the attached truck stop café.

Mooney's exhausted cries finally taper off, and James tiptoes to the closet to tuck an extra bottle into the playpen, in case his son should wake in the night. He will set another in there when he gets home at six so he can catch another twenty minutes of sleep after the kid wakes up. Only when the insistent crying becomes too much will James roll off the bed to start his day. He will catch a few more hours for himself during Mooney's afternoon nap. Even with Mooney learning to stand against the furniture, the thrill James thought he would have raising his son by himself is waning. He had pictured himself teaching him to ride a motorcycle and shoot a mean game of pool, but now he is just praying that the kid won't learn to walk before he's two. But he sure as hell won't take him back to Sari, that quiet little emasculator. *Did you apply for that job at the shoe store? Did you get the unloading job at the recycling depot?* Turning those accusing doe eyes on him. He'll show her. This dead-end job at the Shell station is temporary. Tem-po-rary! He is going to Vancouver where he knows there's work for the taking. Hollywood North, they call it. He will get a job there as a stunt double or a set builder. Whatever. And he'll get a nanny for Mooney—a Filipina who cooks and cleans and looks after the baby (and his father) for a buck a day and says thank you for the privilege. Life will be very sweet very soon.

IV

BUNNY IS IN THE LIBRARY returning the decanter of scotch to the liquor cabinet when the phone rings. She carries her glass, ice cubes pinging against the crystal, to the coffee table. Only after she is seated and has downed a reassuring mouthful does she answer.

"Yes, Leland," she says listlessly, "my little group has gone." Bunny downs another mouthful between sentences. "Back to their little lives, their little families." She jabs at the speakerphone button until it works, then crosses the room to freshen her drink as Leland addresses his conversation to her back. "No, Leland," she yells, compensating for the distance, "I am not being disdainful. Compared to you, my darling, we are all little people with inconsequential lives." She closes the liquor cabinet with the toe of her shoe and thinks herself very adept as she also knocks back another shot of not-yet-cold scotch. "Yes, I am on the speakerphone and no, Leland, I am not drinking." She picks up the handset again, cutting off the artificial amplification. "How could a good scotch replace you, my sweet?" Bunny swings her feet onto the coffee table, crossing her legs at the ankles. "When *are* you coming home, anyway?" Her legs uncross, her feet drop to the floor. "When?" She reaches for the calendar and a pen. "That's lovely. For how long?" she asks brightly, then circles five days in a row. "Your line is fading, Leland. Where are you calling from? Hello? Hello?" She looks at the receiver for an answer then replaces it on the cradle. "Five whole days the first week of September. Well now, that calls for a celebratory drink." If she can still say *celebratory* without stumbling, she can certainly have another. "A celebratory celestial drink to celibacy." The amber-filled glass goes with her as she turns off the lights and climbs the stairs, depending heavily on the banister.

∞

MARIAH STUBS OUT HER CIGARETTE and sets the handbrake on her Honda. Looking through her mother's bedroom window, she's pleased to see the cover is on the birdcage. Sometimes when she's home this late, the damn thing is still up and squawking. Once Mariah is out of the car, the clear night air carries the sound of hollow laughter to her from the television inside the house. "Speaking of up and squawking," she mutters, pocketing her keys. A smack of heat hits her as she shoulders open the kitchen door. A red-hot element on the stove glows in the darkened room and beyond, in the warm spill of light from the table lamp in the living room, she sees her mother's head above the back of the chesterfield.

"Flora!" Mariah barks, peeling off her jacket as the heat from the room and a full-blown hot flash surge toward incendiary impact. Desperately she fans her face, her glasses fogging. "Flora!"

"What?"

"You left the burner on again."

"I did not."

"Come and look then." Mariah tosses her jacket onto a kitchen chair and stomps into the living room. "The burner is screaming hot."

"It wasn't me," Flora says, never taking her eyes from the television.

"OH FOR CHRISSAKE!" Mariah yells. "You make me so goddamn mad."

"I don't think Jay Leno will ever be as good as Johnny Carson."

Mariah rolls her eyes and throws her hands in the air, stomping back to the kitchen to turn off the burner. "Pointless, bloody pointless." She escapes to the back porch to cool off and wishes she'd brought her cigarettes.

Returning to the kitchen ten minutes later, Mariah sees that her mother is inside the closet hanging up her cast-off jacket. She's wearing only furry slippers, pantyhose and a tank top that ends at the waist. Her withered backside inside the nylon casing looks like failed bread dough. Mariah doesn't know whether to laugh or cry. "Flora?"

Hearing her name, Flora emerges from the closet but looks at her daughter as if seeing her for the first time. "You're—" she says as she closes the closet door. She approaches Mariah, hands reaching. "You're still a great lump of a girl, aren't you?"

Mariah grasps her mother's wrists, surprised at the thought that with little effort she could snap them like twigs. "It's almost eleven o'clock. Why don't you go to bed? You've been up since—what was it? 6:15?"

Flora's arms drop to her side, her mouth tightens. "I'm going to make a little something to eat."

With a dramatic sigh, Mariah goes in search of Flora's dressing gown, a striped cotton shift with a mismatched belt. She hears her mother rummaging through the contents of the fridge looking for the makings for a blue cheese and honey sandwich. Had she been banging through the cupboard it would have meant sardines and mango chutney on the menu. So far she's as constant as the Greenwich clock in her taste in sandwiches, only a slight variation every hundred years. But dinner is another matter. Anything is fair game: tuna and marmalade casserole, Chinese-Serbian stir-fry, chili with canned spaghetti. Mariah looks forward to the day it will be Axel, the African Grey, served up with Greek olives.

∽

ON THE WAY HOME FROM Bunny's, Jemima's car approaches the walled entrance to the trailer park where Sari lives. She asks to be let off at the gate but Jemima is uneasy with the look of the place. "Let me take you to the door. You can't be too careful at night, even in a town like this."

"No, no. I'm fine. I need the walk."

Jemima stops the car, its headlights throwing harsh shadows along the pitted blacktop road. Slinking through the high-beams, a fat-bellied cat carries dinner home. "No way you're walking into that place by yourself." Sari's partly open door snaps shut as Jemima suddenly lurches the car into the compound. "Yours is which one, Sari? Number twelve? Thirteen?"

"There is no thirteen." Sari points to the driveway as they approach. "That's me, twelve."

The trailer is dark although the porch light is on. And Jemima watches another resident cat scurry beneath the mobile. "James not home?"

The question has been asked.

Now Sari cannot muster the strength to unclasp her hands and get out of the car. Her chin won't lift from her chest, her legs will not respond. Even breathing is an effort, something she must think about doing. *In, out. In, out.* And it hurts.

A chained dog stands spread-legged at number fourteen, yapping at the idling car. The door to the trailer behind the dog opens and the silhouette of a man fills the doorway. He yells at the dog, which ignores him.

"Sari? What's the matter?" Jemima asks with concern. Sari's chin trembles and fat tears roll, leaving shining tracks down her face. "Sweetie, what's wrong?"

Sari gulps, holding back, but Jemima's genuine concern is too much, and the racking sobs that have been lodged like a burr behind her ribs are finally released.

Jemima is alarmed at the pain she has caused the girl. She should have just let her off as Sari asked. Now she's hip-deep in misery. "Better tell me what's going on," she says, resigned to hearing a litany of woes. She's quite used to this—her daughters-in-law phoning to tell her how big the bills are, their children's need for orthodontics, the car in for repairs. She pats Sari on the back, offering a comforting, "There, there," and pulls a crushed Kleenex box from beneath the driver's seat. "What's happened?"

Sari blows her nose into the wad of tissue, folds it and wipes her eyes with the dry part. She's not nearly finished crying, Jemima feels, but getting her stopped for now is good. "Do you want me to come into the house with you?" she asks, suspicious of the neighbour who is still evident in the doorway of number fourteen.

Sari shakes her head and her long blonde hair swings forward, hiding her face. Jemima flips back the hair and turns Sari's face toward her.

"Atta girl," Jemima says, as Sari attempts a smile.

The girl takes in a ragged breath and straightens her shoulders in some sort of resolve. Later Jemima will tell Joe that "all of a sudden this sodden mass of weeping child just pulled herself up by her own bootstraps."

"James is gone!" Sari says bitterly, pounding her fists on her bony thighs. "James has not been home since last Thursday." Her legs will be bruised in the morning. "And," she continues, "the son of a bitch took Mooney." Her good resolve and her bootstraps collapse. "He took my baby," she says, her chin quivering. She pulls another handful of tissue from the box.

"Took him where?"

Sari shakes her head slowly, her face lost in the Kleenex.

"You don't know where he's taken him?"

"No," comes the muffled response.

"Did you call the police?"

"I've called the police, his mother, his brothers, the police again. And again. And again. Nothing."

"He can't just disappear," Jemima says, disbelieving.

"He has."

"My God, Sari, why didn't you tell us?"

"It wasn't your problem."

"But we're your friends," she says, as if that could move mountains. "Aren't we?"

"I couldn't. You'd all look at me differently." She gathers up her papers, which had fallen to the floor, then opens the car door. She slips out without another word and runs up the steps to her trailer.

Jemima stays until the lights in the mobile come on and Sari gives her a wave, then she backs the Buick out the same way she came in. The man in number fourteen has closed his door, but he hasn't gone inside. She can see the white of his tee-shirt in the darkness as he sits on the bottom step, the dog between his knees.

⁓

"YOU'RE LATE TONIGHT," JOE CALLS from the bedroom as Jemima closes the kitchen door behind her. He's propped up in bed, newspapers scattered across his legs, the television blaring.

"You wouldn't believe—" she begins, sitting on the bed to remove her shoes.

"Yankees won," he says. "Beat Chicago 4–3 in the tenth inning."

"Sari's husband has taken the baby and—"

"I don't know what the hell they're paying the umpires for. They made a call at first that—"

"—the police can't find them."

"Whatt'a'ya talking about, police?"

"For God's sake, Joe, I'm trying to tell you something," she says, cranking down the volume on the television.

He crosses his arms over his chest and sighs. "Go ahead, Mother. I'm all ears."

"Sari's husband took the baby and ran away."

"Why?"

"I don't know," she says irritably as she unfastens a stocking and rolls it down her leg. "I didn't ask her *why*."

He pulls together the newspapers, shuffling them into a workable order. "Musta had a good reason." He makes a production of folding the paper.

"Don't you get it? He stole her son."

"His kid, too, is he not?" He drops the newspaper onto the floor beside the bed, hits the television remote and reaches over to turn off the lamp on his night table.

She throws up her hands in exasperation and pivots on her heel to return to the kitchen. By the glow of the refrigerator light, she scoops rum and raisin ice cream into a bowl and, from the bucket in the pantry, tops it with a dripping spoonful of liquid honey. She needs comfort food at a time like this.

⁓

JEMIMA STIRS, FEELING FOR JOE with her foot, but his side of the bed is empty. She lifts her head to see the clock and is surprised to read it's 9:12. She hasn't slept this late since—since she can't remember when. The cup of coffee Joe left for her is room temperature. She stretches and yawns, luxuriating in the summer-smelling cotton sheets, but guilt soon takes over and she eases out of bed to carry the cold coffee to the kitchen. The back door is open to the morning air and through the doorway she can see Joe working in the shop. She waves to him and he returns the salute. She'll make something nice for his lunch. Maybe he can test that lovely Lima Bean Casserole from the *Watkins Cook Book*. She'll have time for that. Only has to bake twenty-five minutes. And a plum cobbler for dessert. Plums are ready now. Jemima makes a mental note to ask Bunny for some of her windfall apples so she can try making apple cider again. Her first effort was a disaster, she recalls as she pads to the bedroom to get dressed. Joe said it was more like rust remover than apple cider. Maybe she won't tinker with the recipe this time.

It's 9:45 before last night's incident with Sari revisits Jemima. She'll have to phone everybody to let them know. It doesn't count as gossip if she's looking to help the girl. Nothing in her newspaper column, of course, but friends should be aware of Sari's fragile condition. They could be extra nice to her during the week and especially at their next meeting. She and Joe could have her here for dinner, and why, she scolds herself, didn't she think of it sooner?

※

"YOOHOO, JOE! LUNCH," JEMIMA YODELS from the back porch. She returns to the table and surveys the casserole, shaking her head at it, convinced that Joe will turn thumbs down. It called for dried lima beans but she substituted frozen. It won't matter, dried or frozen. There's no disguising a lima bean. She just won't tell him.

"What the hell is it?" Joe asks a few minutes later, pushing the mass with his fork.

"Don't you think the colours are nice? Pale green against the red of the ketchup?"

"I recognize the bread crumbs but what's the rest?" He plunges the fork into it and resolutely sticks it into his mouth. He scowls as he judges what he's eating. "Is this lima beans?"

"Don't speak with your mouth full, dear," Jemima admonishes, ducking her head as she samples the food on her own plate. "There's a lovely plum cobbler for dessert." Perhaps for her column she'd better go instead with the Chow Mein Meat Loaf. She is trying to give her reading public economical meals but maybe a lima bean casserole is carrying it too far. "Do you know, Joe, the *Watkins Cook Book* has a recipe for soup from leftover cereal? You take two cups cooked cereal and add a quart of milk and—"

Joe holds up his hand to stop the process. "Colour for this stuff is a five," he says, answering her question before it's asked. "Taste is a ..."

"A what, Joe?" she pumps, then looks up to see the change of expression on his face. "Oh, it's not *that* bad," she says.

Joe's face has sagged and his fork falls, clattering to the table then to the floor. His great square hand clutches at nothing and he tilts forward, mouth open.

"Very funny," she laughs.

Joe sounds like he has a slow leak. The air keeps coming and coming and with it the pale green and red casserole. His hands drop to his lap and he tips to the side, propped up only by the arms of his wheelchair.

"Joe? Joe?" she repeats, scraping back her chair. "Oh my God! JOE!" She shakes his shoulder and his head jogs with the movement. Quickly she wheels the chair into the bedroom next to the neatly made bed. She attempts to transfer him from the chair but she cannot hold onto him and together they fall across the bed. She scrambles off and around to the opposite side to tug him across the quilt. Once he's arranged from corner to corner, his head on her side of the bed, his feet on his, she tells him, "It'll be okay, Joe. Have a rest now." Jemima takes off her apron as she dogtrots to the kitchen telephone. She finds it difficult to see the numbers for the ambulance.

⁂

SARI SLIPS SOUNDLESSLY FROM THE bed, picks up her terrycloth robe from the floor and wraps it around herself before stealing a look at Ace, one thick arm flung over his eyes. Satisfied there's no break in the steady rhythm of his gentle snoring, she gathers up her beauty salon clothes and tiptoes into the adjoining bathroom, locking the door behind her.

"Idiot," she mutters, lowering the toilet seat and flushing his floating condom.

When she comes out, he's propped against the pillows drinking coffee from James's favourite mug.

"Coffee here for you," he says, throwing back her side of the covers and patting the bed. His tanned hand is dark against the white sheets. "I don't know whether you like cream and sugar, but I will for tomorrow."

Swiftly she coils a rubber band around the tail of her damp, freshly braided hair, hating that self-satisfied look they get, that cat-and-canary look. "There's no tomorrow, Ace," she says and returns to the bathroom, sitting on the toilet to tie the laces of the sensible nursing shoes she wears at the hair salon. When she comes back, Ace's smile has been replaced by a wounded look as though she's stolen his marbles. She grabs the cup of coffee, blowing on the surface to test the heat. He's found the jar of instant and it's double strength.

Ace rolls the blankets down to barely cover his groin and sucks in his stomach, puffing out his woolly chest. He works up a smile. "What do you mean there's no tomorrow? Like for you and me?"

"No. Like for you." She feels mean this morning. "There's no future in this, Ace. Once is enough." *Once is one too many.* Her uniform smells of permanent wave solution. She really must do the wash.

He flings back the covers, spilling coffee onto the pillow in his haste to stand.

She clears a spot on the steamed bathroom mirror and applies her lipstick while Ace bangs around in the bedroom, dressing in the clothes he dispatched onto the floor. She is going to be late leaving for work and she'll have to run partway, but after last night she is too sore to run far.

"Hey," he says, "you didn't seem to mind me last night."

That is true, but then last night he was just suddenly there, leaning against the door frame and looking warm and edible.

"You crying?" he had asked from the bottom step of number fourteen as the tail lights of Jemima's departing car disappeared over a rise. "Somebody give you a bad time?"

"My friend just dropped me off from my writing group."

"Oh, you're a writer, eh?" he said engagingly, following her into her trailer. He issued a stay order to his dog, who dropped to the porch, and closed the door behind him with his back. "I thought I'd write me a book on motorcycles or the manly sport of golf some day." He gave the place a quick once-over before he asked the question he already knew the answer to. "Your old man back yet?" There had been no laundry on the line, no diapers. He'd even checked her garbage can and as far as he could see, she hadn't eaten anything but Shreddies.

She couldn't meet his eyes. "Not yet." He waited while she left the room to wash her face. Her nose was red and her eyes trailed mascara.

"How long's he gonna be gone?"

She re-entered the room and shrugged her response, asking if he would like a beer. There was still one bottle in the fridge.

"A pretty little gal like you shouldn't be left all alone," he said, accepting the beer.

Now how many corny movies had that line been in? she wondered, almost smiling. She slid him a look and found he wasn't too bad. Laundered tee-shirt over a well-built chest, nice butt, good clean teeth. His size made the trailer look small as he circled, checking it out as if to catch James lurking nearby.

"Pretty quiet here without that baby?" he probed.

She didn't care to discuss James and Mooney with someone with whom she'd only had a passing acquaintance, so she sidestepped his queries by asking if he'd finished working on his motorcycle. For months he'd been taking it apart in the living room of his double-wide. Once he had come over to ask James for a spoke wrench. James collects china, so his tool box held only porcelain bonder and a clamp, but he'd gone over with Mooney on his hip to help—to thump the tires and do the guy thing.

"Sit down, Ace." He sat close enough to Sari on the same sofa that she could see the dog hairs on the legs of his jeans. He smelled like fresh air. "That girl finally move out?" Sari asked. "The one you were living with?" James had told her that the "girl" was actually an older woman in black leather aspiring to be a motorcycle mama.

"Toni? Left a long time ago. She wanted to hit the open highway on the back of my Harley but the damn thing still isn't up and running." He shrugged Toni off and tipped back his bottle of Labatt.

"Well," Sari began wearily, toeing off her shoes, curling her legs onto the couch, "it's been a long day and I have to work tomorrow."

Ace finished the beer, placing the bottle on the table next to the arm of the couch. "Before I go," he said, pulling her bare foot toward him, "let me give you a foot rub."

She protested until he actually started, then said to herself, *What the hell*, and turned to put both feet into his lap. She dropped her head against the arm of the sofa and closed her eyes, clamping her arms over her chest. She woke ten minutes later when the massage went beyond her ankles, but by then she didn't need too much convincing—a little neighbourliness in a lonely world. He was a distraction against the panicked feeling of waking at 3:15 or 4:10 thinking she heard the baby crying. James could go straight to hell. She just wanted her son back. She remembered Mooney as angelic, never cranky or unmanageable. The perfect child—and she desperately wanted him home. Somebody knows where he is. *Yes, officer, it's me again. Any news? He's ten months old now, probably needs a haircut. Yes, red hair, brown eyes. May be walking.* Oh God, and I'm not there to see it. *Have you checked the hospitals? Nothing?*

∽

NOW IN THE COLD LIGHT of day they are both dressed and avoiding one another. Ace places his empty cup on the counter and leaves without looking back.

"Same to you," Sari says, dumping the remains of her coffee over the dishes in the sink. She grabs her purse and slams out the door, locking it before bounding down the stairs. Her braid bouncing on her back, she runs until out of sight of the trailer park, then slows to a brisk walk. She has two tints and three haircuts before 10:30 at the Belle Mode Beauty Bar, then a rinse, set, and manicure on Old Lady Cannell at Grimaldi Sisters Funeral Home this afternoon. Whatever it takes, the Grimaldis told the Cannell family, Sari Button will do. Sari wonders who will do *her* when the time comes. She'd like ... a polished aluminum coffin with a champagne-coloured silk lining, she thinks, and a brown paper bag over her head. She'd also like her middle finger pointing rigidly upward. She's enjoying her unusual little mean streak.

In silent disapproval, the owner of the Belle Mode, Mrs. Bahadoorsingh, hands Sari a note before she can catch her breath. Sari checks the clock before looking at the note. She has one minute to read it. The note says, *Call Bunny.*

"Sari, child," Mrs. Bahadoorsingh smiles tightly, "Mrs. Tomaso needs your attention."

Bunny's call will have to wait. "Morning, Mrs. Tomaso," Sari says evenly, bracing herself for the woman's usual complaints about her chronic toenail fungus and her exultation in Mr. Tomaso's lingering impotence. Mrs. Tomaso just can't see what the big deal is about sex—she'd be satisfied with a piece of peanut butter pie with double-vanilla ice cream. "You want the same new-penny colour, Mrs. T?"

∽

ACROSS TOWN, AS SARI GREETS Mrs. Tomaso, Bunny and Gerda are having a row in the kitchen. Bunny is waving a shrunken pink sweater in Gerda's knotted face. "How many is this? How many?"

"Ach, who has time to count? Not me, Missy," Gerda grouses, dismissing Bunny with her one good eye.

"This is the third cashmere sweater you've ruined. How many times have I told you they go to the cleaners?" Bunny is sure Gerda is deliberately setting out to ruin them.

Gerda flaps her hands as if preparing for liftoff but remains grounded, muttering as she slops away in her broken shoes.

"Don't you dismiss me. I'm not going to disappear." Bunny, still grasping the matted sweater, cuts off Gerda's escape. "You are the one who is going to disappear." And raising a finger to the end of Gerda's cauliflower nose, she announces, "You're fired!"

Gerda snaps, biting down on Bunny's accusing finger.

With a surprised shriek, Bunny yanks her finger from Gerda's clenched jaw, bringing the housekeeper's upper dentures with it. They skitter, grinning, across the floor to end up beneath the butcher block island. Bunny whisks her tooth-dented finger into the closest bathroom and plunges her hand under cold running water. Finding no broken skin, she washes thoroughly with soap and hot water. Then with the pink sweater under her arm she marches back to the kitchen where Gerda is pushing her wayward and now cracked teeth into her apron pocket.

"Za Mister vill pay for new one," Gerda says defiantly, untying her apron and rolling it into a ball. She clamps her remaining natural bottom teeth over her top lip, looking very much like a Pekinese.

"Out! Out!" Bunny orders, swinging open the back door.

Gerda's chin quivers, and behind her wire glasses her rheumy eyes fill with tears that spill down her cheeks. "I vas so happy here." She shuffles past Bunny's arm, which is now stiffly pointing to the bicycle tilted on its kickstand in the backyard. Gerda mops her face with the apron, then clings onto the railing to remove her broken shoes and replace them with the red rubber boots standing stoutly on the porch. She marches down the steps without looking back.

Bunny's arm gives out and falls limply to her side. She can just hear the phone calls now—"Delores, dear, this is Mother deLore. Poor Gerda is sobbing in my conservatory about being fired. Enlighten me, Delores." The name "Bunny" would never cross Mother deLore's disapproving lips. Then Leland will call, huffing and puffing about Gerda being "family and anyway, what the hell do you think you're doing? Did you get Mother's permission? What's the old woman to do, live on the streets and beg?" Not dear old Mother, of course, but Gerda, she edits, and realizes she is thinking in misplaced modifiers.

She watches the old nanny cock a leg over the bicycle, stuff her apron with its pocketful of teeth into the handlebar basket and rock the bike off the kickstand. *God, all that's needed now is a Rottweiler to chase her down the road.* "Gerda!" Bunny calls after her. "Come back! I'll make us a nice pot of tea." Bunny follows down the stairs and tries to catch up, but Gerda pumps around to the front of the house and Bunny is left watching her zigzagging down the driveway.

V

SARI HAS A FEW MINUTES between customers and dials Bunny's number. It can't be that she wants an appointment at the Belle Mode. Not here. "Hi, Bunny. You were looking for me? It's Sari."

Bunny has almost forgotten why she'd called. "I think I'm losing it, Sari. Too much going on," she says, flustered. "I called earlier to tell you Jemima's husband, Joe, is in hospital."

"Oh, no! What happened?"

"Jemima says a stroke brought on by her lima bean casserole."

Sari pauses, gathering her thoughts. "Is that possible?"

"I don't think so. He's in pretty tough shape, but so's Jemima and I thought she might need a shoulder. I'm going over after lunch. She's waiting around in the hospital for word. I think one of her boys is on the way from Nelson but until he gets here—"

"Did you call Mariah?"

"I did. Ended up having a spirited, mostly one-sided conversation with her mother. Mariah is working a dog show somewhere."

"I'll get over there after work. Will you phone and let me know if Jemima's still going to be there?" From the shampoo sinks Mrs. Bahadoorsingh taps her watch face with pink lacquered nails. "I won't go see her husband because I don't know him." Sari turns her back on the owner and faces the street. "Give her my love." She settles the phone on the cradle and watches the passing cars until Mrs. Bahadoorsingh clears her throat, noisily interrupting Sari's preoccupation. "Yeah, yeah, I'm coming," she says, jamming her hands into her uniform pockets.

While Sari applies the thick paste to Miss Mitford's thinning hair, Ace, her neighbour and one-night stand, is approaching her trailer. He slides an expired credit card between the door and the lock until it clicks. "You should get a better lock, Mrs. Button," he says, giving the door a push. He picks up the cardboard box at his feet, checks around the neighbouring mobiles for prying eyes, then enters the trailer, booting the door closed behind him.

&

MARIAH SWELTERS IN HER SERVICEABLE dog show clothes—tweed skirt, oxfords and leather apron—her cheeks flushed and upper lip damp. She wipes her fogged glasses before spraying the final fixative to the puff of white hair ballooning above the shaved pink legs and pompom ankles of the miniature poodle known as North Shore Terraces' Sunshine Jubilation. The dog is in a vile mood, lips bared over freshly brushed teeth.

"You nip me again and I'll shove this hairbrush up your arse." Mariah and the dog snarl at one another until the dog's owner, Chloe Hook, arrives at a trot, proffering the leash she has been searching for in her van.

"I found Juba's lead under the seat and guess what else?" she says, waving a studded dog collar. "It's the one we've been looking for since God knows when." Chloe turns her attention to the dog under Mariah's care. "Juba, you look beautiful," she says, cooing into the dog's perfect face. "You want this lovely green collar, sweetie, or the gold one?"

Mariah checks to see if she's the "sweetie" Chloe is referring to. When the dog doesn't offer an opinion, Mariah does, nodding in the direction of the emerald green collar.

Chloe worries a hand through her own bleached white hair then tucks combs into the upsweep to keep the brittle strands from breaking loose. Next she digs into a travel bag, shaking the clanging contents to one end, jouncing the bag until her hand surfaces with a belt for herself to match Juba's collar. She is driving Mariah to distraction, fussing, fussing, fussing, but Mariah continues to primp the dog, staying clear of her. Their biggest rows always happen at this time, just before the poodle judging.

Finally Juba's category is announced and Chloe tightens the green studded belt on her white jumpsuit. "Give us a kiss for luck, sweetie." Mariah dutifully pecks Chloe's cheek, keeping her head low after the contact should anyone have seen the affectionate display. Chloe breathes deeply before her green deck shoes begin skipping along the concrete walk leading into the ring. Jubilation, trailing at the end of the leash, suddenly skids to a stop and hunches over, his groomed tail held high. Chloe looks elsewhere until he's finished.

"You did that on purpose, you feckless little fur-piece," Mariah grinds as she follows behind, pulling a plastic bag over her hand to scoop up his mid-path droppings. She tosses the bag and its warm contents into a garbage can, its lid left swinging long after Mariah has left to repack the equipment.

⁓

"I'M BUYING," CHLOE ANNOUNCES AS she glides the van's side door closed on the caged dog. When she slides behind the wheel, she pins the dog's winning blue ribbon onto the sun visor before starting the vehicle and backing out of the parking stall. "Good judging today, don't you think, sweetie? And Juba was on his best behaviour." She adjusts the mirror to see into the back. "You were a good boy, Juba," she calls over her shoulder. "Mama's good boy."

"Of course, the grooming played no part in it," Mariah charges, rolling down her window before lighting a cigarette.

Chloe pinches her mouth disapprovingly and fans her face, but she thinks better of making disparaging remarks about the perils of second-hand smoke and instead forces congeniality. "Oh, honey, you were wonderful, too." She squeezes Mariah's chapped hand in hers. Mariah's fist relaxes and her fingers entwine with Chloe's on the bench seat. "Do you want to go out for dinner or eat in?"

Mariah, feeling more appreciated for her efforts, responds less rancorously. "In. How about Chinese?"

Chloe makes a face.

"Italian? Mexican?"

"Greek," Chloe says decisively, withdrawing her hand to change lanes. "Wouldn't you love to go to Greece, sweetie? All those white-washed houses set against the blue, blue ocean." Chloe's thoughts drift to a sidewalk cafe in Salonika where she counts the waves polishing a sugar-sand beach. "Sorry. What did you say?" she asks, reluctantly pulling herself back. "I was having an out-of-body."

"Greek's fine," Mariah repeats, "but you have to order. All I know is ouzo."

Chloe casts a mischievous look.

"What?" Mariah says suspiciously.

"Are you staying over?"

Mariah throws her hands in the air. "I don't know. It's my mother."

"Tell her you're staying at a friend's," Chloe says before bursting into her braying laugh. "Tell her I'm having a pyjama party."

"It's not going to be that easy." Mariah feels a flush rise from her chest and she bellows her shirt in the breeze from the open window. She takes one last drag on the cigarette and drops it onto the street. "You don't know my mother."

"And whose fault is that?"

Mariah hears the elastic snap of opposing wills. Two middle-aged menopausal women, aging lovers—one closeted, one with a who-gives-a-shit-attitude. "She wouldn't understand."

"What's to understand? If she doesn't like it, she lumps it." Chloe signals left, gunning the van across two lanes of oncoming traffic to pull in before the blue-stuccoed Greek Taverna Take-Out. After setting the handbrake, she pulls down the rear view mirror, aligning it to reflect the state of her lipstick. "Anyway, mothers have a sixth sense about that sort of thing." She applies a slick layer of Frosted Apricot. "Mine did."

"You were living with what's-her-name then. It was no big secret."

"And you're no big secret. You think people don't know?" she chimes. "Two old gals making goo-goo eyes over the backside of a poodle? Or holding hands in the park? Come on, Mariah. Let go and enjoy life." The door bongs as Chloe climbs out. She shuts it with deliberation then leans in through her open window. "Nobody cares, you know." She blows Mariah an elaborate kiss as she crosses the pitted parking lot.

Mariah scouts the area through her black-rimmed glasses then waggles her fingers in response. Once Chloe is inside the restaurant, she reaches for the comfort of her cigarettes.

∽

SARI'S BACK HURTS DOWN LOW. She guesses it's from shifting old Mrs. Cannell's dead weight, and now she's too tired to even be amused at this unintended pun. The Grimaldi Sisters Funeral Home has all the modern amenities but no extra help for fetching and carrying, and this leaves Sari to do her own positioning, so although the late Mrs. Cannell was just a bag of bones in the aftermath of her stomach cancer, Sari still had a real struggle adjusting her on the portable table to get her head near the sink. The Cannell family wanted her looking her best—a slate-blue rinse and keenly honed waves for Mama's hair and three—not two but three—coats of Silver Twinkle nail enamel for her old-ivory nails. As a result, Sari didn't get her finished until forty-five minutes before the family's visitation at the funeral parlour. But the old lady looked almost cheery, and the Grimaldis, who normally ration their praise, were almost unrestrained: "Oh, well done, Mrs. Button," they had trilled. ·

Now Sari plants one foot before the other on her way home, her purse strap biting into her shoulder. Gripped in a plastic sack is her dinner, a deli purchase of cold meatball stew and another of grapefruit coleslaw. There'll be enough leftovers for lunch tomorrow.

Keeping vigil from behind his drapes, Ace sees her nearing the battered green mailboxes at the entrance to the trailer park. When she comes away with no mail, his heart hurts at her hunched shoulders and scuffling step. "I think we're going to make her day, Mudd, old son," he reports to the dog stretched out on the sofa. Ace's pulse picks up as Sari climbs her stairs and unlocks her door. It whumps shut behind her and he stares at its brown peeling surface, his happiness bubbling into a chuckle. She'll be so surprised, so grateful, she'll probably jump his bones before he even has time to get his clothes off.

The peeling brown door flashes open again and Sari leaps through it and onto the porch. She looks frantically around the trailer park, then abruptly stands stock still, her hand gripping the railing, long braid slung over her breast. She turns slowly, giving Ace's trailer a withering look. Then shoeless, she marches down her steps and across the untended patch of number fourteen's lawn, avoiding Mudd's poop. Ace drops the curtain, his heart drumming on his ribs. The dog's head lifts at the sound of her feet on his stoop.

She gives the door two fast jabs with her elbow. Bam! Bam! The dog's nails skid across the floor and he hits the entrance barking. Ace calls off the animal before peeking out.

Sari stiff-arms her way inside. "What the fuck do you think you're doing?" she yells, dancing on her toes toward him.

"Wha-wha ...?" He backs up at her approach. The dog, seeking safer ground, jumps the dismembered Harley and slinks into the bedroom. This is a side of Sari that Ace has not seen. He didn't know she could yell, let alone use words like that.

"You broke into my home," she says, nailing each word onto his chest with her index finger. "You had no business ..." She feels her chin quiver and her eyes puddle up. She thumps him one more time, then runs, wanting to be in her own place by the time her anger turns to tears. Since she hadn't bothered to close up her place before her assault, her run up the steps and inside is unimpeded. She slams the door, leaning against it for support as she storms her outrage. She sinks to her haunches, head back against the wood.

When she's feeling less fractious, she wipes her nose on her shirttail and sniffs back the tears. That's when she becomes aware of a terrible odour and looks around for the source. It's coming from her right foot. Her tears start anew, this time more from feeling sorry for herself than from anger. "Stupid. Stupid. Stupid," she blubbers, thrusting the offending foot as far away as possible. From this angle, sitting on the floor, she can't see the whole of the table, just the tips of the unlit blue candles and the empty wine glasses. *He had no business doing that.*

When she first walked in to encounter the beautifully set table with the posy of flowers at her place and good warm smells filling the room, she lost it. Her purse went one way and her plastic bag of dinner another. "James? James?" she called as she ran into the bedroom, then into Mooney's room, but nothing had changed. The blue bear in Mooney's crib still waited.

What kind of a life is this? She rolls her head against the door. *Alone and tired and broke with cold dog shit between my toes.*

∽

"I MADE IT," MARIAH SAYS, out of breath from her sprint from the car. "Out of town for the weekend so had to do my writing today and the damned printer was slow," she explains to the group assembled in Bunny's home for its regular Tuesday session. She sprawls into the moss green leather recliner. "What's with all the long faces? Somebody die?"

Bunny, who is standing behind Jemima's chair, flashes her hands at Mariah, signalling her to be quiet.

"What?"

The weight of Bunny's hands on Jemima's shoulders is comforting. "Joe's had a stroke," she explains patiently.

Mariah urges her glasses up the bridge of her perspiring nose. "Who's Joe?"

Bunny clicks her tongue in censure. "For crying out loud, Mariah—Jemima's husband."

"Oh, that Joe." Mariah now tries mirroring the expressions on the faces around her, only succeeding in looking moderately sombre. "Sorry to hear it." She unpacks her paper-clipped pages, her handout for the evening critique. "Is he okay?" she remembers to ask.

Jemima turns her face up to bestow a quick smile on Bunny, who moves away to take her seat and pour from the sherry decanter gracing the antique coffee table. "I thought we could all use a bucker-upper," she offers, giving Jemima the first glass and a flowered cocktail napkin.

Jemima takes it, then finally answers Mariah's inquiry. "Joe's holding his own."

Mariah would love to reply uncharitably, *That's true of most men, isn't it?—holding their own.* She bites her tongue instead and mutters, "Give him my regards."

Jemima nods, knowing Joe would say, *Mariah who?* "Thanks for looking in on Joe, everyone." She purposefully ignores Mariah who hasn't, of course, been near the hospital. "Sari sat with me again during her lunch break yesterday. She walked all the way over from the Belle Mode." Jemima leans to pat Sari's arm affectionately but stops when she notices the bruise pooling around the knob of bone. "What did you do to your elbow?"

Twisting her arm to look, Sari is surprised to discover how discoloured it is. "I'm getting careless, I guess."

"You should be more mindful, dear," Jemima advises. "And you should eat something. My God, Sari, you're thin as a rake! Why don't you come for dinner tomorrow after I see Joe?" Before Sari can respond, Jemima claps her hands to her head, "Then again," she says morosely, "maybe you'd better not. After all, it was my stupid casserole—"

"No, it wasn't," Bunny contradicts.

"Yes, it was," Jemima insists. "It was my cooking."

Mariah scowls, eyes flitting from face to face. "What the hell are you talking about?"

"Jemima thinks her lima bean casserole gave Joe his stroke," Bunny says.

"It probably was," Mariah mutters under her breath.

If anyone hears, they pay no notice.

"Anyway, I have nothing to read tonight," Jemima resumes, "as I didn't really have the time, what with Joe and all. And then my son from Nelson stayed two days to make sure his dad was out of danger. I didn't get any writing done."

"Sari, you want to go first then?" Bunny asks.

"I don't have much either and I haven't made copies." Sari works forward in her chair to brace her elbows on her knees. In steady hands she holds the paper but doesn't refer to the printed words. "I don't have a title for these. I'm not so good at labels."

> Gutted hog on flowered lino,
> Wrested joints akimbo.
> On calloused hands and knees he labours
> assembling scattered pieces,
> hands and knees that last night
> laboured to make love.

Bunny breaks the silence that follows to ask her to read it again. After it's repeated, there's another pause before Bunny asks, "Can you explain what it means?" She taps her temple with her forefinger. "You know I have problems grasping that stuff."

Sari stares at the paper in her lap. "I have three more."

"Better explain this one first, I think." Bunny searches the group, hoping someone will jump in to offer suggestions.

"A hog is a motorcycle," Sari explains solemnly. "It's about a guy taking it apart in his living room."

"I don't get it," Mariah admits, folding her arms tightly against her chest.

Sari crumbles the paper into a ball. "You're probably right, Mariah. It's not very good."

"I didn't say it wasn't good—just that I don't get it. Poetry is so … so emotional."

Bunny gets to her feet quickly to top up the glasses with sherry. "There's more if we need it." When she's seated again, she lifts her glass in a toast. "To Joe," she says. The others join in the salute.

"To Mooney," Sari adds, which has the group suddenly nose-down in their drinks. "It's okay that you know," she states, lifting the blanketing silence. There's not much that goes on in each of their lives now that the rest don't know about. Jemima swore them to secrecy the morning after she drove Sari home, feeling it was in Sari's best interest that everyone know about James kidnapping the baby.

Sari knocks back her third sherry, thankful Jemima will be driving. "Have you any idea how painful it is to lose your child?" she asks, eyes down, fingers knotted in her lap. "I can only pray his father is looking after him." She directs a sidelong glance at Bunny. "Do you think Mooney still remembers me?"

"Your baby remembers you, Sari. You're his mother."

"I don't know," Sari admits. "Babies aren't like dogs, are they, Mariah? Dogs don't forget. I wonder about babies. Do you think way back in their minds somewhere there's a memory of the first face they see? The voice they've heard since conception?" No one is about to interrupt Sari's longest freewheeling monologue that isn't manuscript-dependent. And she still has the floor. Bunny pours the last of the decanter into Sari's glass, electing to wait until she's finished before fetching another bottle. Sari picks up her glass, calming her hands with the task of holding the contents steady. "I'm sure you all know Mooney was—" she sips her sherry then corrects herself, "—*is* not my first child. You've all been in this town long enough to know the whole story. The big news of the day!" She sweeps her free hand to suggest a banner headline. "Grievous Error: Dairy Princess Abdicates Throne."

Mariah clears her throat and pointedly looks at her watch, but Sari misses the signal.

"That's right, the princess was a little pregnant." Sari catches the last dribble of sherry on her tongue from the side of her upturned glass. "On a dark and stormy night," she says theatrically, "I was sent away to my cousin's farm." She holds out the empty glass for a refill but the bottle is empty. "To cut to the chase, I had the most beautiful little girl." She closes her eyes, remembering the birth, and smiles. "Peach fuzz on her tiny head, ten perfect fingers, ten perfect toes. Fingernails like new moons. Do you know that babies at two weeks old recognize their mother's smell and the mother can identify her baby minutes after it's born? How 'bout that?" She opens her eyes and sighs, sitting taller, inspecting her still empty glass. "I held her for a lifetime, for the blink of an eye, then she was gone. Signed away. Given away. Stolen away."

Jemima sniffles into her cocktail napkin.

"Pony," Sari continues. "That's the name I gave her. When I went home again, it was as if it never happened. It was a forbidden subject. But I got around it. 'Think we should get a *Pony* for Celia?' That's my little sister," she explains. "Always hoped they would ask me, 'Penny for your thoughts,' and I could answer, 'Thinking about a beautiful *Pony* I saw for just a moment.' But nobody asked."

"Excuse me, but I have five pages of work here," Mariah says, fanning her papers.

Sari falls silent. The interruption breaks the spell and the others shift in their chairs, quite ready to unmire themselves from Sari's misery.

"And, yes, it's true, dogs don't tend to forget," says Mariah, lighting a cigarette, "and neither will your boy." She smiles tightly to back up her statement then, shifting the cigarette to the corner of her mouth, hands each person her five pages of manuscript. "You'll recall that Derek had taken Willow to the mansion where she met Lady Dunston-Greene. The two women got along famously until Derek left the room, then Lady Dunston-Greene turned on poor Willow."

"I think we said at the time that your plot seemed a touch cliché," Jemima reminds her.

"Cliché or not, it stays. The story will build on that scene—the downtrodden Willow, the high and mighty Lady."

Jemima doesn't quit. "It still sounds like *Sleeping Beauty* to me."

"Fine. Fine," Mariah swells, lurching from her chair to grab the papers. "Give 'em back then."

Bunny, ever the hostess, calms her. Jemima mutters under her breath and holds Mariah's pages to her chest, daring her to snatch them back.

"Go ahead, Mariah, we're with you," Sari adds.

"As I was saying before I was so rudely interrupted, Lady

Dunston-Greene had sent Derek off on some mission, and once he was gone, she dispatched Willow into the black of night. No food, no creature comforts. All but one of the servants, the scullery maid, were unaware of her leaving." Mariah looks up at the intake of breath. "I'm not actually calling her a scullery maid, Jemima. Now, that *would* be too cliché. It's for brevity's sake, okay? The kitchen girl saw Willow limp through the light cast from the kitchen window and caught up to her, and that's where we left off." Mariah eases the moccasins from her puffy feet before beginning.

> "Madam, why are you out in the night air?" asked Rosemary, flinging her shawl over her head.
>
> "I've been cast out by that—that—" Willow cried.
>
> "She-wolf," Rosemary whispered above the sound of her own heartbeat.
>
> "She said I was a hedge-born harlot. And that son of hers is nowhere to be seen. Brings me up here by horseback but now I must walk home on my injured ankle."
>
> "Do you want me to saddle a horse?" Rosemary asked, hoping the girl would turn her down.

"A pony," Sari says thickly, before sliding further into her chair.

Mariah refuses to acknowledge the intrusion but her jaws work, chewing over the remark, before picking up her story.

> "Do you have a bicycle?"
>
> "I believe the groom has one. Come, we must hurry. Madam expects her hot toddy soon." Rosemary aided the faltering Willow to the stables where she discovered the bicycle beneath a canvas. "Here, Miss, take my shawl. It's not much but it will help." She arranged the material over Willow's copper curls, then wrapped the ends around her neck, knotting

them loosely at the back. She helped Willow to mount the bicycle and hung onto the seat while she found her balance.

"Thank you," Willow called back as she slowly started out, testing her ankle.

Rosemary fearing discovery, scurried back to the kitchen.

"Whoops," Mariah interrupts herself, "there's supposed to be a comma after Rosemary."

In the sticky late-summer heat, Mariah's cigarette smoke hangs listlessly. Bunny steals to the window and opens it wider. She notices her eyes getting heavy and forces herself to listen attentively as Mariah drones on. Sari is supporting her head in her hand and even though she's awake, she looks as though she's not even in the room with them. Bunny slides away to the kitchen and takes down a clear decanter and four matching glasses. Into the pitcher she dumps the contents of a package of tea mix then adds cold water and ice from the door of the refrigerator. She cuts a lemon thinly, using a wooden spoon to sink the slices beneath the glacier of ice cubes bobbing on the surface. As she returns to the library carrying the tray, she meets with Mariah's disapproval.

"How can you critique my work when you're not even in the room?"

"Jemima and Sari are perfectly capable," Bunny responds, setting down the tray and moving the empty sherry bottle to the top of the liquor cabinet.

"Look at them," Mariah grouses, aiming a stubby finger toward Sari, who now has her head down on the arm of the chair. "One's asleep," she twists to fling her arm in Jemima's direction, "and the other has her mind elsewhere."

"That's understandable," Bunny responds. "They probably haven't slept for days, but their inattention is no reflection on your writing, Mariah. It's solid as usual."

"My mind was *not* elsewhere," Jemima pipes up. "I was mulling over that last bit about Willow actually losing her way off the path in the woods and conveniently finding a cave. *A cave?* I was also wondering when bicycles were invented? What year does this story take place?"

"Well, how should I know?" Mariah counters. "It's just a story—a piece of fiction, albeit a good one."

Bunny sits back, holding her sweating glass of tea, as she follows the sparring match. She would have stepped in had Jemima been on the losing end, but she takes enjoyment in this one. Sari is now stirring after her nap, hair plastered to her face where it rested on the chair's leather arm. She yawns noisily and shifts her legs, complaining about her foot being asleep.

"Excuse me. Woo-hoo, ladies. We have three people speaking at once here." Bunny draws their attention to the iced tea and lets them help themselves. "What do you say we call it a night? It's too hot and—"

"I didn't get properly heard," Mariah complains as she struggles to return her puffy feet to her moccasins.

"My point exactly. It's hot and we're all tired. I'll save what I've written for next week. By then Jemima will have a better handle on how Joe is and our Sari will be sober," she says. "Mariah will have even more of Willow and Derek for us to enjoy."

"Anybody ever try to enlist you in the diplomatic corps, Bunny?" Jemima says drily, setting down her empty glass and rising.

But before the meeting breaks up, Sari announces, "I've been printing up posters to stick on telephone poles. Maybe everyone can take a handful and do their area?" She distributes the black and white likeness of Mooney. "This picture was taken a week before … before … I just remembered the film was still in the camera and this is one of the prints," she explains. "Please tack them up everywhere. I've done the bus depot and the post office." She falls silent, staring at the poster, recalling James taking that very photo of Mooney.

"Sari, you ready?" Jemima prods.

When the others are gone, Bunny douses all the lights to keep the bugs out, leaves the massive front door open to the summer air and takes a glass of scotch outside to sit on the stone steps, still warm from the day. There's an unwelcome lump in her throat, a sudden sadness that she fights with a double swallow of her single malt. Inside, the telephones ring, a discreet purr from the library and a more attention-grabbing jangle from Leland's study. She lets them ring on unanswered. It would only be Leland anyway, wondering how her day went and *if the girls from her little writing group have gone*. The mosquitoes find her in the dark, but she's determined not to be driven inside and swats at them until her scotch is gone. She tosses the remaining ice cubes into the driveway, then turns her back on the landscaped yard and enters the darkened house to pour herself another drink by touch.

She is in the kitchen rinsing the glasses the others used when the phone sounds again. She dries her hands on the tea towel and slides her glass of scotch along the counter, hoisting herself onto a bar stool before answering.

"Where have you been? I've been phoning half the night."

"Well, hello there." She pulls the almost empty glass closer. "And whom might I have the pleasure of speaking with?" She laughs into the phone. "Whoops, I just ended a sentence with a preposition— unlike *some* people who end their sentences with a proposition."

"You've been drinking," Leland says flatly.

"It's only iced tea, dear." She works her shoes off and they hit the floor. She brings one foot up on the seat then the other to examine her toenails while Leland carries on a stilted one-way discourse. After a couple of minutes of this, she lays the receiver on the countertop and carries her glass to the fridge door for ice water. Remounting the stool, she again engages the phone. "Sorry, dear, you were saying?" The line is dead. "How rude," she says, dropping the receiver back onto its cradle. She carries her ice water as she checks the doors, front and back, then climbs unsteadily in her bare feet to her bedroom.

VI

"YOU GONNA CATCH HELL VHEN za Mister gets home."

Bunny hadn't even heard Gerda's kick at the bedroom door.

"Get up, you. Za Mister is coming home today."

Bunny rockets to a sitting position, shoving her black eyeshade to her forehead. "What are you talking about and why are you here?"

Gerda, with surprising balance, uses her slippered foot to clear a space on the bedside table. With a clatter, she drops the coffee tray onto this space. "Such a lovely day, don't you sink?" Hands on hips, she leans over the bed.

"Tell me again." Bunny cups the hot mug in her hand and inhales the smell of coffee.

"Za Mistress vas mad vhen I tell her I vas fired. Za Mistress phone za Mister and he say, 'No! No! No!' So you see, Missy, I am back. He say, 'Take a few days. Get your teez fix.'" She clacks her repaired dentures inside her jack-o-lantern smile.

"Uh-huh," says Bunny, setting her cup down. "And the part about Leland coming home today?"

"About you he is vorried."

"Now why would he be worried about me?" A flush of anger crawls up her chest.

Gerda backs away to the door and with her hand on the knob replies, "I maybe tell za Mistress so many bottles I see in za garbage here. Scutch, sherry, brandy. No milk, no juice." She clicks her tongue tut, tut, tut and closes the door.

Bunny throws off the covers and steams for the door, coffee in hand. She is out on the landing before Gerda has descended to the second step of the winding staircase. "You're fired, you—you Judas! And this time you stay fired!"

"I don't sink so," Gerda sings, flapping her apron.

Bunny follows and, with a white-knuckled grasp on the banister, hurls her half-filled coffee mug at Gerda, who turns at that precise moment to add one more comment. The cup misses her but smacks the wall above her head, and the shock of it sends her reeling backwards down the stairs, her scream ending only when she slams head-first into the curved railing. Then, rolling and tumbling like a ragdoll, she ends her fall face-down on the hardwood floor at the bottom. Blood seeps from her shattered nose.

Bunny, still gripping the banister, descends hand-over-hand, her lungs sucking in small gasps of air. "Gerda?" she whispers. "Gerda?" Avoiding the blood, she crouches over the housekeeper's broken body, searching for a sign of life. A struggling sigh escapes Gerda's open mouth. Bunny's distressed cry echoes in the great house as she rises from her knees and staggers to the telephone in the kitchen. She gives her name and address to the emergency operator, answering the questions as best she can. "There's been a terrible accident," she reports. "My housekeeper f-fell down the stairs." She hopes they don't notice the stammer. She feels compelled to keep talking. "She wears these run-down slippers, you see, and she must have tripped. I've told her so many times to throw them away. Did I say she's our housekeeper? Gerda. When is the damned ambulance going to get here?"

She stays in her kitchen, shaking hands pressed between her knees until the wailing ambulance turns into her tree-lined driveway. Still in her nightgown, she runs through the house to unlock the front door for the two ambulance attendants. They carry their equipment past her as she points the way to the staircase, but as soon as she catches sight of Gerda's arm extended into the hallway, she turns back and paces to and from the front doors.

After a while the attendants re-emerge, rolling a stretcher toward Bunny who precedes them to the front entrance. Gerda, strapped to a backboard, is locked within a cervical collar. A rivulet of blood runs from her nose into the hair at the nape of her neck.

"What's her name?" asks the male aide, scribbling on a clipboard as they hustle down the hallway. "How old?"

"Gerda von Hauffman." She spells it for him. "She's about seventy. Is she going to be all right?"

"Hard to tell," says the female attendant, changing position to lift the stretcher down the stone steps. "Will you notify her family?"

"She has no family. Only us." The cold stone steps beneath Bunny's feet ground her. She wonders why she feels chilled and realizes she's not dressed. She's suddenly conscious of the black sleeping mask still stuck to her forehead. "Wait! Her purse." She whirls back toward the open doors.

The ambulance driver stretches his arm out the open window ready to take Gerda's bag. "Will you be following us in?" Bunny nods dumbly. He drives away, not turning on his flashing lights until he hits the road at the end of the driveway.

Bunny closes the door behind her, then sinks to the floor in a smothering black void. But almost as soon as the fainting spell hits, it leaves. She feels sick and cold to her core. Hugging her knees to her chest, she thinks she should be crying, but it won't come. In the distance the ambulance whoops at the first sign of traffic, and Bunny, thinking more clearly now, estimates it must already be near the market. Another five minutes and it will be at the hospital. She rolls herself onto her hands and knees and reaches up for the door handle. Standing isn't going to be possible without assistance.

She takes her time showering, and when she's done, she clamps her wet hair behind her head in a tortoise-shell clip. Wrapped in a bath sheet, she stands rooted to a spot in the middle of her walk-in closet and stares up at the top shelf where her sweaters are bagged and stacked. The ringing phone breaks the spell. She blinks, wondering how long she's been there. As Leland won't allow a phone in the bedroom, she must hurry downstairs. Making it as far as the bedroom door, she suddenly stops and turns back. *To hell with it*, she decides. She doesn't want to talk to anybody.

Searching for something sedate enough to go to jail in, she chooses a pearl-grey silk pantsuit, but returns the double string of black coral beads to her jewellery box. If she's going to be taken into custody, the beads would seem too frivolous, although they would show up nicely in the newspaper photo. She slips on her sensible Italian flats and folds her second-best nightgown into a suede overnight bag. Adding a reasonably fashionable jogging suit, clean underwear and a pair of Nike Air shoes, she's packed. Nothing fancy. She certainly doesn't want to stand out amongst the other prisoners. All she needs now is her toiletries and an extra set of press-on nails. As a last measure before leaving the closet, she removes the topaz ring from her right hand and the gold wedding band from her left, inserting them into the proper velvet slots of the jewellery case.

She feels better now that she's organized, but viewing the mess at the bottom of the stairs throws her momentarily. Gerda's blood has skinned over and turned a rusty black. Crumpled gauze wrappers and an empty spool of adhesive tossed aside by the ambulance attendants litter the floor. The brown rivulets of her thrown coffee streak the wall. She wonders who will clean it up.

Bunny parks the BMW in the gravel lot in front of the hospital. There's plenty of space as visiting hours don't begin until 2:00 p.m., four hours from now. She studies the white stucco building for some sign, some signal regarding Gerda—like the flag being at half-mast or a hearse parked with the motor running—but there's nothing out of the ordinary. There doesn't seem to be a police car lurking, but they could be waiting for her inside. She'll hold her head up as she walks in. Leland and PJ will be proud of her decorum. But her resolve crumbles as she approaches the door to the hospital. Digging into her purse, she finds a mint. She waits a moment for the taste of it to fill her mouth before pushing through and into the waiting room. She hesitates, heart racing, anticipating a large plain-clothes cop clapping handcuffs on her wrists, but the only person in the waiting area, a solitary elderly gentleman flipping through a magazine, is only momentarily distracted by the well-dressed woman blocking the doorway. When no one else arrives to show any interest in her, Bunny walks as quietly as possible to the nursing station that serves as both patient information and admitting.

"Excuse me, I'm inquiring about my housekeeper, Gerda von Hauffman."

The nurse sorts through her charts. "Are you Mrs. deLore?"

Bunny braces for the bad news. "Yes."

"From the deLore Estate down the road?"

Bunny nods an answer.

"Lovely place. I often look into your yard as I pass by. All those lovely trees and that lovely house. I'd like to bring the garden club out some day."

Bunny can no longer hold her breath. "Any time."

"That's grand." The nurse smiles then resumes her duties as admitting clerk. "You're her employer, yes? Just fill these forms out the best you can, will you? The doctor will be down shortly."

"Is she going to … to …" *How do you say* die *nicely?* "… pass on?"

The nurse's face softens and she leans toward Bunny, speaking in confidence. "She's in tough shape. She's still unconscious, but you can probably see her for a minute before she leaves for Vancouver."

"Vancouver?" Bunny waits as the nurse answers her telephone. While she listens, she signals Bunny to fill out the papers. Bunny takes them to the waiting room, avoiding the old man still reading his magazine.

When the phone call ends, the nurse waves her over. "The chopper just landed on the roof. If you're going to say goodbye you'd better do it now. Down the hall," she points behind her, "then right at the corner. You'll see the sign for Emerg. Dr. Woolcott may have a few questions."

"Questions?"

But the nurse flags her past the desk and waves her through the fire doors. Bunny drags her feet but still gets there before Gerda's been taken away. A knot of hospital staff surrounds a gurney in front of the elevator. The one giving orders snags her as she slides by.

"Bunny?" Seeing her startled look, he explains, "We met at the golf club. Ron Woolcott." He sticks out his hand to shake hers. "I'm Mrs. Von Hauffman's attending." When the elevator doors open, he stands aside while Gerda's gurney is loaded. "Ride up with us."

Bunny darts a quick look at Gerda, who is swaddled in sheets and blankets and belted to the stretcher. Her head and neck are immobilized in orange plastic blocks. Only her face is exposed, puffy eyes clamped shut, sunken mouth sucking in air.

"Vancouver can deal with the fractures when she's more stable. Right now we have to control the swelling in her brain." Dr. Woolcott glances from Gerda to Bunny, then grabs Bunny's arm as her knees buckle. "You okay?" Not waiting for an answer, he props her against the elevator wall as the doors open. The blades of the helicopter are slicing the simmering summer heat radiating off the rooftop.

As soon as Woolcott, the attending staff and the stretcher clear the elevator, Bunny jabs the main floor button repeatedly. Downstairs again, she bolts from the elevator, clears the lobby in seconds and sprints across the parking lot to collapse behind the wheel of her car. It's not something she's accustomed to—running—but as she catches her breath, she thinks that knocking aged nannies down the stairs is not in her nature either. *God help me but Leland may be right. I may need an analyst. I seem to be developing a character flaw.* So that she doesn't have to do any more self-analysis, she fires up the car and lays her head back against the headrest, appreciating the well-tempered air conditioning. Her eyes follow the rising flight of the helicopter until it becomes a dot and the dot becomes merely a speck and the speck disappears. It takes great effort to sit up and put the car into gear. If she's not going to jail today, then she'd like to go home and have a nap.

⁓

SARI ARRIVES FROM WORK TO find Mudd and a large bag of dog food blocking her trailer's entrance. The dog strains at the leash attached to her door handle, dancing on all fours in his excitement at seeing her.

"What the hell?" She drops her purse to undo the leather loop from the knob. Stuck into the door frame is a folded pizza flyer with a written note on the back. "You stay!" she tells the dog as she unlocks the door. She reclaims her purse and enters the trailer, the dog on her heels.

"The big dumb jerk," she says after reading the note. She balls it and pitches it against the refrigerator. Mudd scrambles across the floor, leash trailing. He tosses the wadded paper into the air, catching it playfully before returning to Sari. Paper clamped in his smile, he sits before her, tail feathering the floor, waiting for the game to continue. "Do you know what he's done?" she says, her voice rising. The dog's ears droop and he sinks to the floor. "I'm not mad at you, you damn dog." Sari throws herself onto the sofa and heaves a shoe at the still-open door. Mudd crawls on his belly and returns with the shoe. Despite herself, she laughs. "Okay, you win. For now." She crosses the room to close the door and removes the dog's leash from his collar. "It appears you are my houseguest for a few days, dog. Your lord and master has fixed the Harley and taken it for a test drive. Jesus, what nerve!"

⁓

FLORA FLINT PLUMTREE HAS A plan. It has been simmering on her back burner for the best part of two days. With Mariah's fifty-seventh birthday approaching, she will have a little dinner party with all her daughter's closest friends. A swish of gaiety through the house will be a treat well worth arranging. She will throw something tropical so that the bird in the back room will blend right in. Crepe paper palm trees, leis, those blue drinks with little umbrellas in them they served at the Briar Rose Seniors' Residence Social Night. She checks her shopping list, adding paper umbrellas to the tally.

"There's certainly not many names," Flora mumbles as she flutters the pages of Mariah's address book. She peers through the window at her middle-aged daughter cutting the patch of lawn with the push mower, her white runners stained green by freshly mown grass. The whole lawn had been matted brown when Flora had first arrived from the home, but with daily watering—standing out there in her dressing gown with the hose in hand—she's revived it. Mariah wasn't at all grateful for the ankle-deep turf that resulted and she was not happy oiling the rusty mower and sharpening the blades. Kids nowadays!

Flora turns her chair to the window so she can keep an eye out and opens Mariah's address book to the As. No As. She flips to the Bs. *Button, Sari/James.*

"Hello, dear, this is Flora Plumtree, Mariah's … uh … social secretary."

Sari puts the grimy dog dish she has found under the tree next door into the sink. She examines her fingers, then waggles them under the hot tap as she clamps the phone between ear and shoulder. "I didn't know Mariah had a social secretary."

"Oh, yes, dear," says the hurried voice. "And I'm also a sort of relative."

"Oh," Sari says, still puzzled. She can hear the woman's laboured breathing on the line and she waits her out.

"What I phoned for, dear—oh, just a minute. I have to check out the window—is that I'm throwing a bit of a surprise soiree for Mariah's birthday and I'm inviting you and—" Flora quickly rereads the address book, "you and James."

"I'm sorry, but James is no longer living here."

Flora catches the flatness in Sari's tone and remembers too late that he's probably the one who left with the baby. She makes a face at her blunder but carries on with forced cheerfulness. "No matter, dear. We'd love to have you. All her friends will be here."

"Um, when is it?" Sari hopes she will be working late.

"Sunday. This Sunday. This very Sunday coming up."

Sari looks around for an excuse not to be there. "Well, I have this dog …"

"Dogs are welcome."

Sari is silent on the other end.

"You're the first one I called," says the shrinking voice.

Damn, damn, damn. "I'd love to come. What time?"

"Good girl. It'll be such fun." Her voice lowers conspiratorially. "It's a tropical surprise party so wear something fruity or Hay-waiian. Say five-ish?"

Sari feels dread. Mariah will be so pissed off.

⁀

JEMIMA SETS JOE'S LUNCH IN front of him and removes her apron before sitting down at the table.

"Oh," she says, bobbing back up. "Forgot the tea."

Joe lowers his head over the sandwich. It's easier to handle than hot soup and the doctor said to give him simple stuff to start with. No casseroles, he said, but she caught the two men making eye contact when he gave this instruction. Joe never cracked a smile. He seems okay but Jemima notices he is much quieter. Won't even argue about how the car should be driven. She'll give him time to settle in then she'll rattle his chain a bit. It won't do to have him an invalid.

"Will you be going out to the shop today, Joe?" She pours a lot of milk into his cup and tops it with tea.

"I'm tired. Going for a lie-down after lunch."

"You've hardly been out of that bed for four days. Maybe that's what's making you tired." She pushes his cup just out of his range. "This Sunday we're invited to a birthday party for Mariah."

"Who?" he says, not raising his head.

"Mariah Flint. You know, from my writing group."

"Mm." His hand directs his sandwich closer to his gaping mouth.

"We'll go then? I think it will be good for you to get out." He looks so old. "I'll give you a nice haircut this afternoon."

"Nuh."

"Yes, Joe, we're going out and we're going to wear something Hawaiian." *And that's final.*

"No, goddamn it!"

Now, she reflects, *that sounds more like it.*

⁀

SEATED AT THE WINDOW IN the library, Bunny watches the taxi approach down the tree-shaded driveway. She has practised being calm and rational but now, despite the three scotches she's put away, her stomach is in knots. She hides her glass behind the velvet drapes and heads down the hallway. Shoulders back, ready to greet him, she throws the door open expansively and faces the cabbie carrying Leland's luggage up the stone steps. He sets them in front of her and palms the folded bill that Leland offers.

"Nice to be home," Leland says, dipping to retrieve his briefcase from the gravel drive. Bunny's forced smile slips as she takes in what he's wearing.

"You look different, Leland. I hardly recognized you." She steps aside to allow him through the doorway, then follows him in. He's never worn blue jeans before, let alone a leather vest that appears too tight everywhere. He's far too short and round for either. And his curly grey hair has been tinted a chestnut brown. He sets his briefcase inside the door and kisses her on the cheek before returning for his suitcases.

"Your razor not working again, Leland?"

He runs a hand over his face. "It's the Brad Pitt look."

"Who?"

"Never mind. Not important." He struggles to get his pudgy fingers into a slit pocket of the vest. "Something for you," he says, offering her a tiny suede drawstring pouch.

Inside is a silver frog pin with one emerald eye. "Oh, darling, it's beautiful," she says, tipping it into her palm.

He waves off the comment.

His look tells her there was no thought given to the gift. *Gotta get a little something for the wife.* Bunny returns it to the pouch.

He picks up a suitcase in either hand and heads down the hallway but stops when he takes in the double sheet spread out at the foot of the stairs. "What's all this stuff?" he asks. "You redecorating again?"

"I have something to tell you but I don't know where to start."

"Try the beginning. On second thought, go straight to the end."

"Gerda fell down the stairs this morning and she's in hospital in Vancouver."

Leland is speechless but his florid face is turning mauve around his nose.

"It's those damn shoes she wears," Bunny rushes on. "She may have swelling in her brain. They don't know yet. That nice young Dr. Woolcott we met at the golf club is looking after her. *Was* looking after her," she babbles.

He drops the suitcases as if his hands won't bear the weight any longer.

He looks so stricken Bunny touches his arm. She hears a sharp intake of breath as his eyes take in the staircase top to bottom. "Our Gerda fell down these stairs?"

Bunny nods and repeats shakily, "Those damn shoes."

"My God! Think of the lawsuit!" He tries to step over the sheet to climb the steps but changes his mind. "Is that blood on the wall?"

Bunny follows his pointing finger to the brown smear halfway down. "Yes. Her shoes …"

"What's under the sheet?" he says, lifting it to peer beneath. He drops it, appalled, then pulls a handkerchief from his pocket to wipe the non-existent blood from his hands. "Jesus Christ, woman, why hasn't this been cleaned up?"

"Who is going to do it?"

"Ohmygawd. That's *her* blood on the floor, isn't it?" He turns and flees to the library, collapsing into the green leather chair. Bunny follows. "I think I need a drink," he says, dropping his face into his hands. Bunny pours two neat scotches. No tap water now that Leland's home. "Poor old Gerda," he moans. "Does Mother know?"

"Not yet," she replies.

He looks at her accusingly.

"I *have* been busy," she says. "The ambulance. The hospital."

"And Joy?" he asks.

She gulps her scotch, spilling some down the front of her grey silk going-to-jail pantsuit. "Our daughter is a busy person with a life of her own." *And she would know her mother is lying!* Her heart begins pounding. "You should phone your mother," she says, leading him from the topic of PJ. "She'll know what to do," she wheedles. *And I'll never hear the end of it.*

He walks his drink into his study to use the phone there.

Bunny heads for the kitchen with her glass. She wipes absently at the front of her suit with a clean tea towel as she looks out the window above the sink. The early apple trees are dropping their crop onto the grass. Her award-winning Japanese iris needs attention, and it looks like the damned blight might be attacking the young dogwoods again. She'll call her gardener and the tree guy as soon as Leland leaves. She can hear his intermittent conversation down the hall and then, in the quiet that follows, his approach.

"Oh, there you are." Leland has removed his vest and rolled up the sleeves of his collarless shirt. Down to business. "Mother is understandably quite upset. She wonders whether the police should be involved."

Bunny stiffens, then turns to face him, stricken.

"I told her it was an accident." He folds his arms across his paunch. "It *was* an accident, wasn't it?" His voice is like butterscotch.

Bunny sniffs repeatedly, trying to fight off the tears but loses. She would have made it had he been nasty, but show a little kindness and she buckles. She sobs into the tea towel.

He encircles her with his sturdy arms. "Sorry, I know you wouldn't have anything to do with Gerda's getting hurt. That was Mother's influence."

Bunny lays her head on his shoulder, minimizing her height advantage and enjoying the closeness.

"Now stop crying," he says. "It's the stress of dealing with this all by yourself. You did a good job," he adds, patting her on the back with moist hands before straight-arming her away.

"Fix your face and we'll go for supper somewhere. I gotta put a call in to my lawyers to see if we're liable." From somewhere down the hallway out of her sight, he calls back, "Have you phoned the Vancouver hospital to get an update on her condition?"

"No," she answers. The warm fuzzies are over.

VII

"FLORA?" MARIAH YELLS, AFTER HANGING up the phone. "FLORA!"

"In here with the bird," Flora replies, bracing herself for what is coming. And what is coming is a flat-footed Mariah chuffing tobacco smoke as she steams into her mother's bedroom, armed for battle.

Removing the cigarette from her face, Mariah barks, "I just got off the phone with Bunny deLore. She says she's sorry but Leland won't be coming to the party."

"Who's Leland?"

"What party?"

"Who's Leland?"

"Her long-lost husband."

"Too bad," Flora replies, pinning open the door to the birdcage. "Come on, baby," she coaxes. "Time to stretch your wings."

"Just what the hell have you done?" Mariah says, looking for a place to stub out her cigarette.

"Poor little guy. Did that Mariah get smoke in your eyes? She's a naughty girl," Flora croons to the bird in the kind of a singsong usually reserved for babies and new puppies. Axel struts up Flora's arm to perch on her shoulder. "I invited a few people for a party, that's all. Your writing friends, the neighbours," she says on her way to the kitchen, "and your sweetheart, that dreadful dog woman."

"My wha-at?" gasps Mariah, trailing her mother.

"You heard me," counters Flora, setting the bird on the back of a chair. "Your girlfriend, companion, partner—whatever you call her."

"She's a friend," says Mariah, chucking her cigarette butt into the sink.

"Right, like you two are having pyjama parties at those sleepovers of yours."

"It's my fucking life, so what of it?" she yells.

"Means nothing to me," says Flora, handing a piece of apple to the bird. "I've known for years. I'm just surprised you're so slow in putting it out there."

Mariah is uncharacteristically quiet. She pours herself a coffee and leans against the counter. "And you're okay with that? Not that it matters."

Flora takes a moment to clean her glasses on a tea towel. "I don't care who you sleep with, dear, as long as you get your rest."

"You're a real piece of work, Flora," says Mariah, trying not to laugh, "but I still don't like parties."

"So don't come."

"I won't," she says as she picks her wet cigarette from the sink and throws it into the garbage.

"Now who will we get to blow out the candles?" her mother wonders aloud.

Mariah tops up her cup with hot coffee and reaches for another smoke.

"Happy birthday to yo-o-o-o," Flora warbles, a full octave too high.

"Happy birthday to yo-o-o-o,

"She won't be here to enjoy it,

"But we'll save her a piece of cake and all the presents,

"And I'll tell everyone how o-o-old she is,

"Happy birthday to yo-o-o-o-o-o."

The bird whistles and squawks in accompaniment, turning in circles on the chair.

As expected, Mariah is back in the conversation. "This party is more for you than for me, right?"

"Nope, it's all about you. You're fifty-seven, remember."

"Fifty-five."

"Who are you kidding?" Flora quips. "*I'm* fifty-five." She picks up Axel and places the bird on her shoulder.

Mariah harrumphs, hating to be the loser in this skirmish. "And who is being coerced into coming?" She flops into the chair next to the window, opening it to drop her ashes into the garden.

Flora sashays over to clamp a hand on Mariah's shoulder. "You know, dear, anyone looking in would think, 'How lovely! A family having a morning chat before setting off on the course of the day.' They couldn't possibly know that the bountiful, caring mother is being rebuked by her ungrateful, thankless daughter. The wonderful caring mother who spent hours planning and phoning—"

Mariah has had enough. She sticks her head out the open window and launches her retort. "People," she heralds. "This woman has interfered with the process of my life, inviting God-knows-who to a stupid birthday party. You be the judge."

"It's not a stupid party," Flora says, her shoulders slumping. The bird slides off and takes flight to avoid hitting the floor.

Mariah notes with sudden regret the tremor in Flora's chin. She has pushed her mother too far. Now she's forced to make an apology of sorts, something she tries to avoid at all costs. "Okay, so a party isn't such a bad thing."

Flora's face brightens.

"Once in a while, that is." She doesn't want to give in too much. "So, when is it and who's coming?"

⸜⸝

"I KNOW, I KNOW, WE'RE late," Jemima says, backing into her usual comfortable chair in Bunny's library. She explains that Mudd had begun howling as they left and Sari had to return to the trailer to shut him up. Sari then has to explain Mudd's existence and confess that the dog has become attached to her this past week, his eyes rolling to watch her every move. She informs them that she has heard nothing from the neighbour who left him tied to her doorknob. "If the dog is still at my place next Tuesday, he's up for adoption if anybody's interested." But Sari looks brighter, not so pale and tired. She's been walking the dog in the evenings after work and last weekend they had struck out together to tack up more "Have You Seen This Child?" posters.

Bunny has made the tea early as she feels it may be a longer session than usual since there is so much news to catch up on from the past week. Jemima leads off by declaring Joe almost back to normal. "He's kind of cranky and his speech is slurred, but he's not doing too badly. He said I was to come here tonight and not to bother myself phoning home to check on him." What he'd actually said was, "Will you for Chrissake get the hell out and quit fussing?" He had even ventured into his workshop as she'd watched anxiously from the window in the back door.

"You're kind of quiet, Mariah," Bunny says, removing the cosy from the teapot to pour Earl Grey into the cups.

"I have nothing to say. It is a writing group, not a quilting bee."

They wait her out. She arranges her printed pages in a cordwood-like stack by her feet, then nudges her glasses up her nose as she sits back. Her bangs hit the top of the frames, hiding her eyebrows and forehead completely. Beneath the frayed hair, her eyes evade the others seated around her.

"Your birthday this Sunday, eh Mariah?" Jemima goads, now that it is no longer a surprise.

Mariah removes her glasses, pressing thumb and forefinger into her eyelids. After a weighty sigh, she rams the glasses back onto her face. "Unfortunately."

"We're looking forward to the party, aren't we, girls?" Jemima says merrily. "Can we do anything for it?"

"Yeah, send a note saying you can't make it."

"Well, if that's the way you feel," Jemima states, "Joe and I can certainly find something else to do." She looks expectantly at Sari and Bunny, hoping they will wade in. *Actually*, Jemima thinks, *Bunny looks like she's lost her last friend*. "What's with you guys, anyway? Faces like bullfrogs."

Sari plays with her braid.

Bunny clears her throat. "I have something to tell you." She steels herself to tell the tale yet again. "There was an accident here during the week."

"Your husband?" asks Sari, concerned.

Bunny shakes her head. "Gerda." Seeing their puzzled looks, she adds, "The housekeeper."

"What happened?" Sari asks.

Bunny suddenly feels quite emotional—a moody mix of shame and guilt. She throws her hand across her mouth and fights back tears. "She fell," she begins, her voice cracking. After pausing to steady herself with a mouthful of tea, she continues, "From top to bottom."

"A ladder?" asks Sari.

"No. No, the staircase," Bunny replies, nodding in the direction of the hallway. She won't explain about the trodden slippers to her friends. They'll understand that old ladies sometimes fall down stairs just on their own.

"And?" Mariah prompts.

"Massive head trauma. They transferred her to Vancouver." Her eyes squeeze shut as she recites Gerda's injuries. "Leland was told she has a torn liver and her collarbone is broken. Both wrists, too."

"Trying to save herself, I guess," Sari says.

Bunny's eyes fly open, "What do you mean?"

"Well, she'd put both hands out trying to save herself from falling, wouldn't she?"

"Instinctively," Mariah offers.

Jemima agrees. "What are you going to do?"

"Do?"

"Is she going to make it?"

"I don't know, Jemima. *They* don't know."

The group falls silent again.

Mariah leans over to put her cup on the coffee table. "Yes, it *will* be my birthday this Sunday." She holds up a restraining hand. "Don't even think about asking how old. This is all Flora's idea. She's a bit of a shit disturber." But her harsh words are tempered with a small measure of affection. "She doesn't understand the word *no*." She's struck with an idea. "Do you think we should cancel it because of

Gerda? With the poor woman clinging to life, it's kind of a slap in the face, don't you think, having a frivolous birthday party?"

"It's up to Bunny," Sari decides, and three heads turn to await her benediction.

"Not having the party won't help Gerda, but having it may help us. Maybe what we all need is a nice day out together," Bunny states with forced gaiety. "A gala affair to cheer us up." She looks to Mariah. "Your mother assured me she is a gourmet cook and she's pulling out all the stops."

Mariah stops groping for her smokes and guffaws. The brief burst of laughter ends in coughing. She pats herself on the chest, then replies, "The gourmet cook wants me to stop at the library and pick up a copy of *Fun Things to Do With Jell-O*."

"Don't bother." Jemima shuffles her writing assignment on her knees. "I have it at home. A little dog-eared but serviceable."

Mariah comes close to praying for divine intervention. *Maybe if Gerda actually dies ...*

"I gotta get home soon," Jemima says, "so let's get on with the work. I'll go first, shall I?" she offers, distributing a copy to each of the others. "I've been researching recipes for folks on a restrictive diet. Like Joe. He doesn't have to be on one, you know, but I thought something light and nutritious would be suitable. Nothing with lima beans. I've devoted a full page to a family recipe named after my mother—Mrs. Shertzer's Steamed Raisin Puffs with Foamy Pudding Sauce. When my mother made it originally, she used three or four eggs and a half cup of butter. I tweaked her ingredients so it could be assembled with a solitary egg and a smidge of margerine." She admits it hasn't yet been tested on Joe but is fairly confident it will work. She weaves a story into the preamble to the recipe about her mother making this same pudding for the son who came home from the war with one arm fewer than what he'd left with. Like Jemima, her mother used food as a cure-all. A nice dish of Steamed Raisin Puffs could probably coax the bud of a new arm. After all, a fresh simmered beef tongue with a zesty Spanish sauce had been known to restore circulation to her Uncle Bert's blocked artery, and the heart of a boiled onion inserted into a child's aching ear saved a trip to town to the doctor. Kitchen miracles. "This is comfort food," Jemima concludes. "Like tomato soup or oatmeal. Everyone has comfort food. Sari, what's yours?"

Sari straightens from her slump in the green leather chair. "Nothing's a comfort right now."

"How about scotch?" Bunny suggests, thinking more of herself.

"I do like a glass of good red wine," Sari offers after a moment's reflection. "Or even better, ice cream with soda crackers crushed on top—"

"Ew-w-w-w," they harmonize.

"—and beans right out of the can."

"Well, to each her own," Jemima says. "Mariah, how 'bout you?"

Mariah has been mulling over her choices. "Coffee and a cigarette."

"That's hardly food," Jemima sniffs.

"Food for the soul." She plants her feet ready to defend her position. "Take it or leave it."

Jemima had been hoping the group's ideas would be fodder for future columns on soothing sustenance but their selections are a jarring disappointment. "Bunny?"

Bunny was ready. "Ginger in dark chocolate, sardines on toast—"

Now this is something Jemima can use and she scribbles "*sard. on toast*" atop her page.

"—and an expensive single malt scotch. Just a taste, mind you."

Mariah snorts.

"Doesn't pot roast or meat loaf count anymore?" Jemima questions as she gathers the copies of her column from the others. "Along with comfort food, I'm going to jot down personal reflections about the changing season. Leaves and the harvest and the summer heat retreating from the land." She does the same thing for every season's change but each time thinks her idea fresh and original. "I'll add a few words about my Joe. That seems fitting. And if time allows—editors are always wielding the whip—I can do something like a society page item on Mariah's birthday party."

"Over my dead body!" Mariah thunders.

"That could be arranged, right, Bunny?" Jemima is pleased Mariah took the bait.

Bunny blanches. "Why are you asking me?"

"Can we get back to writing?" Coming from Sari as it does, this mild remark carries a stinging lash. "It's late and I have to work tomorrow."

"What'cha got for us?" asks Jemima, aware that Sari had been writing on their drive over to Bunny's house.

"I almost didn't come tonight," Sari says, "because I had nothing done, but when I went back to the trailer to shut the dog up, I had this picture pop into my head. It's probably not very good," she apologizes. "Not polished or even edited, so you'll have lots to tear apart." She reads from her single sheet.

> Grief, despair, course down his sunken cheeks
> and drip from bristled chin unseen.
> To come to this: a box
> that used to house a fridge
> now houses him.
> Tacked to the wall a current
> calendar. Today is Monday, now what?
> Within the box, a box that holds canned heat
> and all the barbecued chicken he can carry
> from back of Safeway.
> Croissants, too.

The words hang in the silence as Sari carefully folds the paper into halves, then quarters.

"For God's sake, girl, lighten up," Mariah snaps. "Can't you write something a little more optimistic?"

"I write what I feel. And, frankly, Mariah, I feel shitty." With her grungy toes, Sari probes for her sandals and rams her feet into them. She pushes her poem into her pocket as she stands, then plunges her arm and head through her purse strap, bandolier-style. "Don't look to me to write about some airy-fairy earl in a castle on the moors when I fight just to get through each bloody day." She looks around for more possessions but realizes she's only brought her purse and the poem. "Don't get up, Jemima. I'll walk." She tosses off a "thanks" to Bunny and heads for the door, her purse bouncing off her hip.

"Now what brought that on?" Mariah asks. "And what's she mean about an airy-fairy earl, I'd like to know?"

Bunny chases after the departing Sari.

"Jesus, Mariah," Jemima says, "the girl has not only lost her husband but her baby as well. I don't know where your head is sometimes."

"I only said—"

Jemima can't bear to look at her. "I know what you said. You were being nasty."

"And that's so unlike me," Mariah states, cupping her wide-eyed face in her hand.

"You really need a good swift kick," Jemima remarks on her way to the window.

Bunny comes back alone. "She's gone." She runs her hands through her expensive haircut. It swings back into place beautifully. "I think she needs to walk it off."

But Jemima worries, "It's dark by eight-thirty and she's cutting across the orchard."

"Siddown, you two," Mariah orders. "She's not a ten-year-old. She'll be okay."

"You want to continue or call it a night?" Bunny looks drawn, ready to bolt for the scotch should they decide to leave.

Jemima and Mariah make eye contact. "We'll stay," Jemima states, easing back into her chair. "The damage is done. I'll drop by the trailer on my way home and see if her lights are on," Jemima promises Bunny. "Want me to call you?"

Bunny nods. "Let's hear your piece, Mariah, if you're up to it."

Mariah hands out her sheets and settles back comfortably. "It would take more than that to rattle my chain. I believe the last episode was where Willow went running home—or, more precisely, riding home—on that bicycle. And, by the way," she says, referring to the notes she has written in a sprawling hand on her top page, "the bicycle was invented in 1645 in France but it had four wheels and then in 1790, again in France, came a two-wheeler. Then the Germans invented their own in 1816." She raises her eyes to make sure she has their attention, especially Jemima's as she's the one who brought up the issue. "In 1839 the Scots developed another one and damned if those French didn't come up with something better in 1865. So you see, I *can* have a bicycle in my story. My time frame is just fine."

"Thanks for that," says Jemima primly. "I thought perhaps it might be pertinent for holding your storyline together."

"We now have Willow at home with her mother. She's still nursing her injured ankle if you'll recall, and catching hell for losing her bicycle, although she did bring another one home that's in better repair."

Willow's mother, Bronwyn, sat knees apart before the meager fire, shelling peas that weighed down her apron. "So, the ill-bred mold warp threw you out, did she? She and her son of a rabbit sucker?"

"Her son is neither a mold warp nor a rabbit sucker. He saved me, Mother. Derek doesn't know she threw me out. She sent him off on a mission."

"Mission, shmission, he's a good little mama's boy. The lad didn't deflower you, did he?" she asked, eyes squinting in the smoke from the fire.

"Mother!" cried Willow.

"Too bad. We could have done something to right the injustice." The room was silent with the exception of the peas hitting the copper pot.

"Right it how?" Willow asked coyly, drawing her stool closer and taking a handful of pods to shell.

"A hasty marriage of convenience. You are of an age, my dear."

Willow dipped her head. "There was nothing out of the ordinary."

Her mother slapped her sharply across the head. "The whole thing was out of the ordinary, you lean-witted whipster. You could have had yourself a manor and a husband had you played your hand right."

"Yes, and a peevish mother-in-law," Willow retorted.

"Do you think the lad will seek you out?"

"He is probably riding hill and dale searching for me. He did look at me with bawdy eyes but unfortunately, Mother, he does not know where we live."

"Get back on your bicycle, girl, and ride. Ride where he first found you. Ride down those lanes and crossroads. Ride to the manor," she said urgently, clutching her daughter's wrist. "Ride like the wind itself."

"But my foot ..."

"Your foot my ass," sniped Bronwyn. "I'm not feeding you forever, my dear." Her arm, still holding a peapod, made an arc. "I could see myself all fat and cosseted in a manor. I could see myself a Lady."

Willow's peas fell to the dirt floor as she abruptly stood. She limped to the door, took down the borrowed shawl from the peg and opened the door without further ado. With not a backward glance she mounted her bicycle, hitched her skirts between her virgin thighs and, avoiding the wagon ruts in the dusty roadway, made for the countryside where she first met Derek of Dunston-Greene.

"That's it," says Mariah triumphantly. "A little goes a long way."

"Her virgin thighs?" Jemima says. "Isn't that just a tad over the top? And her mother saying ... what was it?" She runs her fingers down the lines. "Oh, yes, 'your foot my ass.'" She shakes her head. "I think maybe she would say it differently. Wouldn't you say so, Bunny?"

Bunny, who has no heart for the remaining evening, sighs and says, "That did stand out, Mariah. It sort of stopped the progress of your story." She won't mention the arm holding the peapod. *Serves her right if we overlook it.*

Mariah looks to the ceiling for a long moment but, when she thinks it over, says, "You may have a point."

"I have to confess, ladies, I am suddenly so darn tired that I'd like to call it an evening," says Bunny. "It's been a long day. What I have can wait until next week."

"I want to check on Sari, anyway," says Jemima.

AS SARI CROSSES THE FIELD, she breathes in the sweet smell of windfall apples spoiling underfoot. She tries to spot one in good condition, then says to hell with it and picks a couple from an overhanging branch. She feels much better now that she's left the house and that toad, Mariah, with her stupid black glasses and her big mouth. Sari polishes an apple on her shirt, then bites into the crisp green skin. She wipes away the juice running down her chin. *I could live here,* she thinks, revolving slowly, arms held shoulder high, a stolen apple in each hand. *Mooney and me.*

She arrives home as the last blink of light is pinched from the horizon, and from the mailboxes she sees Ace's Harley parked as close to his steps as he could get it. He must have dismounted on the first stair. She almost expects to see him lolling there as well, but he isn't. She'd love to throw her remaining apple through his window and yell theatrically, "How dare you abandon your dog, you so-and-so" but instead creeps up her own stairs to unlock the door. A shadow crosses the light she has left on for Mudd and she hesitates. Inside, Ace is talking to the dog.

It's another break and enter. She charges through the door and heads straight for the telephone. Ace is at the kitchen sink running water into the dog's dish so the element of surprise is in her favour, and she snatches up the phone, holding the base against her chest, intending to fight him for it if he tries to stop her.

Ace drops the dish into the sink and skirts the easy chair in the living room. "Wait! Wait! I can explain." He jams his thumb on the button, disconnecting her call. She hits his wrist with the receiver. He yelps, yanking back his arm to suck on the welt. She tries for the operator again but Ace pulls the cord from the wall.

"I got him!" he says triumphantly. Mudd sets up a howl. "Shaddup, you silly bugger," Ace commands.

In the sudden silence Sari hears a small cry from the back bedroom. She drops the phone, her hands to her mouth. "What was that?"

Ace rubs his wrist. "That's what I've been trying to tell you. I got him. It's your boy."

Sari's knees buckle but she throws out a hand, catching the edge of the table. Keeping her eyes on Ace, reading his face for some sort of treachery, she feels for the hallway light, then turns and stumbles to Mooney's room. There's a faint odour of gasoline. Mooney sits in his crib, eyes wide with fright, his thumb in his mouth. "Mooney?" she whispers from the doorway. "Mooney! Oh, God, I thought I'd never see you again."

"C'mon, Mudd, let's go," Ace calls, heading for home. But instead of trotting behind his owner, the dog drops to the floor and rests his head on his paws, his rear legs spread frog-like. His sad gaze follows Ace, then rolls to where Sari has disappeared. Ace flops resignedly into a chair, throwing a leg over the arm.

The boy begins to whimper as Sari cautiously approaches the crib. "Mooney? Baby, it's Mummy," she cries. He backs himself into a corner and turns his head away. Sari leans over the crib to pick up his old toy, offering it to him. "Here's Blue Bear, sweetie. 'Member your Blue Bear?" The child's lower lip trembles and he turns his back to Sari, forsaking his thumb long enough to grasp the bars of the crib and haul himself up.

"You're standing!" she says with delight. "He's standing," she calls to Ace. All this extra excitement is too much for Mooney who lets loose with a shriek. "What's the matter with him?" she wails as Ace enters the room.

"Probably scared," Ace says. He is about to provide a comforting hug to Sari's shoulders, but, remembering the welt, thinks better of it. Mooney leaves his corner and works his way around the crib to lean against the railing and hold up his arms to Ace. When he lifts him, Mooney's wet thumb grazes his ear. The baby quiets, staring soberly over Ace's shoulder. "See, he's fine. It'll just take some getting used to. After all," he says, leading the way to the living room, "it's been weeks since he's seen you. Isn't that right, big guy?" He growls into Mooney's neck until the baby chuckles.

Ace snaps his fingers at Mudd, who begrudgingly gives up his space on the couch, then sits, switching the baby to his knee. Sari perches on the edge of the couch facing her son, wiping her eyes with the back of her hand. Tentatively she strokes his cheek. "It's all new to you, isn't it, sweetie? Poor little boy." She drops her hand into her lap. "Where did you find him? How did you find him?"

Ace settles back smugly with the child leaning into the crook of his arm. "Well, a bit of shithouse luck and some leg work. When James left, he took all that stuff—the ceramics and collectibles," he says, pinching his mouth around *collectibles*. "Right?"

She agrees, shifting her attention from Ace to Mooney, who now seems quite content. "Do you think he'd like a bottle?"

"Want a bottle, big guy?" Ace asks.

Mooney gives no indication he's even heard the question.

"Guess not. Where was I?"

"James's antiques," she reminds him, extending her open hands to her son, testing. He snugs his chin into his chest and drops his gaze.

"I knew he'd be running out of cash travelling with a kid and all, so I checked places along the highway that deal in that sort of thing. Second-hand stores, antiques, and," he raises a finger for emphasis, "consignment stores."

Sari gets a why-didn't-I-think-of-it look and slides further onto the couch.

"It was a consignment store in Cache Creek that recognized his picture."

Sari sits up alertly. "What picture?"

"Uh-h-h," Ace says, stalling, "I, uh, got his picture from your album."

Sari swivels to see if the photo albums are still stacked beneath an end table.

"I had Mooney's poster but I didn't have anything of James and since he's the one driving the truck ..."

She folds her arms. "So you helped yourself." She's not really angry with the liberties he's taken but she shakes her head at him.

"If I had told you I was going to look for the kid, you would have gotten all excited, wondering if I'd find him. Wondering what was happening. And what if I hadn't found him?" Mooney's eyes grow larger as Ace's voice rises. "I had to do it on my own. Right?"

Sari responds, "Sh-h-h. It's okay, baby. Mummy's not mad." She lowers her voice. "Fine. You stole a picture, then what?"

"Well, first, let me go back to the beginning. You see, after I fixed the Harley, I had to figure out which way he went. If *I* were gutless and running away from my responsibilities," he squints one eye as he peers at her, "which way would I go? Well, I would head towards Vancouver. More work there and a guy could get lost pretty easy. Having a little kid along would slow things down a bit but, yup, that's the way to go—Vancouver."

Mooney is fighting to stay awake but the pleasant thrumming of Ace's heart against his ear soon soothes him into closing his eyes.

"So, like I said, I stop at these little second-hand places, showing his picture. Around Kamloops there's one old lady who thinks she might have recognized him. Thinks he might have been the guy who traded in a teapot. One with a monkey on it."

"That would be a Minton. He had a yellow one, I think."

"Yellow, that's what she said. She believes she paid him $60."

"It's worth more," she says.

"He'd take anything for a little gas money." Ace checks the sleeping Mooney. "Want me to put him down?"

"Let me have him," she says, reaching out.

Ace transfers the child to his mother and flexes the numbness from his forearm.

Sari eases back, finally holding her baby. She breathes him in.

"He smells so good," she says, her voice cracking. Tears well and she tries sniffing them away. Ace heads for the bathroom, returning with a length of toilet paper, handing it to her before taking his place on the sofa again.

"He'd been there so many weeks ago," he continues, "that the Kamloops woman couldn't really be sure. She didn't see a baby, so he must have left him in the truck." Ace extends his legs, propping them on the coffee table. "After that I just keep going. It was kinda nice, getting back on the road. Wind blowing in my face and all that." He watches Sari run her fingers through Mooney's short red hair.

Aware of his stare, she explains, "He's had a haircut. When it was long, it was so curly my fingers would get tangled."

The sight of Sari cuddling her son causes Ace to jam his fist into his mid-section right where he feels the jolt. "Got a beer?" he says, suddenly standing.

"You know where everything is."

He opens the fridge door, moving aside the milk and ketchup. "Nope." He looks around the kitchen for inspiration. "Want a coffee?"

Remembering the last cup he made, she requests tea instead.

He resumes his story, talking over his shoulder as he fills the kettle from the tap. "In Cache Creek I hit pay dirt. There's this couple running this antique place. You know the kind, they write the name in Old English and spell it s-h-o-p-p-e." He plugs in the kettle and leans against the counter waiting for it to boil. "Anyway, they know him for sure because he's left the rest of his stuff there. On consignment. Which means there has to be a contact number." Ace swishes water through the teapot and looks around for tea bags.

"Above your head and to the left. In a jar," Sari directs.

"They suggest I purchase a 'dear little reproduction of a motor-cycle.' It's made of tin but, jeez, the price I paid you'd think it was gold." He waves away her offer of repayment. "I kinda like it now. It's an Indian. A real old-timer. Anyway, one of these guys leads me to the door. He points way down the highway to a Shell station. 'That's her,' the guy says, 'that's where he works.' He swears me to secrecy—Scout's honour and all that." Ace pours water on the tea and replaces the lid. He reaches for two mugs. "You take milk and sugar, right?"

"Neither."

"I knew that. I was just testing." He returns to the couch with the tea, placing hers on the table within reach.

Once Ace is comfortable, he continues. "I scope out this garage from across the street, but he isn't there. 'James working today?' I ask the girl at the pumps. 'Works midnights,' she answers. 'Where's he live?' I ask." Ace shrugs in answer to his own question. "'Dunno,' she says. 'What time's he start?' 'Duh,' she says, 'try midnight.' So I figure I'll just hang around until he shows up." Ace stands to illustrate the next portion of his story. "I back my bike up between these two buildings, see, across from the garage. Then I look for a place to eat supper where I can watch the street. The closest is a truck stop next to the Shell. So over I go and grab a table, get a bite and just hang out. 'Bout eight o'clock I can't drink any more coffee so I go sit on my bike for the next four hours."

"Long time," she says.

"Long time," he concurs. "But, now you won't believe this, around twelve, people coming and going, you understand, twelve o'clock, because my watch beeped, so I know it's twelve o'clock and from the building right next to where I'm parked, James strolls out the door."

"James?"

"Hard to believe, right? Almost in my lap. He doesn't look to right nor left 'til he gets to the highway, then he runs over to the Shell. And he's wearing one of their uniforms. I figure he must live in the building that's holding me up, so I try the door. Locked. Now what? I check the names next to the door and there he is—J. Button, 303. Didn't even change his name. I push all the buzzers but his, and damned if someone doesn't buzz me in."

Sari closes her eyes, resting her cheek on the top of Mooney's head.

"Want me to finish this tomorrow?"

"Sorry," she says, stealing a glance at the clock. "I've been up for almost eighteen hours, but I want to hear the end."

"Okay. Two flights up I go looking for 303. There it is, right in the corner. You wouldn't know it first hand," he grins, "but I'm pretty good at breaking and entering. A flick of the credit card and, ta-da, like magic, it opens up." Ace bounces back onto the couch now that the heavy action has taken place. "I scan the hall, then walk in as if I own the joint. It's only one room and the kid isn't there. Then I hear him sucking on the last of his bottle. Guess where he is?"

"Where?"

"In the closet! In the goddamn closet," he says fiercely. "The door's open a crack but he sure as hell doesn't like it when I look in on him. Raises a big stink." He smiles at the memory.

Sari doesn't smile in return. "He left him alone in a closet?" she says.

Ace nods. "Yeah," he says.

"The dirty bastard!"

Ace agrees with her assessment of James. "But I pick him up 'cause he's just a little kid and I talk to him and sing to him, and he's okay with that."

"You sing to him?" she asks, trying to erase the image of Mooney's isolated confinement.

"Yeah, stuff my dad used to sing. 'The Cowboy's Lament' and 'Rye Whiskey' and 'Bullfrog Sittin' on a Lily Pad'—you know, stuff like that."

"Guy songs," she says.

"Right! Wasn't any time at all and the kid and I are conversing man-to-man. Then I figure it's about time to hit the road. Test-drive the Harley he's heard so much about. I look around the apartment a bit. There was food in the fridge. They weren't starving and he's got twelve hundred dollars in the bank."

"Wha-a-t?"

"Bank book says twelve hundred and some-odd change. No TV, not much in the way of furniture, just one of those futons that pulls out to a bed. There's toys and a walker and things like that. The kid probably isn't hard done by but the son of a bitch still shouldn't be leaving him in a closet all night by himself."

Sari pulls Mooney closer and he stirs in his sleep.

"I forget to bring a bag for his clothes, so I use a couple of grocery bags, toss in a few little toys and put them all by the door. All this time, I'm still holding him. I find his jacket in the closet and he starts to cry, thinking maybe I'm throwing him back in the crib. He's still got a full bottle left but I wash a couple more and fill 'em up. By then I'm getting pretty good at working with one hand. Then I leave a Dear James."

Sari lets her shoes drop to the floor and curls her legs onto the couch, trying not to disturb Mooney. "What did you write?"

"Word for word? Can't remember. Something like, I'm returning Mooney to his mother. Go to the authorities if you want because they'd love to see you about a kidnapping. Let them know he'd been abandoned in a fuckin' closet."

She extends her bare foot to give a reassuring touch to his leg. "Do you think he'll try to get him back?"

"No."

"What makes you so sure?" she asks, studying his face.

"Well," he admits, scratching the stubble on his chin, "I tacked the note to the wall with six inches of steak knife. He'll get the message."

Mooney opens his eyes, raises them briefly to his mother, then crawls to Ace's lap.

Ace gives him a kiss on the top of the head and says, "Come on, little man, bedtime." He carries him down the hallway to his room and tucks him into bed. Mooney sets up a protest but Ace settles him down again, promising to stay right in the doorway.

Sari follows but stays out of sight, leaning her hip against the wall.

"We spent a couple of days on the road, this little biker guy and me, not hurrying, just taking our time. He sleeps in the sidecar and I ride, then when he wants out, we hang at playgrounds or gravel pits and other neat places like that. I phoned you twice but you weren't home. End of story. It's okay, little feller, I'm still here. Lie down."

Sari moves toward Ace, sliding her arms around his waist. She lays her head against him and hugs him tightly. "Thank you," she whispers. "Thank you." He hugs her back.

"You go to bed, too," he says. "You're asleep on your feet. I'll hang around for a bit and keep an eye out."

She peeks in at Mooney, then turns and heads for her room.

A few minutes later, Ace hears a shout and rushes down the hall, almost colliding with Sari, now returning in her baggy night tee-shirt. "What's the matter?" he asks, seeing the stricken look on her face.

"I've got to work tomorrow," she says, waving her hands.

"Yeah. So?"

"Mooney's back. James was always here to watch him."

"Not a problem. I'm right next door."

"I can't ask you to babysit," she says, appalled at the idea. "I'll call in sick and phone around for someone." She slaps a hand to her forehead. "After I fix the phone."

He grasps her shoulders, twisting her to face him. "You'd get a stranger to watch him when I'm right here? Good old Uncle Ace?"

She covers her face, thinking. "Okay. Okay," she concedes, her hands falling to her sides. "But only until I find someone reliable."

"I am reliable," he shoots back.

"A daycare, maybe. You know what I mean."

"We'll be just fine," he says, turning her to face her bedroom. "Now goodnight," he concludes, giving her a little push. "See you in the morning."

During the night she dreams Mooney is back and, waking, slips from her room to check his crib as she has so many times before. In the living room, Ace, snoring gently, one hand trailing into her discarded shoe, shares the couch with Mudd, curled in the space where Ace's legs rise to cross themselves on the arm of the couch. Sari continues down the hallway to Mooney's room. He's on his stomach, thumb in his mouth, backside in the air. She luxuriates in his being there, then covers him to his ears. She picks up a Winnie-the-Pooh quilt from the nearby rocking chair and returns to the living room to cover Ace from shoulder to knee. "Thank you," she repeats, before tiptoeing back to bed.

VIII

ON SUNDAY MORNING A TRIO of women from the Briar Rose Home—Mrs. Stubbs, Mrs. Dickie and Miss Toomey—arrive to bang on Mariah's back door even before the automatic coffeepot has turned itself on. They cluck and chirp around the kitchen, unpacking aprons and card tables and supplies. Flora scuttles away in her nightie to get dressed while the visitors begin the business of decrusting the long loaves of white bread for rolled cream cheese and asparagus sandwiches. They will also construct ribbon sandwiches of ham, Swiss and eye-watering homemade mustard. At Flora's request, Roquefort and honey and a recent favourite, cheddar cheese and jam, have been added to their list of things to make, but once the women assemble them, they plan on burying them at the back of the fridge.

After collaring her mother in the hallway, Mariah demands, "What are we going to do with those women once the sandwiches are made? They'll be sitting around for the rest of the day with nothing to do."

"Leave the girls to me," Flora snaps. "These ladies know how to throw a party, and, I might add, how *to enjoy* one."

Mariah throws up her hands defensively. "I'm going to enjoy this party too, Flora. Even if it kills me."

"Why don't you go write something? I've got work to do." Flora returns to the kitchen to start another pot of coffee, then, shears in hand, departs to slash daisies from the roadside. These and a generous armload of wild oats from the same source will stand sentinel in buckets around the yard. Orchids came under discussion with the ladies she calls her birthday committee, but they were ruled out as unnecessary because pulled-apart gladiolas come close enough in appearance to be an excellent substitute.

Up until two days ago Mariah had been dreading this event. She had been waking in the night with her stomach in knots, knowing it would come to pass but wishing for something dreadful to happen— Bunny's housekeeper could die, she herself could catch something highly infectious, her mother could slip into a coma. But with her mother so consumed by this party, Mariah has finally had a middle-of-the-night change of heart. And after all Flora's work and enthusiasm, Mariah decides, God help anybody who doesn't show up.

Although Mariah has talked her out of making kidney and plum upside-down cake, she has encouraged her to make the *pièce de résistance,* a stunning blue Jell-O lagoon with too-large sunken fish and a fringe of paper palm trees, which is now displayed in all its glory beneath the patio umbrella borrowed from the neighbour. Flora, however, won't let her see her birthday cake. All in all, Mariah suspects, she might just be able to endure this thing with the generous helping of overproof rum she will slide into the pineapple punch.

Flora, in a flash of artistic inspiration, has adapted an idea from a 1994 home decorating book. Covering two scruffy tables with bed-sheets from the house, she yawns open a variety of small suitcases on the table tops, overflowing their interiors with colourful scarves and glass beads. Her helpers then load these valises with plates, glasses, pitchers of cold lemonade and pineapple punch. In a wicker suitcase that no longer locks, Flora piles leopard-spotted napkins and the silverware. Plugged into a long extension cord snaking across the lawn, a portable stereo holds two Hawaiian tapes—one an eight-string guitar medley and the other a syrupy Don Ho—that will entertain the revellers throughout the afternoon.

The last item for the party, with the exception of the cake Miss Toomey is finishing, is Axel. With the bird still enclosed within his cage, Flora attaches a shoelace to his scaly leg while she warns him that ladies are present and he is to watch his language. Then she carries the African Grey in one hand, perch in the other, out the door and across the yard to shelter beneath the striped sheet she has pegged to the clothesline. Two raised poles hold up the opposite corners to form a canopy over the assortment of tables and chairs pressed into service. Flora rams the perch into the grass, then ties the dangling shoelace to it. The bird hunches on his dowel, head pulled into his turtle-necked feathers.

When Mrs. Stubbs appears, resplendent in a scarlet and lime muumuu, she takes a gladiola blossom from a moss-lined basket and wedges it over Mariah's ear. Now the party can begin.

IT'S A VISION IN A pink orchid-print dress, slit both sides to the thigh, who greets Ace and Sari as the Harley stops on the grass and gravel driveway at the side of Mariah's cottage. "Aloha! I heard you coming. Who might you two be?" says the vision.

"I'm Sari Button. I'm in Mariah's writing group and—"

"Sari! How nice you could come. We talked on the phone. I'm Flora, Mariah's—"

"Social secretary, right?" Sari teases.

"Right."

"I hope you don't mind that I brought my neighbour, Ace Wilde?" Sari says, "My son is quite attached to him and I'm having to ease him back into life with Mom." She steps from the sidecar with Mooney in her arms, shifting him to her hip before removing her helmet. Mooney casts about for Ace, holding his arms out as he climbs off the Harley. Sari hands him over and rolls her eyes at Flora. "See?" Ace settles the baby on his hip.

"More the merrier," Flora beams, taking Ace's free hand in both of hers. She opens his palm, sweeping her index finger across the map on it. "Shows a love of the open road," she reads, "and a long life line." She drops his hand to take Sari's. "We were so happy to hear you got your son back. Don'tcha just love happy endings?" Flora clings to Sari's arm and leans in. "Thanks for wearing that nice tropical skirt. Mariah thinks I'm out of my mind trying to get a Hay-waiian atmosphere but just look at you. And that beautiful baby. Thanks, honey. Everyone's out that way," Flora points. "There are name stickers to fill out on the table and Mrs. Stubbs is in charge of the pineapple punch."

"Aren't you coming?" asks Sari.

"You go ahead, dear. I see dust rising down the road. Must be another car and I'm official greeter."

Sari leads Ace and Mooney toward the only face she knows–Mariah's—but Mrs. Stubbs halts the procession to tuck a gladiola blossom behind Sari's ear then thrusts glasses of punch at the couple. Each drink is adorned with a paper umbrella, its stem frozen into an ice cube, which unfortunately bobs around the glass making drinking hazardous.

In the driveway the new arrival coasts her BMW into the space beside Ace's motorcycle. On the passenger seat is her contribution—silk leis purchased from the dollar store.

"You must be Mrs. deLore. Aloha! Oh, how lovely," she coos when handed the leis. "Just the thing." *There are perhaps fifteen or so*, she thinks, *and I've invited just that many people, including the three ladies from the Home, Sari, Mrs. deLore …*

"Is that Sari?" Bunny inquires as she alights from her car. "With the baby?" She smiles broadly and excuses herself, hailing Sari as she nears.

Flora begins her count again. *The three gals from Briar Rose, Sari and her neighbour, Mrs. deLore, Jemima and her husband in the wheelchair, that dog woman, Chloe, the neighbours on either side and Clive if he can get away …* "Naw, Clive won't show," she says to herself as she picks up her skirts and heads for the party. Clive doesn't visit his mother and sister. "He'll phone an hour after everyone's gone home to say how sorry, how very, very sorry he is but something came up." Of course, Roland, her other son, had pooh-poohed the whole thing as tiresome.

Flora regrets there is no closeness between her kids, but this is not something that could have been her fault. She assigns blame for this family dysfunction to the fact that each of her children had a different father. Mariah's was the heroic Nigel, a guy whose face she can't recall; Roland's she remembers only as Houdini because he vanished when her pregnancy became very evident; and finally there was Clive's daddy, dear old reliable Dodge. That is, reliable until he missed Clive's first birthday by turning up his toes and dying after falling from his mother's roof. Flora stops, lost in thought for the moment; recovering, she begins searching the faces in the gathering for her daughter.

Mariah has her back turned, speaking with that girlfriend of hers, that dreadful dog woman, Chloe, whose starched blonde hair spikes above Mariah. Chloe bellows a laugh, throwing back her head, then flinging her arm around Mariah's shoulders and rubbing between her shoulder blades. Flora is about to break up this tête-à-tête and get her daughter to mingle but turns instead at the sound of another car crunching the gravel. "Well, I'll be damned," she exclaims as the Jeep driver throws her a crisp salute. "He did show up."

"Hi, there, Mater. Long time no see." He unfolds his long thin body from behind the wheel then reaches in to retrieve his oiled leather Australian bush hat.

"Now whose fault would that be, I have to ask myself."

"Uh-uh-uh," Clive says, wagging a finger at her. "This is be-kind-to-darling-Clive day." He lifts Flora in a fierce hug, swinging her round in an arc. "You look as good as ever, you gorgeous wench, you."

"Put me down, you'll hurt yourself." When her feet return to the ground, she gives him a smack on the chest. "You stay away forever then all of a sudden show up expecting me to fall all over you." Despite her harsh words, she kisses him on the cheek and takes his arm, wanting to be seen on it when he makes his entrance on the back lawn.

"Did you not leave a message on my machine saying the Great Lump is having a birthday party and to bring a very expensive gift?"

"Clive," Flora warns, as she walks him toward the stereo, "be nice to your sister."

"I'll try."

Flora turns down the music, clears her throat and announces, "Everybody, can I have your attention? Woo-hoo!" Faces turn toward her expectantly. Axel, indifferent to Flora's demand for attention, emits a series of wolf whistles that end up bridging into the first eight notes of "Oh, Canada."

Mariah mouths, "Oh, for Chrissake," when she spots the newest arrival.

"Everyone," Flora trumpets, "I'd like you to meet my son, Clive. He drove all the way from the Island to be here."

After a patter of polite applause, he gives a wave and a tip of the hat, then excuses himself to lope to where Mariah is shrinking into herself. She looks for escape but her feet are grounded. "Happy birthday, sister dear," he booms. He gives her the same enthusiastic hug he gave Flora but without the whirling liftoff, and when his chin hits her ear he whispers, "You look none the worse for wear, Lump." Then, straight-arming her, he inspects the goods. "You stacked on a little weight? Coloured your hair? Suits you. So where's the girlfriend?"

Mariah splutters as he darts around her to confront Chloe.

"You must be that 'dreadful dog woman' Mother told me about. What's the name?"

"Chloe," she says coldly.

"I'm pleased to meet you, Chloe. She didn't mention that you were such a stunning piece of work." He wraps an arm around her shoulder and leads her toward Flora. "Flora?" he calls. "Flora, you didn't tell me Mariah's friend here—" he squeezes her to him in another of his animated hugs, "—is so—so divine." He bestows a charming smile on Chloe who is now looking into his face with uncertainty.

"Nice to meet you, Clive," she finally utters. She looks over her shoulder to where Mariah is standing.

Clive follows her glance, quickly releasing Chloe from his grasp. "Uh-oh," he says, feigning fright, "she's got her bullfrog face on. Come on, I'll walk you back."

Now that she no longer has Clive's attention, Flora cranks up the music.

"Is he for real?" Chloe asks Mariah once Clive is a safe distance away, engaging Mrs. Stubbs with his winsome smile.

"As real as polyester and capped teeth and hair replacement therapy can make him." Mariah drains her tumbler, the red umbrella in it hitting her glasses. "Oh God, he's coming back."

"Mariah, love," Clive says temperately, "come with me to the Jeep. I have a little something for your birthday."

"You weren't supposed to bring gifts, Clive," she reminds him, but she breaks into a trot to keep up with his long legs.

"This is special. Just for you," he calls back without looking.

Mariah braces for something completely awful—a bag of briquettes, a new toilet seat, something totally practical and devoid of emotion. When Clive hands her an immense, heavy, gold-papered box tied with lacy metallic ribbon, she almost drops it. "It's nothing alive, is it?"

He smacks his forehead, knocking his hat askew. "You wanted a pot-bellied pig, didn't you?"

Mariah stumbles a few steps, not being able to see around the box.

"Take it into the house," he directs. "The rest of them don't have to know."

She looks at him suspiciously. "You're scaring me. Why are you being nice all of a sudden?"

"Here, let me take that," he offers, removing the box from her arms. "You don't have to be brave for me."

"Brave? What are you talking about?"

They reach the back porch and Mariah moves ahead to open the screen door. Miss Toomey is at the sink making fresh lemonade. "Howdy-do?" she says, turning off the tap. "Thirsty bunch out there." She throws a few slices of lemon into the pitcher, then stirs the mixture, ice cubes pinging against the glass. She gazes out the window, humming as she stirs. The humming and pinging continue until Clive pointedly clears his throat. She gets the message and picks up the pitcher, holding it against her daisy-print apron while she heads for the door.

He opens the screen for her before continuing his conversation with Mariah. "Flora told me," he says, his long face now showing his years.

"Told you what?"

"About your ... you know ... your female ... um-m ... your female problem."

Mariah guffaws. "My what?" She stands with her hands on her hips, a stance that always annoyed Clive as a boy. It usually meant he was about to get jumped on by his older sister. Even now he holds out his hands placatingly.

"You're p-probably in denial, and that's okay," he stutters. "I know lots of people who have had tumours removed and lived. Lots of people."

"Tumour?" she says, puzzled. Her expression changes to one of sudden understanding. "Ah-h-h, that's how she got you here, isn't it? Poor old Mariah has a monstrous tumour. On my ovaries, is it?"

"Some kind of tubing," he replies.

"Sorry to disappoint you, Clive, but I'm in the pink." She walks to the window, tipping on the ball of one foot to take in the whole back-yard. "Want me to call her in? We could really do a number on her."

"She hasn't changed all that much, has she?" he says, picking the box from the stove top. "She's still manipulating us."

"Does that mean I don't get the present?"

He snorts a laugh. "Nah, it's still your birthday." He places the package next to her. "I would have come anyway, you know."

"Sure, Clive." She tugs at the ribbon, pulling it free to drape it around her neck. Very carefully, she lifts the sticky tape from the gold foil, then folds the paper neatly, delaying the outcome. At last she opens the flaps of the box, pulls out reams of lilac tissue paper, then tilts the box to see what's inside. She frowns. "What the hell is it?"

Clive steps up, saying, "You hang on to that red thing there, and I'll pull the box off." He discards the box and the rest of the tissue drifts onto the floor.

Mariah is left holding a time-worn carousel in her two hands. The red top has faded to a warm shade of adobe and the chipped white paint shows its primer beneath. She holds it at eye level and comes face to face with a black horse, his mane flowing behind him as he races the music. "It's beautiful, Clive," she breathes.

He's relieved at her approval. "It's an antique music box."

"I love merry-go-rounds," she says. "You remembered that?"

"Sure, old girl, why wouldn't I? Here, let me wind it up."

Mariah places the gift in his hands and plants a self-conscious kiss on Clive's cheek as he turns the brass key. The merry-go-round starts hesitantly then the swans and horses begin gliding to a tune she can't place. "What's it playing?"

He shrugs. "Nothing Hawaiian, I can assure you."

"It'll come to me when peace and quiet return to this place." She picks it up. "I love it. I'll put it in my room so it doesn't get broken. Thank you." Even after Mariah takes it to her bedroom, the music continues to play. She shuts the door on it to return to the kitchen.

Clive has left the house but the box and scattered tissue remain. She squats to gather the paper, shaking her head first at the audacity of Flora's statement, then at the occasion of Clive's visit. She suddenly sits back on her heels. "Oh God, you don't suppose she got everybody here the same way?" She abandons the box and slams out the screen door just in time to see Jemima's old Buick pull in behind the other cars. But Flora has seen it first and she's hustling across the lumpy lawn with her skirt in hand as Jemima exits the driver's side and steps to the back of the car. Joe opens the passenger door in readiness as Jemima wrestles the folded wheelchair from the trunk. When Jemima sets it beside him, he eases into it.

Mariah clunks down the stairs and marches over to where her mother is chatting up the new arrivals.

"Happy birthday, Mariah," Jemima says dutifully. "Give her the present, Joe."

"You shouldn't have done that," Flora scolds sweetly. "Your being here is gift enough. Isn't that right, Mariah?" When she doesn't get an answer, she looks into Mariah's face.

"Want a hand with the chair?" Flora says, hoping to get away. "Everyone is out back."

Jemima smiles at Flora's quick thinking. She's caught the look between mother and daughter and, having seen Mariah's thunderous looks before, knows that soon the *fit will hit the shan*. "We'll manage with the chair. It's all downhill from here."

Mariah catches Flora's shoulder and spins her around as she tries to follow the new arrivals. "I've got a bone to pick with you," Mariah proclaims, hands on hips.

"What?" Flora replies hotly, taking the same stance.

"The only way you could get Clive here was to tell him I had a tumour?" She hears the familiar wheeze in her chest and begins deliberately breathing as evenly as possible.

"Is that what he said?" She flaps her hand dismissing Mariah's accusation. "Must have been the message machine acting up. Now why would I tell him a thing like that? A tumour, you say? Huh!" She hikes up her skirt, the slits on either side exposing her spindly legs to the thigh, then tramps toward the back yard.

"Does everybody at this party think I have a tumour?" Mariah says, loud enough for Flora to hear.

"Now you're being melodramatic," she calls back, but she soon stops to see if Mariah is following. "Well, come on. Everybody's here. We can bring out the cake." She frees a hand to shade her eyes. "Wipe that look off your face, dear. After all, it's your party."

"And I'll cry if I want to," Mariah concludes under her breath. She doesn't immediately follow Flora but stands looking over her guests. If she were invited to a party like this, she'd leave. She's surprised that people seem to be having a pleasant afternoon. Sari and Bunny sit cross-legged on the lawn with Mooney between them, playing with a bucket of small toys. Mariah's neighbour is adjusting the strap on her sandal while enduring Chloe's complaints regarding the declining quality of judging at dog shows. Joe, Clive and Ace balance paper plates and talk without looking at one another. Jemima is feeding cheese to the bird. At the house Miss Toomey is emerging backwards from the kitchen, butting open the screen door with her rear end. She holds before her what looks like a portly pink dog balancing on the platter. "What the hell?" Mariah mutters, her curiosity leading her on.

Miss Toomey's legs are bowed under the burden of the platter and Clive leaps up to relieve her of the thing. She clutches her chest dramatically and pants her instructions to set it on the table. "Don't look! Don't look!" she squeals, before retreating to the house. When she emerges with a knife and a bowl she hustles directly to the cake table to repair the damage done in transit. "Okay, now you can look," she announces proudly as she steps back, arms spread wide, bowl in one hand, icing-covered knife in the other. "Sur-r-rprise, Mariah! It's a pink poodle cake. Flora told me how you love dogs."

Mariah doesn't argue the point or dare to raise her eyes from the table. She digs her nails into her thumbs. Her walleyed birthday cake stares back, sturdy on the legs angled to his body. Right where it should be, a stubby tail juts ninety degrees from the dog's square back end. "I baked the cake mix in soup cans to make the legs. And the body is like a jellyroll—well, actually it is a jellyroll," Miss Toomey reveals. The jostling and the heat of the day are taking their toll and the melting cream cheese icing has begun to slide from between the poodle's ears, oozing over the forehead and cheeks, wrinkling under its own weight to settle jowl-like around the dog's clove-studded muzzle.

"Thank you, Miss Toomey, it's … it's …" Mariah struggles for words.

But Miss Toomey is sagging as fast as her icing. Her lip trembles and her brimming eyes enlarge behind her granny glasses. "It's awful, isn't it?"

In the awkward silence Chloe steps forward to give Miss Toomey a comforting hug. "It's wonderful, Miss Toomey. Isn't that right, everybody? Let's give the cook a big hand." Chloe gives Mariah a piercing look and Mariah stumbles through another appreciative thank you.

"Okay, folks," Flora says, picking up a paper plate, "who wants a piece of this fine-looking cake of Miss Toomey's?"

"We didn't sing 'Happy Birthday,'" Sari reminds them.

Flora replaces the paper plate and reaches into the depths of her muumuu. "Anybody got a match?" she asks, holding up a sparkler.

When it's lit, she plunges it into the cake. "Now!" she instructs, raising her hands to conduct the group in a discordant chorus.

∞

LATER, WHEN THE LOWERING SUN is in their eyes and the body and legs of the cake have parted company, Flora wraps leftovers in waxed paper, urging the departing guests to help themselves. First to leave are the neighbours who lent the patio umbrella, then Chloe, complaining behind her sunglasses of a sinus headache, followed by Sari, Ace and the sleeping Mooney, his cheeks flushed with too much sun.

Having insisted that a woman Flora's age must have her rest, the cheery trio of helpers from the Briar Rose Home clean up the disarray. Flora, unhappy at the reference to age, glumly burps cream cheese icing and drops onto a chair, collapsing inside her muumuu. She always feels down after one of her famous parties, during the period she calls her post-party-um blues. What she needs, she believes, is another pineapple punch, but Miss Toomey has dumped the remainder on the garden, saying it just won't keep, then rinsed the bowl with the hose. Mariah has withdrawn to the eastern corner of the lawn. She lights a new cigarette from the stub of her last.

Clive pushes Joe's wheelchair uphill to see Joe and Jemima off before returning to the lawn chairs to go knee-to-knee with Bunny. He tries his best to charm her with a travelogue of his past tours—the Arenal Volcano of Costa Rica, the Mayan ruins of the Yucatan, the new subway tunnelling beneath Athens. Bunny braces, overwhelmed by Mariah's lanky bombastic brother, and she's relieved when one of the Briar Rose Trio woo-hoos at Clive. Bunny interrupts his monologue to point this out. He gives her knee a friendly pat, saying he'll be right back to tell her about Down Under. Then while he's toting card tables to the trunk of the appointed station wagon, she strikes out to thank Flora and Mariah for the wonderful time. It hasn't been as wonderful as she is about to make out, but it has certainly taken her mind off her own problems. "Mariah, honey," she says, feeling a compassion that probably won't surface again for a while, "Thank you for the lovely party."

"It was the shits," Mariah says thickly, not even turning around.

"It was grand. Those ladies did an amazing amount of work. All that food and the lovely cake ..." She trails off.

Mariah turns slowly, peering from under her bangs. "Bunny deLore, always saying the proper thing." She grinds the cigarette into the lawn, then stares past Bunny to the remnants of the afternoon's affair. "You're right," she admits, her tone softening. "They did outdo themselves. But that's not what I'm moping about." Mariah removes her glasses to clean them on her shirt. She heaves a theatrical sigh. "I'm lamenting the passing of time. I'm fifty-seven years old and look at me." She replaces her glasses.

"I know the feeling," Bunny commiserates.

"How the hell could you possibly know?" Mariah shoots. "You have a big, beautiful house, a rich husband, a grown daughter and no worries."

Bunny doesn't know whether to laugh or cry. "Is that how I look to you? All surface stuff?"

"What other way is there?" Mariah gropes for another smoke.

Bunny decides that this is not the time to lay bare her soul. "You're right," she says lightly, throwing away the argument. "I have it all." She turns and begins to stride across the lawn.

By the tone of her reply, Mariah realizes that she's probably gouged Bunny's thin veneer, and she goes after her.

"I have to thank your mother," Bunny says, spotting Clive closing the trunk and dusting his hands.

"She's asleep. See?" Mariah thrusts her chin in the direction of the chair Flora is slumped in, head back, mouth open, drinking in the afternoon sun.

"Are you sure?" Bunny asks. Flora appears more dead than alive, much like the unconscious Gerda laid out on the stretcher.

"I'm sure," Mariah snorts. "She got an early start this morning."

"Walk me to my car," Bunny says, pretty sure that Mariah's presence will deflect Clive.

IX

BY TUESDAY EVENING BUNNY HAS run the mop around the parts of the house that her group will see and ragged the dust from the furniture in the library. Once they are assembled, Sari makes a point of telling Mariah that Ace and Mooney enjoyed the birthday party.

Seeing as Sari has brought the subject up, Jemima asks, "What's with this neighbour of yours, Sari? Is he going to be a permanent fixture?" When she picked Sari up, Ace had been holding Mooney, encouraging him to wave bye-bye to Mummy. Jemima still doesn't like the looks of him. A biker.

"He's my babysitter."

"You trust him to watch Mooney?" Jemima persists.

"Trust him, Jemima?" Sari replies sharply.

"I seem to remember you complaining because he broke into your trailer once."

"Matter of fact, he broke in three times."

Now Sari has everyone's attention. Mariah pushes her glasses up and waits expectantly.

"The first time," she says, holding up a finger, "was when he wanted to set the table to surprise me. He knew I was all alone and walking into an empty house." She pauses, shaking her head in disbelief. "I sort of overreacted." She holds up a second finger. "The second time was when he took a poster of Mooney and a picture of James from my album. He didn't want me to get my hopes up that he would find them. And third was the wonderful night he brought Mooney home. Three times. And third time lucky." She crosses her arms, expecting to field some questions.

"So," Jemima says, still suspicious, "has he moved in then?"

"No, he hasn't, thank you very much. He's my babysitter, like I told you."

"So he goes home at night?"

"That's right, Bunny, he goes home at night."

"Too bad," Bunny responds. "I was looking for a little romance."

"Well, you'll just have to get it elsewhere." Sari isn't about to tell them how things are progressing with Ace. And they are progressing. She is finding him a good listener. He usually has Mooney fed by the time she gets home from work and has supper on for them, though he isn't a great chef. He overcooks the vegetables and tries to get her to eat liver, but she doesn't care. He is making the effort and that pleases her.

"How come he doesn't have a job?"

"He's on a year's sabbatical."

"From what?" Jemima asks, without adding *bank robbery*?

The phone rings and Bunny says, "Don't answer that question until I come back."

"Come on, what does he do? You can tell us," Jemima coaxes.

Sari refuses.

Mariah loses interest and fusses with her manuscript pages, then asks bluntly, "Are we having a writing session here tonight or what?"

Bunny replaces the receiver. She takes a moment to reflect on the call before she rejoins the other three, who are getting out their pages.

"That was the hospital," Bunny reveals.

"Oh, rats, I meant to ask about your housekeeper and forgot," Jemima admits.

"Yeah, me too," Mariah echoes.

"Is there something wrong?" Sari inquires.

Bunny wanders to the window and parts the curtains. She feels quite buoyant. Like a weight lifting from her body. *Gerda doesn't remember the accident.* After absently straightening the curtains, she turns. "I've come to a decision," she says firmly. Then, as if only just hearing Sari's question, she says, "No. No, nothing's wrong. In fact, it's the opposite. Gerda is out of her coma."

"Hey, that's great," Sari tells her.

"Well, it's good and bad," she tells them. Mariah tempers her impatience to begin the evening's session. "She's out of her coma," Bunny continues, "but it seems for the moment that she has some brain damage. She responds to her name but remembers nothing about her accident."

"What's this momentous decision you've come to?" Mariah inquires, with an edge of sarcasm.

Bunny paces in front of the liquor cabinet. She would love to pour herself a large scotch but feels the group would think less of her. She'll try to end the evening early. "When the time comes, I'm going to bring Gerda back here to this house and nurse her back to health."

"Martyrdom just coursing through those blue veins, eh, Bunny?" Mariah sallies.

"I think you're out of your mind," Jemima says. "I've been looking after Joe and it's bloody hard work, and he only had a stroke. Is this woman able to walk on her own? Feed herself?"

"I don't know. Probably not."

"Then you'd better rethink this decision of yours."

"Are we *ever* going to start?" Mariah says tartly.

Bunny taps the back of Sari's chair. "What were you going to say before the phone rang? Something about Ace—such a funny name—enjoying a sabbatical."

"It's not important."

"Oh, please," Mariah says, sweeping her hand dramatically, "we're all ears."

"Well, since you asked, Ace is not unemployed." Sari pauses for effect. "He's a golf pro—"

Mariah and Jemima snort.

"—at a course in Saskatoon." She gives a look that dares any disparaging remarks.

"Lovely," Bunny answers automatically. *I can put Gerda in the music room and then there wouldn't be those damn stairs to climb. Those killer stairs.*

"Who wants to go first?" Jemima inquires. The first spot is not an honour. It gets the most scrutiny. "No takers? Then I'll start. I thought I'd write something about manners and serving afternoon tea." She begins to read aloud.

Emerson states that "Manners are the happy way of doing things." Things have changed since Emerson's time. Today's diners are bereft of even the most fundamental manners. Elbows on the tables, napkins tucked into collars if they are picked up at all. Children are moving constantly, eating with their little mouths jammed full of food, yelling or carrying on with the fond indulgence of their parents.

Back in the 1920s manners were given due regard, and civilized people judged others by their etiquette. Etiquette tends to establish conduct and good conduct is welcome everywhere. I believe today we lack this essential courtesy. Children run amok and parents wring their hands in dismay or scream obscenities at them from a distance. Perhaps the problem today with young people is the lack of manners and the total disregard for the feelings of others. Starting when babies are strapped into their high chairs, they should be taught please—

Jemima emphasizes this point with a thump to the arm of the sofa.

—and thank you. Expect great things from them and they will live up to your expectations.

"You have your grandchildren visiting last week?" Mariah asks, peering over her glasses.

"Yes," Jemima replies shortly.

"Thought so."

Her cheeks a higher colour than usual, Jemima complains, "I'm still cleaning up after them. Jell-O stuck to everything." Her arms flail as if to describe her kitchen dripping green ooze. "After they leave, there's nothing like a nice quiet cuppa, and that's how I got to thinking about afternoon tea." She switches pages and the others do likewise.

When I did my research into afternoon tea, I read a 1926 book on etiquette. In it the author describes two forms of tea—"a tea" and "tea." The difference is significant. A tea is an affair and begs formal decorations with a lady dressed in her best afternoon gown complete with white gloves, whereas tea is a break from the rigours of the everyday world. The formal afternoon tea calls for the invitation to be written on the hostess's visiting card. She may be forgiven for overextending her household's capacity to house the tea guests as too many is better than too few. The hostess who must scrape by with only one maid may hire another for the day to open the door—before the bell rings if possible—and to guide the guests into the correct area for removing coats. It's a ceremony where just the right foods are served—tea, of course, and chocolate or coffee, baskets of skinny bread-and-butter sandwiches, trays of plain wafer-thin cakes (so as not to soil the gloves), and, if the kitchen help is willing, toast or scones. The food is not to be overdone. Simplicity is a point of pride. Guests who weigh their hostess down with conversation is considered bad form. Just a few moments of her time is ideal so as not to slow the receiving line. It's an orderly ceremony where rules govern how one should conduct themself. There's a measure of comfort knowing what is expected.

"Is that it?" Mariah blurts, turning over the page.

"That's enough for a column. If there's any further interest, I will continue."

"That's really good, Jemima," says Sari. "There's a lot of history to tea. But I'm glad we don't have to go through all that rigamarole today. White gloves and tiny sandwiches?"

"Give me slabs of roast beef and horseradish between hunks of white bread any day," Mariah states.

"Things were different back then," Jemima says. "Girls had chaperones. I read that under no circumstances could a girl younger than her early twenties attend the theatre with a man unless she was chaperoned."

"You think they were still virgins when they got married?" Sari asks.

Mariah laughs. "Can't you just see the wedding night? The new Mrs. Smedley in her proper nightgown. 'Oh, one moment, Mr. Smedley, while I check with Mummy.'" Mariah pretends to hold the phone to her ear. "'Mummy,'" she says in an affected falsetto, "'must one remove one's gloves before coitus?'"

There's ribald laughter until Bunny, even though she likes to see Sari laughing again, leads them back to the purpose of being there. "I like your piece, Jemima, but is it replacing your usual recipe or are you still going to have one?"

"Still going to have one. Maybe currant scones, like they would have served at tea back then. I just haven't got it written down yet what with Joe *and* the grandkids. Currant scones with butter," she mulls to herself, confirming the perfection of her choice.

"Okay, I have a problem with …" Mariah runs a finger over the lines, counting. "Two lines up from the bottom … *where rules govern how one should conduct oneself*, not *themself*. And that line about *Guests who weigh their hostess down* is probably better written, *It is considered bad form for a guest to weigh her hostess down*, et cetera, so you don't have that problem with the verb."

Jemima corrects her copy then collects the rest of them from the others. "Sari, you're next."

"I'm finally getting back to a little writing now that Mooney's settling in. Here's one I wrote last night after he'd gone to bed and I had time to sit."

> Listen to the purring, a hum of life,
> The belly-slinking cats in the grass,
> Or baby's sweet breath
> Or the tinkerings of nature
> As she makes a slight adjustment
> To the hem of her velvet night gown.

"Something wrong there," Mariah says. "I can't get the rhythm."

Sari agrees. "I did seem to lose it, didn't I? Let me read it again." She does but Mariah is still not satisfied.

"There's more where that came from," Sari says.

> Reflection in a mirror
> Doesn't lie.
> Bold lines, the long crevasses
> Splitting the once flawless planes and features,
> Leaving the gazer wondering
> Where she's been for eighty years.

"That's better," Jemima exclaims. "I get that one! Heck, it could have been written about me."

"Did you have us in mind, Sari?" Bunny inquires.

"I was describing myself, actually. I'm very self-centred."

"Yeah, like you have to worry," Mariah scoffs. "Any more?"

"A couple."

> Stolen memory,
> A flash of smile, a look
> that summons itself uninvited …

Sari's poetry is brightening but not yet back to the impossibly happy, pre-James-losing-his-job standard. It was establishing a nice rhythm despite the occasional poem the group just didn't get.

> ... Patchwork memories,
> Pieced together,
> Quilted...

Bunny's thoughts drift again. She's finding it difficult to stay focussed. She sees herself dressed in a crisp white uniform while she patiently nurses Gerda. Linen-covered trays with nourishing soup. *I'll use my good Gien dinnerware. That will perk her up. It always works for me.* "And a dinner party with the girls."

Sari peers over the top of her paper. "Pardon?"

"What?" Bunny says, confused. They're all looking at her. "What?"

"You said something," Sari coaxes, "about a dinner party?"

Bunny's hand flies to her mouth. "Did I? I was thinking out loud."

"You're losing it, sister," says Mariah.

"Should I keep going?" Sari asks hesitantly.

"Yes, dear," Bunny says, looking contrite. "Sorry to interrupt. I guess I was woolgathering."

Sari smoothes her page on her leg and gets out one word, *indolent*, before being interrupted yet again.

"Would you come to a dinner party here when I bring Gerda home?" Bunny blurts. "It might do her a world of good, being surrounded by friends."

"Bunny," Jemima reminds her, "she doesn't know us from a hole in the fence."

"But she knows *of* you," Bunny says brightly. "Knows your names." She turns to each of them in turn. "Knows you write."

"Yeah, sure, we'll come," Mariah says sullenly, "if it means so much."

"And bring your mother. She's such a dear soul."

"Don't get carried away."

"Your husband agrees with this—having Gerda living here?" Jemima asks.

"Oh," Bunny says, her gaze travelling to a far corner of the room. She thinks for a moment before she says almost to herself, "I guess I'd better tell him, hadn't I?"

It's unusual for Bunny to be so distracted. The group feels ill at ease. Mariah's shoes suddenly feel too tight. Jemima needs to go to the bathroom. Sari folds her paper, tucking it into her purse. "I'm all through," she says.

Jemima jumps to her feet, bumping into the table, rattling the bone china basket of roses. Her heart hammers to think how much that would cost her should it fall to the floor. She stops the rocking motion of the ornament, then carefully removes her hand. She doesn't breathe until she straightens and walks away.

When she returns, she asks to use the phone to call home. Bunny takes this time to make the tea, apologizing for not having done it sooner. Jemima holds a brief conversation with Joe and returns to Sari and Mariah.

"Joe's fine," she says, although no one has asked. "He's in bed reading."

Sari remembers her manners. "How's he doing now? He looked pretty good at the birthday party." She actually thought he looked like death warmed over.

Jemima shrugs. "I really don't know. He feels kind of useless 'cause he can't hold onto his tools. Only the screwdriver—it's light enough. But the hammer, forget it. He sits in his damn workshop but doesn't work. Sits at the table and doesn't eat unless I prod him. Doesn't get dressed unless I lay out his clothes. Just not himself, you know?"

"Quit mothering him," Mariah says

"Smothering him?" Jemima asks.

"Smothering, mothering—same thing." Mariah lights her first cigarette of the night.

When Bunny returns with the tea tray, she sets it down, then threads her way to the window to open it. *There'll be no smoking when Gerda gets back.*

"Why don't you back off and let him do whatever the hell he wants," Mariah persists. "If he doesn't feel like getting dressed, so be it." She draws in a quick lungful and steams it out her nose. "If he sits in his shop, it's probably because he wants to get away from you. No offence."

Bunny steps in when she see Jemima's jaw working. "She may be right, dear. Although it could have been more subtly put."

Mariah squints in the smoke wafting up from her cigarette. She loves a little friction. The best compliment anyone ever gave her was to call her a shit disturber. Her epitaph and proud of it. "Bunny, your kick at the can."

Bunny dutifully distributes three pages to each and clears her throat. "You'll remember that last week," she says, "Tiara Ballestaire was tracking down the man who she thought might be the hit man for hire. She'd left a message on his answering machine and when he finally returns her call, she catches the phone on the fourth ring." She begins reading.

> "Yes?" she said breathlessly. Tiara had been on the Stairmaster with concert music turned loud enough to take her mind off the tediousness of the exercise. "Oh, Mr. Smith." She carried the phone to the stereo and turned down the volume. "Yes, I left a message two days ago." She emphasized the span of time. I wanted to speak to you about a ..." She groped for the right word. "... an assignment." Tiara heard a click. She removed the phone from her ear and looked at it before hanging it up. "What a rude man," she said and jogged back to her Stairmaster. But within ten minutes he had called again, wanting to know where she got his name. "The detective agency that was tracking down my husband said you were available for ... for ..."
>
> "Listen, lady, I don't discuss business over the phone." He dragged audibly on his cigarette. "Where do you live?"

She sure as hell didn't want him here. She didn't even know him and besides that, he smoked. "Pick a place to meet. Somewhere central."

"You gotta car?" When assured that she did, he continued, "Then be at the bus depot in half an hour."

"The bus depot!" she spat. "That's not the nicest place in town."

"For Chrissake, whaddya want, Chez George?"

"You needn't yell. I'll be there. Should I ask at the desk for you?"

"That's not the way it's done. I'll find you."

"I'll be the tall blonde in the Versace coat. Lavender and green with a black fur collar. Black Italian boots with silver spurs."

"Oh yeah, you'll blend right in. You got jeans and a sweatshirt?"

She clicked her tongue in annoyance, "No, of course not."

Bunny sneaks a look over the top of her paper to see the reactions to her story. Jemima is reading ahead, caught up in the dialogue, Sari is sitting back with her eyes closed and Mariah meets her glance.

Tiara parked her Volvo in the car lot of the bus depot but before she gathered her purse to exit the car, there was a jarring rap on the window next to her ear. She opened the window an inch, no more.

"Tall blonde in the Versace?" he said acidly. "Unlock the other door." He walked around the back of the car, scanning the lot. As he opened the passenger door he ordered, "Turn off the dome light." When it winked out, he slid in.

Tiara was wrong about the cigarettes. He reeked of cigars. And leather. "You're Mr. Smith?"

"Right." He shifted into the corner where he could better check her out. "State your business."

"I'll come right to the point, Mr. Smith. I want my husband to meet with an accident."

He reached into his jacket and produced the stub of a cigar followed by a plastic lighter. He rammed the cigar into his mouth, working it from one side to the other.

"Don't you light that thing in this car!" she warned. "I have allergies."

He flicked the lighter, shielding it so it revealed little of his face, and lit the butt.

Bunny continues her story to the point where money is discussed and it ends when a completion date for the murder is set. She feels pretty good about what she's written. *Seems to be going well.* "So, what do you think?"

"Kind of wordy," says Mariah directly. "Tiara is perfect, isn't she? Small ass, great legs?"

"Well, yes. What's wrong with that?"

"No flaws so far," Mariah says in a self-satisfied manner, harking back to her own earlier drubbing.

"You don't think having her husband killed is considered an imperfection?"

Jemima raises her hand as if she's in school. "Excuse me," she interrupts. "Dialogue is okay. You could cut a bit." When she sees Mariah open her mouth to speak, she points a finger in her direction. "One moment, Mariah, I'm not finished." Jemima rattles through the papers. "Page forty-seven, halfway down. When Mr. Smith gets into the car, would he not get into the back seat rather than the front? That way he can see her but she can't see him."

Bunny mulls this over. "That's a good point," she says slowly. "I'll rework it."

"Why?" begins Sari. "Why does she want to kill her husband?"

"Because he's fooling around with his legal assistant," Bunny reminds her.

"Is there no other way to go about this than to kill him?" Sari looks wounded.

"She wants it to end," Bunny says heatedly. "It's not the first time and it certainly won't be the last." Then she adds quickly, "At least that's what Tiara thinks."

Sari examines Bunny's face and a slight frown pulls at her eyebrows.

Bunny perseveres, "Sometimes women can only take so much before they crack."

The telephone rings, startling them all. Bunny answers it, then turns to give Sari a questioning look. "It's for you." She holds out the receiver.

"For me?" Sari says, bringing her hand to her chest. "Who is it?"

Bunny mouths, "I don't know."

Tentatively Sari takes the phone. "Hello?"

The rest make no attempt at conversation. They're involuntary listeners to Sari's half of the call.

"Where's Mooney?" Sari's voice is rising. "He has no business—"

Bunny realizes she's listening intently and tries to engage the others in small talk. It falls flat.

"Okay. I'll be ready." She hangs up without the usual goodbye, and she is pale and agitated.

"Trouble at home?" Jemima asks.

Sari gathers her papers from the floor, stuffing them into her handbag before slinging the strap over her shoulder. "Trouble?" she echoes. "Guess who showed up as big as life at my place?" She strides to the library window to see if Ace is coming down the road.

"Not James?" Jemima says.

"One and the same." Sari again peers out through the glass then turns to lean her back against the sill, arms folded across her chest. "He walked right in as if he owned the place."

"Doesn't he?" Mariah retorts. "Half his, by rights, isn't it?"

Jemima reaches over and slaps her on the thigh.

"What?" Mariah responds, rubbing the spot.

"Shut up, for Pete's sake," Jemima admonishes. "Always got your big foot in your mouth."

Never one to back down, Mariah plows on. "He has rights, too, ya know."

Bunny leaves the two of them to hassle it out and joins Sari at the window just as they hear the throbbing sound of the Harley approaching, its single headlight tracking toward the house.

"Sorry about this," Sari says urgently as Bunny follows her out onto the porch, "but I've got to go home and deal with James." Sari drops her purse next to Mooney in the sidecar, checks to see that he's strapped in, then climbs onto the seat behind Ace. She wraps her arms around his waist and lays her head against his back, keeping Mooney in sight.

Ace gives Bunny a nod as he revs the motor, easing out, taking care not to spray gravel. In his haste he's forgotten to insist Sari wear a helmet and she's not about to remind him. The thought crosses her mind that they, the three of them, should just strike out—Mooney contented behind the windscreen in the side-car, Ace's broad leather-clad back against her cheek. Just strike out, poking a hole in the darkness. She works her hands beneath the front of his jacket to clasp her fingers over his flat stomach. Despite the knowledge that James awaits, she feels deliciously happy right now. This could be her world, small and manageable.

Before she can fully exhaust the daydream, Ace is pulling into the trailer park.

"You have any money?" she asks, still clinging to him.

"How much you want?"

"Enough to just leave and not look back." She removes her hands from the warmth of his jacket and climbs off the bike.

Ace figures she's not looking for a response so doesn't give one. He unstraps Mooney and lifts him out. "You want me to take him to my place so you can yell at that asshole at top volume?" Mooney drops his head onto Ace's shoulder but still watches his mother with his serious dark eyes. He pops a consoling thumb into his mouth. "Or do you want me to come with you? I could kill him if you'll help me hide the body."

Sari straightens, tracing a finger down Mooney's nose. "Take him home and put him to bed. This may be a long night." She turns away and climbs the stairs to her place, taking a deep breath before slamming the door open.

Ace swallows hard against the lump in his throat. "It'll be okay, big guy. Your old man's a jerk. Mummy knows that." He hooks Sari's purse from the sidecar. "Mummy will remember that."

TO JEMIMA, THE RIDE HOME seems longer without Sari in the car. She turns up the radio but doesn't really hear the local baseball game being broadcast from under the lights at Judge Packard Field. Her mind is going over the evening at Bunny's. *The nerve of Mariah, saying James Button had a claim on that damn trailer. And her storyline taking that impossible twist. I hope Derek dies with his head up his arse.* She turns off the highway onto her half-mile of deserted narrow back road. The white-painted pole fences on either side of the road glow in the headlights. Past the Johnsons' Horse Farm, and the Stolzes', then she brakes quickly, pumping the pedal. There's something big on the road ahead. One of the horses must be out. She brings the old car to a stop a safe distance from the object and blinks at the sight, unbelieving. She climbs out of the car, leaving her door open. A wheelchair is coming toward her at a slow, steady pace. Joe's head bobs with the motion of his hands driving the wheels.

"What are you doing out here?" Jemima shrills, stomping toward him.

"Was goddamn tough going 'til I hit the blacktop."

"Joe! Are you crazy?"

"Yup." He makes an adjustment so the wheelchair misses the front bumper of the car and jerks past the open door.

"You stop right this minute!" she demands, hands on her hips. "You hear me?"

"Who's winning?" he asks in his slow manner, the result of his recent stroke.

Jemima slams her door and follows him into the glow of her tail lights. "If you don't stop, Joe, I'm going to hook a bungee cord to that chair and drag you home behind the car."

"Always did like listening to the games on the radio."

"You hear me, Joseph Albert Spooner?" Jemima opens the trunk of the car to pick up two cords from the spare tire well. "Last chance! I'm warning you."

Joe's arms drop and his big hands hang against the spokes of his wheels. He sags in his chair.

Jemima flings the cords back into the trunk and slams it. "Tell me what's going on. What's happened?" She approaches the chair and crouches beside it. "Look at your poor hand, Joe." She brushes the dirt from his bleeding palm.

His head lifts and he looks down the road. "You remember those young guys who played ball here for a couple of summers? Brothers, they were."

"No, can't say's I do." She places his right hand in his lap and turns the chair to reach for his other hand.

"Damn good ball players, Mother. Wonder what happened to them?"

"I'm wondering what happened to you." She places his left hand over his right, then stands. "How did you get so far?" Joe doesn't answer. "Let's go home," she says, dragging the chair to the side of the Buick. "I'll make you a nice cup of tea."

Joe begins to cry.

X

AFTER POURING THE LAST OF the milk from his fridge into Mooney's bottle, Ace carries him and Blue Bear into the bedroom, where he tucks the child into his double bed. After all the nightie-nights are over, he parks himself in front of the television in the living room. Mooney reappears less than five minutes later holding out his bottle, asking for more. Once he's re-bedded, Ace jabs the remote, killing the TV. He wants to be able to hear any loud noises coming from next door. Any bangs or crashes or—God forbid—screams. He's ready to rush in and save her. But it's very quiet—too quiet. He signals Mudd to stay, then tiptoes to the front door so as not to alert Mooney and slowly turns the knob, letting himself out. From the porch the only sound is a distant truck gearing down as it takes a hill. Not even the trailer park cats are serenading.

Standing next to James's truck on the sparse grass in front of Sari's trailer, Ace strains to hear what's going on. Nothing moves inside. He skirts the side of the trailer to see if the bedroom light is on, but the only light seems to be coming from the spill of illumination from the living room. He crouches beneath the window, then takes a deep breath to calm himself. He's prepared for the worst, prepared to find them naked as jaybirds, sweating to the old and familiar. But when he rises to look inside, he sees her bed is still made and undisturbed and his breath releases in a rush. He steals back home, feeling a little foolish but more than a little relieved. This is something he can keep to himself, his inclination to be a Peeping Tom. Anyway, it won't happen again. Probably.

Ace lies down fully clothed next to Mooney. Just has to throw on his socks and boots should she need him. But he's asleep before he can complete his next thought and doesn't wake until hit with Blue Bear. "Holy Jeez," he says, blinking in the bright morning light. "What time is it?"

Mooney giggles his answer.

"Oh, man! I blew it." He rushes barefoot to the door and charges out onto the porch. Mudd follows close behind and trots down the stairs, straight for his favourite peeing spot. James's truck is still there. Just as he feared, he has spent the night. Ace slaps a hand to his head and slumps against the door frame.

"Baba," says Mooney, knocking last night's bottle against Ace's knee. "Baba."

"I'm all out, big guy." Ace directs Mooney toward the untidy kitchen and ties him onto a chair at the table before opening the fridge. "We've got beer. Want beer on your oatmeal? Olives? Chinese food from a year ago?" He grabs a partial loaf of bread and flings it onto the counter. "Toast and jam." Before he begins to search for the toaster, he pulls back the curtain to stare dejectedly at trailer number twelve and leaves it open so he can check minute by minute. Plunging bread into the toaster, he remembers there's a carton of juice somewhere and starts another search.

"Baba?" Mooney reminds him, banging the bottle.

Ace absently takes the bottle and rinses it, urging Mooney to wait a minute while he finds the juice. The apple juice he uncovers is outdated by two weeks, but he plunges two knife slits into it and sniffs the contents. Judging it okay, he fills Mooney's bottle and hands it to him. Ace casts a quick look out the window before returning his attention to the toaster, then does a double-take back to the window, slow to recognize what he's just witnessed. A tousled head is rising from the front seat of the truck. "By Christ, that's ..." He turns to point this out to Mooney. "... that's your old man. He slept in the bloody truck." Ace is beside himself with delight. He picks up Mooney and the chair he is tied to and polkas them around the room, blissfully unaware that the toast is smoldering, curling thin grey smoke beneath the upper cupboards.

∽

"SO WHAT HAPPENED?" HE ASKS when Sari comes for her son half an hour later.

"Not much," she admits. She sits with her head in her hands, her elbows on the table. Mooney has finished his toast and is now mashing the banana she has brought for him into the crusts. "All I got out of it was a headache." She folds her arms onto the table top and drops her head onto them.

"Poor you," Ace commiserates, grasping her shoulders to grind his thumbs between her shoulder blades.

She squirms from beneath his grasp. "That hurts." Sari would like to go back to bed and sleep off her headache but instead begins scraping Mooney's food mess into her open hand, then looks for a place to toss it.

Ace opens the cupboard door beneath the sink with his toe and Sari finds the garbage can. While at the sink, she checks her trailer through the window. "I'm just waiting for James to have a shower and clear out. He's heading back to Cache Creek. They made him assistant manager of the service station." She rinses the dishcloth under the tap and wrings it out before throwing it to Ace, who's waiting to wipe Mooney's face. "For what it's worth," she elaborates, "there was no screaming. It was quite civilized. I just don't care enough about him to yell."

"Did he come back for Mooney?"

"I don't think so," she says, drawing each word out slowly. "He asked about him, of course, but didn't seem too upset that he was back with me." Sari takes the dishcloth from Ace, who had done nothing with it, and wipes Mooney's face and then the table. "Have you got an Aspirin?"

While Ace rummages through his medicine cabinet in the bathroom, Sari continues her narration from the kitchen. "He wanted to know if we were sleeping together."

"If we were what?" Ace exclaims, returning to hand her two tablets.

Sari steps to the sink and runs the cold water. She pops the Aspirin into her mouth, then cups a handful of water, drinking enough to wash them down. "Sleeping together," she says, drying her hand on her jeans.

"Whad'ya tell him?"

"Said yes."

"You wh-a-at?"

"You're bigger than he is," she says as if that explains everything. Seeing the look on his face, she says, "Telling him we're sleeping together lets him know there is no going back to the way it used to be. That he should just move on." Sari unties Mooney from the chair and lifts him onto her knee, brushing the crumbs from his lap onto the floor. "Is he still in the same diaper?"

"Aw, jeez. I forgot. Here," he insists, "let me do it."

"Don't worry about it," Sari says, swinging Mooney onto her hip. "You've already done more than enough."

"He was so bloody hungry, I just fed him," Ace continues to explain, trailing her into the bedroom.

"It's okay." She flops Mooney onto the unmade bed. "Have you got his diaper bag?"

While he collects the bag, she strips Mooney of his pyjamas, dropping them onto the floor then adding the sodden diaper to the pile. "You are wet, wet, wet, Moonshadow. Hold still."

"So what did he say to that?"

Sari tickles the baby's tummy before doing up his diaper. "Sorry, you lost me."

"James. What did he say about us sleeping together?"

"Not much," she says, setting Mooney's feet onto the floor and releasing him. "Wondered how long it had been going on and had it happened while we were still together."

Ace shakes his head from the doorway. "You think it's a good idea saying that? He might get you declared an unfit mother or something."

"It's probably a saw-off. After all, he did kidnap Mooney and the police would still like to have a talk with him."

"True," he concedes. "But now that you've brought it up, when are we gonna ... you know ... sleep together?"

She clicks her tongue and rises from her knees.

"Mooney didn't think it was so bad," Ace presses. "He slept with me all night with no complaints."

"Uh-huh." Sari rolls Mooney's sleepers and stuffs them into the diaper bag, then picks up the diaper and heads for the garbage. "Thanks for watching him. Much appreciated." She leans over the sink to look out the window. "James is leaving now." She scoops up the baby and again settles him on her hip, wrapping her sweater around his naked back before heading to the door. "We'd better go wave bye-bye. Coming?" she asks Ace, a playful grin taking over her face.

"You're working today?" he asks, walking them to the door.

Sari nods.

"Then I'm going back to bed for an hour." He chucks the baby under the chin, "See you later, Moon Man." Ace allows the dog inside before closing the door.

⁓

BUNNY IS PUTTERING WITH A specific purpose in mind—to find the right room in which to house Gerda. It has to be on the ground floor and within hearing distance of the library. That leaves Leland's study, the music room, the living room, the formal dining room, the solarium, the kitchen and the pantry. She stands at the bottom of the staircase looking up, wondering if Gerda will be traumatized by seeing it. She wonders also if Gerda could be housed upstairs and transported with a lift unit attached to the banister. Bunny feels overwhelmed dealing with all this herself. "Maybe it will have to be the music room after all," she says aloud, heading there again.

She leans an elbow on the piano to concentrate on the sunken sitting area three steps below. "If I leave the piano here and move those chairs into storage, there might be enough space for a bed." She tips her head, previewing the room as it might look a week from now. "Some window shades, a bedside table, a little radio. Oh, I don't know!" She throws up her hands and, turning on her heel, heads for the liquor cabinet in the library. "I need a leveller," she says, "then I've got to get some writing done. Everything else can wait until tomorrow." Once she has loaded her glass with scotch and ice, she heads for Leland's study and settles before her computer to listen to it whirr and hum into life. She brings up the story of Tiara Ballestaire. She checks the corrected copy of her work against the onscreen manuscript and, after making her corrections, sits staring at the monitor with her chin in her cupped hands. She watches the flashing cursor, forgetting everything until the melting ice cubes clink in her glass. The words begin to come.

> Tiara Ballestaire was feeling lower than a snake's belly. Delete.
>   Tiara Ballestaire sat perfectly still, her hands gripping the wheel of her car, which she had parked in the triple garage of her palatial home. Mr. Smith had made one attempt to kill her husband and had failed, and she wondered whether she shouldn't just close the automatic door and keep the car running. Carbon monoxide is supposed to be painless but she's heard it turns you a funny colour.

"Red, I think," says Bunny, reaching for her now diluted scotch. "Something in a person turns red. Maybe it's the blood. Bright red."

> "No," Tiara told herself as she alighted from the car. "Lance is supposed to die, not me." If Mr. Smith couldn't do the job properly, she figured she would have to do it herself. On her way to the side door of the house, she plotted ways. Poison mushrooms? Maybe. But how do you go about obtaining them? Safeway doesn't have a poison mushroom section.

Botulism? She could leave a potato salad sitting out in the sun for the afternoon, then serve it for his dinner. A lovely dose of salmonella. Perfect, she thinks. That's very doable. Just to be sure, she'd leave it out for two days and put in lots of chopped eggs and shrimp. She would phone Mr. Smith and tell him to forget about shooting Lance. Too messy. "Where was my mind?" This was much more reasonable. No suspicion cast upon her. Well, maybe his family would have their doubts, but just let them try to prove she did it on purpose.

"Hm-m-m. Now does Tiara have Mr. Smith's number? Or did he call her?" She scrolls up the manuscript to an earlier passage. "She left a message for him on an answering machine," she reads.

The number Tiara had dialed previously was now disconnected, which wasn't surprising, she thought, with the career path he'd chosen. In the morning she would just go back to the office above the service station and call the deal off. Mr. Smith wouldn't try shooting again so soon.

She liked the idea of the deadly dinner so much she continued working on the plan. Lance's dinner would be waiting, as it was whenever he was not home in time. They hadn't had a meal together for over a week. If she served it the evening she volunteered at the hospital, she could admit later, should anyone inquire, to running late and just grabbing an apple on her way out. This is so doable, she told herself.

Bunny pushes away from the desk, unhappy with the way her writing is going. "They'll hate it. Mariah will find something wrong."

She returns to the library for the bottle of scotch and pours more than usual before taking the drink to the kitchen for fresh ice cubes. As she passes the phone on her way back, it rings and she answers immediately.

"That was quick," says Leland. "You must have been sitting there waiting for my call."

"Well, I'm glad you called," Bunny says, perching on a stool. "I need some help with Gerda."

"How can I possibly help, my dear, when I'm at the airport?"

"Are you coming or going?"

"Going. Heading to Hong Kong."

"Big oil strike there?" she asks caustically. In the silence following, she hears muffled airport din as if he's covered the receiver.

"No," he says, sounding tired.

Bunny regrets being bitchy and tries to lighten up. "Something wrong, Leland? All this travel getting you down?"

"I have a lot of things on my mind." He clears his throat. "Since Miss Spring-Dunning left."

Her reach for the sweating glass of scotch falls short. "Excuse me?"

"Miss Spring-Dunning terminated her employment," he says flatly. "Yesterday morning."

Bunny wants to laugh, to chortle, to gleefully say, "Miss Spring-Dunning has done springing?" But instead she keeps silent for a moment or two.

"Are you still there?" His voices breaks.

"Yes, Leland. Why don't you just come home? Nothing can be that important."

"It's a conference. They're all important," he informs her. "So you're taking Gerda in then?"

"*We're* taking Gerda in, as we discussed, and I'm trying to arrange a place for her. I thought maybe the music room?"

"You know best about that sort of thing, my dear. I leave it in your hands," he says, a bit rushed. "They've just announced my flight."

"I'll have to buy a bed and hospital things to keep her comfortable."

"Whatever it takes. Give Mother a call, she'll be a great help. Gotta go."

"Leland?"

"Yes?"

"How will you manage without Miss Spring-Dunning?"

"With difficulty," he says dully. "Must run."

"'Bye."

"'Bye." Then the line is dead.

"I love you, too, Leland," she says, releasing the receiver to drop the foot or so to its cradle. Quickly she grabs her drink, spilling some down the front of her tee-shirt, and swallows the rest of it in gulps to wash down the lump in her throat.

⌘

THIRTY-SEVEN MORNINGS AFTER GERDA'S FALL, the same ambulance attendants who had wheeled her out return her at 9:45 a.m. and install her in the music room. Awaiting the arrival with Bunny is Josephine Rosella, a home care worker assigned to visit twice a day. She fusses over the inert form strapped beneath the grey blanket while Bunny distances herself from the activity. Only after Gerda is transferred to the hospital bed and the attendants have packed up their equipment and left does Bunny tentatively approach. Miss Rosella crooks a finger from the bedside, coaxing her closer.

"Come on, Duchess, she won't hurt you."

Bunny squares her shoulders. "I know that." She expects to see the bloodied face that had been mashed at the bottom of the stairs but is somewhat surprised to see the same face she's always seen— Gerda's. "Where are her teeth?" she whispers, gesturing toward her own mouth.

"Can't wear them, they said." Miss Rosella dips into a freshly folded paper bag to hold up Gerda's upper dentures. "They make her gag." She drops them with a plop into a blue plastic container, then marches off to the bathroom to cover the teeth with water.

Bunny ventures a step toward the bed, leaning over the railing to whisper, "Welcome home, Gerda."

"You don't have to whisper, you know," Miss Rosella says. "She apparently lost quite a bit of hearing with her fall." She places the denture cup on the bedside table and claps a lid on it. "Now, Duchess, you know how to put on her Attends?"

"Attends?"

"It's the box under the bed. Diapers. Adult diapers. You ever do one before?"

Bunny shakes her head.

"Well," Miss Rosella says, enthusiastically rubbing her dry palms together, "let's get started." She reaches beneath the overhanging duvet, hauls an Attends from the open box and hands it to Bunny, who takes it with two fingers. "Let's see if she's wet," says Miss Rosella, flipping down the duvet. She hollers into Gerda's ear. "We're going to change you." When she receives no reaction, she raises the hospital gown far enough to feel the plastic crotch of the diaper.

Bunny turns her face away.

"It's time anyway." She rips the Velcro tabs on either side of the Attends and pulls it from beneath Gerda's body. "Here you go," she says, handing it off to Bunny who draws her hand back in revulsion. The sodden diaper plops to the floor. "You really gotta do better than that," Miss Rosella admonishes. "Get your rubber gloves on. Dive in."

Bunny helps herself from the box of rubber gloves, picks up the new Attends again and carries it to the bedside, trying not to look at Gerda laid out like a scrawny hen on a butcher block.

"Drop the bars and roll her toward you by grabbing here and here," the home worker instructs, grasping Gerda's shoulder and hip. "You paying attention?"

Now that she's forced the issue, Bunny snaps to.

"Once she's balanced," Miss Rosella resumes, "drop the open Attends behind her, like so, then ease her back onto it. Voila! Now bring it up between her legs, making sure there's nothing to irritate her and zip, zip, you're done." She folds her arms over her flat chest and asks, "Think you can handle it?"

Bunny stoops to the floor. "Of course," she says shortly, retrieving the soggy diaper. She looks around for a place to put it.

"Over there in the plastic bag. Just put it out with the regular garbage and zip, zip, it's gone."

Dropping her rubber gloves in as well, Bunny bunches the top of the bag.

"She gets her pills at twelve-hour intervals," Miss Rosella instructs. "So you get to administer either morning or evening. Which one do you want?"

"I don't care," Bunny says.

"Are you a morning person, Duchess, or an evening person?"

"First of all," Bunny says coldly, "my name is Bunny or Delores. Or Mrs. deLore. Or even Hey You! I'm not a duchess nor have I ever aspired to be one. Is that understood?"

Miss Rosella sucks in her cheeks, then says crisply, "Understood."

Bunny draws in her horns, "Secondly, if I have to be up for Gerda anyway, I may as well give her the morning dose."

"Fine. Seven a.m. and I'll do her when she's ready for bed at night." Miss Rosella locks the bedrail into place then checks the bedside table, tapping the jug of imported bottled water, the denture cup, the pills, the thermometer in its case, the flashlight, the notepad and pen. "All set. Tonight I'll show you how to care for her wrist splints and how to wash her. I'll bring a bedpan back with me and we'll do that, too." She gathers her large shoulder bag and, rummaging for her car keys, heads out of the music room. Before reaching the door, she snaps her fingers and does an about-face, returning to the bed. "See you about six, Mrs. Von Hauffman," she says, patting Gerda's chest. "They always like to know when I'm coming back."

Bunny changes into her newly purchased pastel nursing uniform and begins her first day's vigil at Gerda's bedside. The radio is tuned to an easy listening station with few commercials, and the new sheers filter the late morning light.

"Just you and me now, Gerda." She checks her watch, then leans over to speak into her housekeeper's ear. "Are you hungry?" she enunciates slowly. "It's lunch time."

Gerda's eyes snap open and glare directly into hers. No adjustment from sleeping to waking—just an immediate heart-withering, laser-like focus.

Bunny backs away. "I'll go get some lunch then, shall I?" She's only too happy to be out of the room assembling the food Gerda will be served. When she returns with the tray, Gerda has her eyes closed so Bunny settles the tray on the bedside table and proceeds to crank up the top end of the bed, jerking Gerda slowly to a sitting position. Bunny has practised this but the delivery isn't as smooth as she'd hoped. Retrieving the tray, she clunks it down on Gerda's wrist splints concealed beneath the sheet. "Time to eat!" She tries to sound cheerful, upbeat, as if she knows what she's doing. It's not like she's never fed anybody before, she thinks, as she spoons up puréed green beans. She touches the spoon to Gerda's mouth just as she used to do when feeding PJ as a baby and receives the same reaction—a clamping of top lip to bottom. Gerda squints her a look that lets Bunny know she has met her match.

"You have to eat something. You want to get better, don't you?" She doesn't shout into her ear but doesn't whisper either. She tries another smile, this time with less anxiety. "Come on, Gerda. Be a good girl." She raises the spoon and this time Gerda accepts the contents. "That's it," Bunny coos, scraping up more green beans from the saucer. As she raises her eyes from the tray preparing to inflict the spoonful of beans, Gerda lifts her head from the pillow and sprays her with the first mouthful. Bunny is horrified, dropping the spoon onto the tray and fleeing from the room to wash her face. She knows the loud crash she hears midway through her cleanup is the tray hitting the floor.

She returns with wet spots on her pink uniform and her face wiped clean of beans. She carries a glass—a weak mixture of half scotch and half water—and a roll of paper towels. She promised herself she wouldn't drink on duty but this is a little much. Approaching the bed to deposit her glass on the bedside table, Bunny is convinced Gerda is smirking. Bunny gathers the broken dishes, throwing the pieces onto the tray, then smears up the colourful remains of lunch with the paper towels. She takes it all to the kitchen and reappears in the music room to finish the job. "I know what you're thinking, Gerda. It's nice to see me on the end of a mop." She pokes at the last of the food on the floor and carries the mop back to the kitchen, dropping it into the bucket of Pine-Sol and water. When she arrives with another tray of lunch, she puts it on Gerda's lap before leaning right into her ear so she won't miss a word. "We can do this the easy way or the hard way." Standing back to gauge the old woman's reaction, she scoops up a bit of cottage cheese, but when she reapproaches with the spoon, Gerda has hooked her seven remaining bottom teeth over her upper lip. "The easy way is, you eat this stuff nicely," Bunny conveys. "The hard way is, if you don't eat it nicely, I'll give it to you rectally." Gerda's jaw drops and Bunny seizes the chance to pop in the cottage cheese. Gerda's eyes dart from side to side as she makes her decision. Bunny raises her index finger in warning.

Gerda swallows.

AT SIX, MISS ROSELLA ARRIVES to get Gerda ready for bed. After giving her a wash, a change of nightgowns and her pills, she tucks Gerda in and pulls the new blinds, promising to return the next day between 10 and 11 a.m. "You do realize how much work is involved in being the primary caregiver?" Miss Rosella asks Bunny, as they stand on the front porch.

"I'm beginning to," Bunny replies.

"Well, I gotta give you credit for trying." Miss Rosella descends the stone steps. "Don't be too disappointed if you can't make a go of it." She climbs into her Volkswagen van. "Toodle-doo," she calls, waggling her fingers.

Bunny responds by quietly shutting the door. She walks back to the music room and leans against the piano with her arms folded, listening to Gerda's breathing. *I can pull this off.* She absently wipes at the fine dust powdering the piano. Her thoughts are interrupted by the front door chimes. She checks her watch. "Now what does she want?"

She's surprised to see Ron Woolcott in shorts and a tee-shirt on the other side of the door. "Dr. Woolcott? What brings you here?" She stands aside to let him in.

He hands her the newspaper. "I met your papergirl in the driveway," he says as he enters the house. "I'm still assigned to Mrs. Von Hauffman so I'll be looking in on her from time to time." He glances around the hallway with appreciation. "Quite the place."

"Thanks," Bunny responds, suddenly noticing the house needs a good airing. "She's in the music room."

"Music room?" he repeats, switching his medical bag to his other hand.

"It's the only spot I had available without putting her upstairs. It's not too bad, considering."

"Nice," Ron says appreciatively. Bunny has purchased sunshine-yellow sheets for the hospital bed and added a cheerful floral print duvet to make it look more like a guest suite than like a sickroom. "Can we get a little more light in here?"

Bunny raises two of the blinds and Ron waves his thanks. "Do you want me to leave, Dr. Woolcott?"

"No. No. I'm just giving her the once over. Her records were faxed this morning. I'll go over them and see what's what. This is more a social call," he says, bending over Gerda and lifting her eyelids. "You in there, Mrs. Von Hauffman?" Levelling his gaze at Bunny, he asks, "She say anything yet?"

"About what?" Bunny responds nervously, thinking he is referring to her fall down the stairs.

"Anything! The weather. Where am I? What's for lunch?"

Bunny is suddenly embarrassed by her blunder. She stutters out a no.

"Well, when she does say something, it's a good indication she's on the way back." He throws his stethoscope into his bag and snaps it shut. "You do realize this is quite a commitment, don't you?" Before she can respond, he fires off another query. "You have help?"

"I have a home care worker, Miss Rosella, coming in twice a day."

"Good. Your husband willing to give you a hand?"

Bunny turns to lead him out of the room. "He's away a lot."

But the doctor has folded himself into one of the stiff French provincial chairs near the fireplace. "Yeah, I think I knew that. Just slipped my mind." He stretches his thick suntanned legs, crossing one ankle over the other, his Nikes twitching out his excess energy.

Bunny, flustered that he seems in no hurry to leave, asks, "Um-m-m, would you care for a drink, Dr. Woolcott?"

He lunges from the chair in one motion, swooping to catch up his bag. "Maybe next time. I booked the racquetball court for eight o'clock so I'd better be off. You play racquetball?"

"No," she exclaims, as if he's asked if she'd ever climbed Everest.

He grins at her answer. "It's not too late, you know. There are a few women your age taking it up."

Women my age? He breezes out and Bunny locks the door before his Jeep has left the driveway. *That man is very annoying.*

XI

"FLORA?" MARIAH CALLS ANXIOUSLY FROM the back door where a man with a beer gut tucked inside his muscle shirt is leaning with one hand against the door frame. "Flora!" Mariah doesn't want to leave the man standing there with only the screen door between them. You never know what sort of crazy person he might be.

"What'd'ya want?" Flora responds from somewhere in the house.

"There's somebody here to see you." Mariah gives the man a reassuring look.

"I'm watching *Wheel of Fortune*."

Mariah gives him a what-can-you-do shrug. "I'll get her," she promises. "Just a minute." As she trots through the kitchen, she scans it for anything of value. Should it go missing, she'll be able to relay the information to the police along with the man's description. If she lives that long.

Flora is in her bedroom parked in front of the television. Axel is attached to her shoulder. "There's a man at the door," Mariah hisses, expecting him to have snuck up behind her with a chainsaw.

"What's he want?" Flora asks, not removing her gaze from the screen.

"How should I know?"

"Go find out."

Mariah grabs Flora by the elbow and pulls. "Get off your bony butt and deal with him yourself."

Axel shakes his feathers, puffing himself into a formidable foe, then tiptoes down the arm of Flora's housecoat toward Mariah's big rough hand.

"Hey, lady!"

"It's him," Mariah stage-whispers. "Move it."

Flora throws her a look of exasperation and struggles to get out of the chair.

"You want this bike or not," he yells from the porch. "I haven't got all day."

"Oh, it's the bike guy. Why'n't you say so?" Flora shoves her purple-veined feet into her slippers and shuffles out of her room, Axel scrambling up her arm to resume his perch on her shoulder. "It's Caspar, isn't it?" she calls from midway across the kitchen. "Come in, come in. My daughter has no manners, leaving you to stand outside."

Mariah rolls her eyes and leans against the wall to watch.

"The bike outside?" Flora asks, peering around him as he comes through the doorway.

"In the pickup," he indicates with his thumb. "You still want her, don'tcha?"

"I sure do," Flora assures him. "How much was it again?"

He tips his ball cap back enough to scratch his scalp, then pulls the hat snugly over his forehead. "Twenty-five and five for delivery. Thirty all together."

"Make yourself at home while I get my purse."

Mariah pushes off the wall and darts into Flora's room ahead of her.

"Now where did I put it?" Flora asks herself as she enters.

"You're buying a bicycle?" Mariah asks incredulously.

"As a matter of fact, I am," Flora says loftily as she remembers where she hid her handbag. She fetches it from beneath the pillow on her bed and does an about-face to head for the kitchen again. Axel adjusts to accommodate the sharp turn.

Mariah lowers herself into Flora's chair as *Wheel of Fortune* rewards a screaming young woman with a trip to New Mexico, but she can hear the slip-slop of Flora's slippers returning above the forced cheerfulness on the TV. "You got twenty-seven fifty?" Flora asks, shaking her purse as she peers into the bottom.

"What for?"

"I'm a little short. I just need another twenty-seven fifty." She snaps the handbag shut before tossing it onto her bed.

"Not for a bloody bicycle, I don't," Mariah states, thrusting out her jaw.

"That's fine," says Flora sweetly. "I'll just tell Caspar that he came all the way out here for nothing." She shakes her head sadly. "I hear tell that you shouldn't make him mad. Oh well," she says airily, "you do have the place insured."

Mariah lets her get halfway to the kitchen before calling her back.

"Here's your money, Caspar," Flora says, a self-satisfied smile tweaking the corners of her mouth.

He thumbs through the bills and hefts the change before sliding the money into his pocket. "Nice bird," he says.

"I bought the bicycle mostly for him," she says, offering Axel her finger as a perch. As soon as he steps onto it, Flora seizes him and tucks him into the crook of her arm. "He needs to get out into the fresh air. See the world." She trails Caspar out the door, following him to his truck. "Just set the bike next to the porch."

He hefts it from the back of the truck, setting it down on its balloon tires. "I found those old training wheels we talked about. You did want me to stick them on, right?" The bike squeaks as he rolls it to the porch. He gives her a nod in passing, then hops into his truck and leaves the yard in a plume of oily smoke.

As Flora leans over the porch railing to admire her new purchase, Mariah joins her, lighting a smoke before offering her opinion. "Well," she exhales, "she's a dirty old thing, isn't she? I learned to ride on one of those, right?"

"It'll do just fine."

Mariah's glasses slip down her nose and she peers over them. "The basket on the front has seen better days."

Flora straightens. "The basket is serviceable. It's only for carrying the bird."

"What's with the training wheels? Do you even know how to ride a bicycle?"

Flora clicks her tongue in response, then re-enters the house to put Axel into his cage. She'll put on her shameful old walking shorts and go outside again to apply a little spit and polish to the bike, to oil the chain, shine the chrome fenders, put a few silk violets on the wicker basket. Then, and only then, will she teach herself to ride.

∽

WITH FLORA OUT SERVICING HER bike, Mariah takes the opportunity to give Chloe a call and make arrangements for the weekend. They are to attend a dog show in Kamloops, which gives them the excuse for a weekend away. This hasn't happened for a while.

"Will your mother be okay by herself?" Chloe asks.

"Normally I'd say yes." Mariah hesitates before ploughing on. "Do you know what she's done?"

"Eloped?" Chloe whinnies.

"It could be serious."

Chloe falls suitably sombre as she catches the tone of Mariah's voice. "What's she done now?"

"Bought a bloody bicycle," Mariah replies, "with training wheels, no less. She's just traipsed through the house in those God-awful plaid walking shorts and there's rags over her shoulder and a pail full of soapy water in her hand. She's outside washing the damn thing."

"And the bad part of all this is?"

"I'm pretty sure she can't ride."

"So, we should cancel our arrangements because your dotty old mother might pedal off into the sunset, so to speak?"

Dotty old mother? Mariah feels a rise of anger. "My mother may be a bit eccentric, Chloe, a bit forgetful now and then, but she's not nuts."

Too far. She'd gone too far. "Mariah, sweetheart, don't take it the wrong way. I love the old dear, you know that." Chloe waits for a response but none is forthcoming. "Dotty doesn't means nuts, it's— it's an affectionate term. See," she continues, realizing she's balancing on the fine edge of blathering, "I would consider anyone who eats Roquefort cheese with buckwheat honey on a daily basis a little … what's the word I'm looking for?"

"Idiosyncratic?" Mariah suggests.

"That will do for want of a better one. Can we consider the matter closed?"

Usually if she's mad, Mariah can enjoy a good two days of sulking and long silences, but not with Chloe. "I suppose." In the silence, each expecting the other to fill the void, Mariah hears Chloe's dogs playing in the background. Mariah breaks the quiet. "Flora will be okay. I'll call her when we get to Kamloops and leave a number just in case."

"We're on then. A whole weekend!" Chloe whoops. "The dogs and I will pick you up Friday just after lunch. That suitable?"

"Flora's back," Mariah conveys then half-covers the receiver as she speaks to her mother. "You finished yet?"

Flora bangs open the cupboard doors beneath the sink. "You have any car wax?"

"Does my car look like I have car wax?"

"Floor wax? Furniture polish? Never mind," she says, rising from her knees. "I found it."

"A wash and wax won't make it run any better," she calls as Flora slams out the screen door. "She's always going off half-cocked," Mariah tells Chloe. It's okay for her to comment on her mother's idiosyncrasies. "Last time it was my birthday party. Remember that? Could hardly hold her back."

"Gotta go, sweetheart," Chloe says, sounding rushed. "The dogs are barking about something. See you Friday."

Mariah hangs up, then saunters out the door to see what her mother is up to. She finds her squatting in the gravel, rubbing small circles of paste wax onto the frame of the bike. "Wow. I didn't realize it was red," Mariah says, impressed with the work. "And it has whitewalls? Could be a real beauty, Flora."

With the back of her hand, Flora pushes her hair from her eyes. "We're both real beauties, I'd say. I clean up real good, too."

"I know you do." Mariah wonders how to break the news to her mother that she is on her own for the weekend. May as well tell her right out. "Chloe and I have a dog show in Kamloops this weekend."

"I'll bring my bike."

A look of alarm spans Mariah's broad face. "Uh, I don't think you'd be happy travelling with us. The van only holds two people and with the dogs' cages in the back and all our stuff ..."

"I don't mind. I won't even take the bike. Just throw some clothes in a bag and you won't even know I'm there."

Mariah, hissing a jet of smoke, flips her cigarette off the porch and into the grass. "We've already booked the room and the place is full. It's a big show weekend, you know."

Flora takes up where she left off, buffing the frame of the bike.

"Did you hear me?" Mariah demands. "I'd love to take you but—"

"Oh, don't get your shirt in a knot. I was just kidding."

Mariah looks visibly relieved. "Flora, anybody ever tell you you're a pain in the ass?"

Flora runs her polishing cloth through the spokes, jabbing at the last of the rust spots.

"We'll be gone Friday and Saturday night. Home by noon on Sunday. They have the pretrial Friday and the final judging late Saturday. Too late to drive all the way home."

"Why are you rambling on? I got the message."

"I'll take you on the next trip, okay? Maybe in a month or so." Mariah steps down off the porch to stand behind her mother and place her hand on Flora's shoulder. "You hear what I said?"

Flora shrugs off the hand and sits back on her heels. "How's she look?"

"Great," Mariah says distractedly, her mind already working on the weekend ahead.

⁓

IN THE BELLE MODE BEAUTY Bar, Sari Button's gaze is fixed on the pile of clean folded towels as her hands move automatically on the old head beneath them. *How can I still feel all alone when I'm not? Ace loves me. Mooney loves me. But I don't love me.*

"Ow!" her customer says. "You're scrubbing too hard."

Sari apologizes as she rinses the shampoo from the woman's thin hair, but her thoughts still stray from what she's doing. *Why do I feel so hollow and heavy all at the same time? I want to cry myself to sleep then not wake up for hours, days even.*

"The water's cold!" the woman protests.

Sari turns off the water, which has gone cold just as the woman has broadcast. "I'm sorry, Mrs.—Mrs.—" She can't even remember who her client is. "I won't charge you for the shampoo." She wraps the dripping head in a clean towel, then directs the woman toward an empty chair facing the mirrored wall.

Mrs. Bahadoorsingh, the owner of the Belle Mode, bustles up to the customer in Sari's charge. "Is there a problem, madam?" she asks in her clipped accent.

"The water ran cold," Sari answers.

"I am seeking a response from Mrs. Katz, if you please," Mrs. Bahadoorsingh says, glaring at Sari over the woman's head.

Katz! Mazie Katz.

"No," says Mrs. Katz, making eye contact with Sari, "everything's just lovely."

Mrs. B turns on her heel without another word and waddles back to the reception desk.

"Thanks," Sari says, leaning over Mrs. Katz's shoulder to reach for her comb. "It's not one of my better days."

"I noticed that right off, my dear. You spent ten minutes just washing my hair. I didn't think there'd be anything left."

Sari sighs theatrically. "I just feel so sad."

Not wishing to be involved in her hairdresser's emotions, Mrs. Katz changes the subject.

At five, when she's cleaned up her station, Sari leaves the shop and walks listlessly to the grocery store as Ace has asked her to pick up something for dinner. For ten minutes she stands, lost in thought, in front of the rotisserie in the deli section as the sizzling barbecued chickens spin like Ferris wheels behind the glass. She finally hears the clerk as he repeats, "Can I get you anything?"

"One of those," she stammers, pointing to the chickens. It's the third one this week and she really doesn't want it. She's seen a program on street people—dumpster-divers—who push aside the barbecued chickens they find in the garbage. They're sick of eating them. Tired of the same greasy, salty meat falling off the bones. "And maybe a medium container of coleslaw." Mooney won't eat coleslaw and Ace won't either so she'll end up taking it for her lunch or throwing it out. "And a loaf of garlic bread." God, she'd give anything to snap out of these doldrums. "And some of that fruit salad with the marshmallows." As she reaches the checkout stand, she spots Ace, with Mooney in the side carriage of his motorcycle, looking for a parking spot. She picks up her bag of groceries and exits the store before he can locate her. She doesn't want to deal with Ace right now. She'd either be weepy or nasty and she just wants to sort herself out on her walk home.

XII

ON TUESDAY NIGHT, AFTER GERDA has had her supper and Miss Rosella has helped push the hospital bed out of the music room, down the hall and into the library, Bunny explains to her housekeeper, "You'll probably find our group sessions quite entertaining. You've never met any of them but they know about you. Sari is the poet, Jemima the newspaper reporter, and Mariah's the one who takes on romances."

Gerda snaps her eyes around the room as if she is familiarizing herself with its weighty velvet draperies and the endless books she had to dust once a month. "You remember Leland's library?" Bunny hopes this is a big step forward. "Come on," she urges, "nod or something." When there's no response Bunny becomes exasperated. She's sure that there's life behind Gerda's rheumy eyes. She's even had the housekeeper's broken glasses repaired and put them on her just to see if that would make a difference. It hasn't. The housekeeper can just as easily ignore her with her glasses on as off. The previous day Bunny had also tried putting Gerda's teeth back into her mouth, but the old woman clamped her jaw, and Bunny decided not to force the issue. "Look at me, Gerda. If you get tired, I'll take you back into the music room but for now …" As Bunny folds the sheet down neatly across the bony ribcage, she is aware of how quiet the house is—aware the only living sound is Gerda's mouth breathing. "You like show tunes?" she calls back as she looks through her music selections at the stereo. "How about *South Pacific*? *Cats*? No, you wouldn't like *Cats*." She chooses *South Pacific* and cranks up the volume so Gerda won't miss a note. "I'm going to get changed out of this uniform. Be right back," she tells her patient.

Bunny is surprised to hear a banging on the door as she's returning down the hallway to the library. She hadn't heard anyone drive
in. It's Jemima and Sari at the door and they leave it open for Mariah,
whose car has just turned into the long, tree-lined driveway. "Were
you two waiting long?" Bunny asks, leading them toward the library.

"A minute or two. We didn't think you could hear us over the music."

"Just a sec. I'll turn it down." She leaves it playing softly enough
that it becomes background.

When the two women encounter the hospital bed, they are taken
aback. "So you really did it?" Jemima says.

Bunny introduces her writing companions to the housekeeper.

At the front entrance Mariah hip-checks the door closed.

"Does she understand what you're saying?" Sari asks, leaning
over to look closely at Gerda's face.

"We don't really know so we have to assume she does."

"What's all this?" Mariah huffs, stopping short when she almost
collides with the hospital bed.

"You remember Gerda, don't you?" Bunny adjusts the bed slightly.
She leans to speak into Gerda's ear. "This is Mariah. She's the fourth
member of our writing group." There's no response. "She's the smoker!" The small green eyes scan Mariah, and Mariah feels a chill in
the air.

"I don't know whether I like being identified by my only bad habit."

Jemima smiles. "Are you saying that other than your smoking,
you're perfect?"

Mariah dumps her bag to the floor and collapses with a grunt
into the nearby chair. "Damn near perfect," she replies cheerily, getting comfortable. "So, what's with her?" She indicates Gerda with a
jerk of the head. "We on a death watch?"

Jemima gasps at Mariah's rudeness, uncertain about whether
to sit or stand to voice her opinion. She elects to stand. "Do you
have no regard for other people's feelings?" she says passionately.
Embarrassed, Sari looks out the window.

"Sorry," Mariah says in a mock-serious tone to Jemima. "Sorry,"
she says in turn to Bunny, then Sari, and finally in Gerda's direction.

Jemima is mollified enough to sit with a measure of dignity in her chair. She tilts toward Bunny. "Why did you do it?" she asks in a whisper. Her usually placid face has taken on an intense look. "Do you realize—"

Bunny raises a hand, "I know. I know. Do I realize how tough it's going to be?"

"That's not exactly what I was going to say, but it's close enough. Well, do you?"

"How would I know until I've actually tried? And keep your voice down."

"Maybe," Mariah interjects, "Bunny's striving for martyrdom."

Sari, who can stand it no longer, slams her palms on the arms of the leather chair. "It's no goddamn wonder I'm depressed! Can't you people ever give a person credit for doing something nice? Jemima," she says, toning down what she really wants to say because she's still dependent on her for a ride home, "Jemima, I'm surprised at you. You look after Joe day in and day out. Does Bunny give you a bad time?" Her look says she expects an answer.

"No, she doesn't, but then I didn't have a choice in the matter."

"You did have a choice. Joe could have gone to a home or something."

Mariah rests her head against the back of the chair and closes her eyes. No doubt her turn will come.

"Joe isn't going to any home while I'm alive. It'd kill him."

"My point exactly. It's okay for you to be noble but not Bunny? She takes in her housekeeper and you both get your hackles up."

"The thing of it is," Jemima says, shaken by Sari's attitude, "Bunny has a perfect life. She's rich, good-looking, has no encumbrances, can travel anywhere she wants if she has a mind to. Should I go on?"

Bunny just shakes her head. They have no idea and she's not about to get into it. "I'm going to put the tea on. I hope this senseless argument will be over when I get back." On her way out she checks Gerda, but the housekeeper has turned her face from the light and appears to be asleep, her mouth gaping slightly, lips puffing with every exhalation.

In the kitchen, leaning over the sink to gaze out of the window, Bunny has to laugh at how the others see her. But it's her own fault, she reflects, because she does tend to act as if to the manor born. Sometimes she would rather be back in Calgary in the cute little two-bedroom apartment that overlooked the park. Leland was just starting his career with Mega-Oil then. Those were such good times. Her bubble had burst when Leland's mother had bought them this too big, too showy house in Grievous. Mother deLore had wanted her little Leland back along with her new grandchild, and Leland had assured Bunny that he'd fly home to her and PJ every weekend. And he had—for a while.

Back in the library Sari is trying to put a cap on the rebuke she has just delivered. "That's all I have to say," she tells them, then lowers her voice so it won't carry beyond the room. "Bunny has not got a perfect life. It looks good from our side of the fence, but I think she's as miserable as I—as any one of us on a bad day," she corrects. "We don't know what her motivation is—love, compassion, guilt—who knows? And anyway, it doesn't matter."

"All right, already," Mariah moans. "Sari Button is 100 percent correct. Will that do?" She is in too good a mood to let Sari bring her down. The weekend with Chloe and the dogs was terrific and even the sight of Flora sitting on the back steps waving forlornly as she left had not interfered with her having a good time.

"We seem to have gone beyond a writing group tonight, and if I had wheels I'd be packing up and heading home," Sari says, staring at the floor between her knees. She has run out of steam.

"Guess you'll just have to do your time then, dear." Jemima smiles tightly.

Sari rises and moves to the hospital bed. She leans over the bar and tucks the spiky grey hair behind Gerda's ear. "Want me to come over soon and cut your hair? Maybe do your nails?" She checks the small knobby-knuckled hands sticking from the splints. "It would make you feel better. And maybe you feeling better will rub off on me." She slides Gerda's hands beneath the sheet and returns to her chair as Bunny brings in the tray holding her musical teapot.

After pouring the tea, Bunny leans in conspiratorially. The others follow suit. When their heads are together, she speaks just above a whisper. "We don't know how much Gerda comprehends so be careful what you say. And she's not dead so don't speak as if she is."

She sits back and the rest follow. "Now," she says brightly, "who's first?"

"I have a couple of poems I need help with," Sari offers. "One just doesn't have the rhythm and I can't finish it. And the other? Well, let's just see." She distributes her hand-written, carbon-copied work to the group.

"With angel wings I'd rise from here," she reads, nodding her head to establish the rhythm.

> and soar to greater heights,
> The lift and rise of sucking wind
> that carries me aloft
> would gently drop me down again
> to somewhere warm and soft
> where only noise is ruffled fronds,
> a bird, a child's laugh,
> bare toes sink into sugar sand
> my back shrugs off the weight,

Her voice falters.

> Of—of home and job—and ...

"See what I mean?" she says, balling the paper. "I can't get it right."

"What are you trying to say, dear? In your poem, I mean. Just read it again for us, will you?" Bunny says, stalling for time.

Sari smoothes the paper over her knee and rereads it. "I'm trying to say I'd like to ...to ... oh, I don't know."

"Maybe that's the problem right there," Mariah points out. "Can't put your thoughts down clearly if they're not clear to begin with."

Sari looks so disheartened Bunny encourages her to read the next one.

> The skeleton in the closet
> is no relative of mine
> but I carry her around as if she is.
> Clean yellow bones, long dead, chink
> and clang in the wind of bitter change
> but cease their restless chatter when I listen to them.

Sari likes this poem and she sets her face so it won't reflect disappointment should the rest not like it as well.

Mariah is first to voice her opinion. "I'd say drop the last two words and read it again. I think I like the sound of this one."

After the rereading they all agree with Mariah's editorial comment. Sari, buoyed by their optimistic reviews, says she'll rework the initial poem.

"You'll finish that last one, too? It could go on longer," Bunny remarks. "There should be more to it."

"More? I don't know. Let me think about it, okay? With so many things going on at home, I don't feel inclined to write. I actually did these," she says, pressing her pages to her chest, "on my lunch break at work."

"What's happening at home?" Bunny asks, slipping off her sandals and tucking her legs beneath her.

With a drawn-out exhalation, Mariah sinks back in her chair. And so they don't miss her intent, she rolls her eyes skyward.

Sari picks at her cuticles. "I think I'll be looking for a new babysitter."

Bunny tries to fill in the blanks. "Ace not working out?"

"Ace is fine. It's me that's not working out. He—well, he wants to be thought of as more than a babysitter." She clamps hands and poetry between her knees. "He'd like to move right in and play house."

"You sleeping with him?" Mariah asks, as she dips into her bag to search for smokes.

Sari thrusts out her chin. "And if I am?"

"Hey," Mariah says, spinning the wheel on her lighter. "No skin off my nose." She secures the burning cigarette between her teeth and throws the lighter back into her purse.

"Would that be so bad, Sari?" Bunny asks. "He seems a nice enough guy."

"Well, he is a nice guy, yes. He's reliable, considerate and Mooney thinks he's his daddy … but I don't love him. And by the way," she announces to everyone, "I'm not sleeping with him."

"Ha!" Mariah expels a smoky exclamation, which Sari disregards.

"I thought young people slept around at every opportunity," Jemima states. When she's the recipient of Sari's unflinching stare, she adds, "I wasn't referring specifically to you, you understand. It was a generality. The love generation or something," she ends lamely.

"Jemima, that was the sixties. I wasn't even born then. You were probably the right age for free love. Did you spend the sixties flat on your back with your legs in the air?"

Bunny and Mariah laugh at the thought.

Jemima's face flushes. "No, I did not," she states hotly. "I was raising my boys and there was no time for love. Free or otherwise."

With this admission the room falls silent. The other three are suddenly very interested in their tea cups.

"I guess I'd better explain," Jemima says resignedly. "After Joe's accident—"

"You don't have to do this," Bunny counsels.

Jemima waves her off. "I'm among friends, aren't I?" She receives a murmured lukewarm response and takes it as an affirmation. "Joe's accident killed more than his ability to walk, if you catch my drift." She pinches her bottom lip. "His last kick at the can was the night Robert was conceived. He's our youngest. The following day was when the tractor overturned. That was the end of the—you know," she shrugs, "the hanky-panky, the old bump and grind, the Saturday night special, the—the—"

"Beast with two backs," Bunny adds.

Mariah throws in her two cents' worth. "Roll in the hay? Hide the weeny?"

"Nooky night," Sari chimes in, laughing. "Poontanging. Um ... lunch at the Y?"

"Hey, hey," hails a voice from the doorway. "Is this a party and I wasn't invited?"

The laughter drops of its own weight and all heads turn.

Bunny jumps to her feet as if she's been caught doing something naughty. "Oh, Dr. Woolcott, I ... I wasn't expecting you." She looks confused. "Was I?"

"I knocked, but you girls were having such a great time I guess you didn't hear. No, I wasn't expected, but as I was in the vicinity, I thought I'd pop in and see my favourite patient here." He makes his way to Gerda's bedside. "Are you telling these ladies dirty jokes?" He leans over her upturned face and says out the side of his mouth, "Did you tell them the one about the doctor who ...?" He scrutinizes the group fidgeting uneasily in their chairs, then, realizing at last that his entrance hasn't been such a big hit, straightens. "Sorry for the interruption. I'll just be a moment. Can I have a word outside?" He crooks a finger in Bunny's direction.

Barefooted, she trails him into the hallway and leans against the wall with her arms crossed. She's enjoying his look of contrition. *Serves you right, you cheeky bugger.*

"I'm sorry for barging in," he says, ducking his head.

She feels this may be a practised move.

"I saw the cars outside but I never put two and two together. You having a meeting?"

Bunny shoves herself off the wall. "My writing group."

"You're a *writer*?" His eyes widen in surprise.

It's as if she'd said she was a serial killer. She clicks her tongue. "We're all writers, the whole group." She doesn't give him time to ask how many books she's written before she adds hastily, "We meet here once a week, every Tuesday."

"Gerda part of the lineup?" His cockiness re-emerges.

"I thought it would be good for her to get out and see something different. If she had shown any signs of distress, I would have returned her to the music room, of course."

"I'll run her back there and just check her out." Like pulling a rabbit from a hat, he pops his stethoscope from somewhere inside his jacket. "If it's okay with you," he adds with what she would later think of as a twinkle. A definite twinkle. *Cheeky bugger.*

She sweeps her hand toward the library door. "Be my guest."

All eyes follow him as he pushes Gerda's bed toward the doorway and zigzags it into alignment. As he passes Bunny who is standing aside to make room, he sallies, "No, no, don't bother. I can handle it."

She hides her quick smile behind her hand and turns on her heel to join the others. "Sorry," she says. "I didn't know he was coming."

"Who is he?" says Sari, drawing out her words.

"Dr. Woolcott. He's a bit of a smart-ass but he's very good with Gerda."

Mariah crosses her heavy ankles. "What's his bedside manner like?" she teases.

"Don't get carried away," Bunny warns.

Jemima nods solemnly. "He's got a nice bum. And I know my bums."

"Yes, and good teeth and great hair and legs with tennis muscles but so what? He's simply Gerda's physician and somebody I know in passing from the golf club."

"Is he single?" Sari asks coyly.

"I don't know. He's never mentioned anyone but then why should he?"

But the group has decided: he has the look of a single man.

"All I can say is it seems a shame that my Joe has old Dr. Freeze. It would be much more comforting to cry on the sturdy shoulder of your Dr. Woolcott. Oh well," Jemima sighs theatrically, "such is life."

"Okay, who's next? Mariah?" It will be a shorter evening than usual as Bunny has had a limited chance to write. Taking care of Gerda is time-consuming. The laundry, the minced food, just being there twenty-four hours a day. Even with the home care nurse, it's very confining. The best thing for her would be to have Gerda get better quickly. She'll have a talk with her in the morning. Inspire her to get healthy. After all, it's only the first week. Things are bound to get better.

"Bunny?" Sari summons. "Bunny?"

She breaks from her preoccupation. "What?"

Sari tilts her head toward the doorway where Dr. Woolcott is braced.

"Don't get up," he says, raising his palm. "I'm on my way. She's looking pretty good." Bunny, slipping into her shoes, stands anyway to show him out. "One thing, though," he says forcefully, "if someone in here is smoking, get Gerda out."

Like kids on a playground pointing out the troublemaker, they all turn toward Mariah.

The doctor waits for Bunny and together they walk to the front door. "You shouldn't be in the same room as a smoker either."

"Not to worry. We're used to it." She grasps the handle, opening the door with a flourish.

"If you have any problems, give me a call. Otherwise, I should be back tomorrow. I like to run so I'll change my route and jog past here before supper. That okay?"

She watches him bound down the stone steps and stride toward his Jeep. *Jemima's right*, she admits. *Nice bum.*

"When's he coming back?" Sari inquires. She turns from the window where she has been monitoring Dr. Woolcott's leave-taking.

"That sounds a little predatory," Bunny says, amusement on her face. She kicks off her shoes again and folds into her chair, dropping her head against the high back. On the wall facing her is the painting—not her favourite—of a pair of drooling bloodhounds in a straw-filled barn. Leland had wanted it above the fireplace in the music room but she convinced him it would be more apropos among leather books and sturdy armchairs. "He should be back sometime before supper tomorrow, if you're interested. You said something to Gerda about doing her nails?"

She turns her gaze to Sari, who is sitting cross-legged in the green leather chair chipping flakes of deep purple polish off her toenails. "I'll do what I can to get over here. After all," she says impishly, "no effort should be spared to make Gerda's life a little more tolerable."

"I visualize this open hole in the ground," Mariah says, holding her arms wide to illustrate. "And sticking up inside this hole are sharpened stakes like those little orange sticks you use, Sari, to push back cuticles." Her arms fall to her wide lap. "You know the kind." Her hands rise and limply wave at shoulder level. "And impaled, struggling feebly, is the good doctor." She repositions her sliding glasses. As she has their attention, she continues. "I don't mind the chit-chat about everybody's love life, but can we wrap it up? He's only a guy, for Chrissake. Let's get on with it." She picks up her papers and fans her moist face with them. "My God, it's hot in here."

"You still have the floor, Mariah. It's your turn," Bunny orchestrates, leaving her chair to check the thermostat. "Anyone else too hot? It's about seventy-two degrees." When no one else complains, she leaves it as is and returns to her seat.

Mariah hands out four typewritten pages, explaining where she left off. "Willow rode off on the borrowed bicycle, you'll recall, and as it was mostly downhill, made her way to where she'd met Derek of Dunston-Greene."

> Willow dismounted and set the bicycle aside. She had fled in such haste from her mother that she hadn't brought bread nor water. Her mother could be such a harpy that Willow decided she would enjoy this time alone and proceeded to lay down in a patch of daisies. The clouds overhead were moving slowly and thinning into wisps. Birds resumed their song and Willow soon fell asleep. She woke at the sound of an approaching horse with the sun much lower on the horizon. She raised herself to sitting and looked for the rider. As she hoped, it was Derek.

"I have been searching for you since yesterday," he lamented as he dismounted. "I spent the night here in case you returned but to my sorrow, I awoke with the dawn all alone, except for my steed."

"I am here now, sire."

Jemima chortles at the word *sire*.

"What!" says Mariah.

"Sorry, that word just struck me as funny for some reason."

"Get over it." Mariah pulls her neck into her shirt and dons her bullfrog face. She continues:

"You are indeed. Why did you desert me, Miss Willow? Why would you leave my home, my refuge from the world?"

"I was evicted, sire. Thrown into the night like a common serf."

Derek drew her to standing. "Who would do this?"

"I cannot say, sire."

"Do not call me sire, Willow. I am Derek."

Willow felt tears building and turned away. Derek clasped her elbow and turned her back toward him. He held her at arm's length, then enfolded her in an embrace, his chin resting atop her head. Willow slid her arms around his slender waist and laid her face against his chest.

"Now, tell me, love, why you fled into the night. I promise no harm shall come to you."

Willow hesitated for dramatic effect then haltingly spoke. "It—it was your mother, Derek."

He released her to look into her tear-streaked face. "My mother?"

"Yes, Derek, your mother. As soon as you left, she threw me out into the night. I had to borrow a shawl and bicycle to get home. My ankle ..."

Derek was visibly upset and paced past his grazing horse. He returned a few moments later with dust on his fine leather boots. "Willow, that will never happen again. I want you for my wife."

A smile played around Willow's lips. "Are you asking, sire?"

He picked her up under the arms and swung her around him in a dizzying circle. "I am asking, Willow." He set her down gently, then dropped to one knee and held her hands. "Will you marry me, Willow, and be my wife? Will you be the Lady of Dunston-Greene manor?" He stood to await her answer.

"Yes, Derek, I will. However, I must seek the counsel of my dear mother. She would want the best for me but would miss me terribly should I leave her alone." She blinks back tears with her thick dark lashes.

"I will speak with her also, my love, and perhaps convince her to live with us. Do you think that she would mind?"

"You would have to be very convincing indeed, dear heart, for Mother is single-minded about being dependent upon others. She may balk."

"When we marry, we can put our two beloved mothers together in the east wing." He laughs as he recalls the distance between the east wing and the main house. It would take them days to figure out the maze of rooms.

"That's all, folks," Mariah says, pleased with herself. "Always leave 'em wanting more. At this point you should hear the swell of violins and smell the dewy roses."

Jemima and Bunny exchange glances. How the hell are they going to tell Mariah that this is swill?

"Mariah," Jemima says, tapping her fingertips together nervously. "Mariah, do you seriously think this kind of story will sell? I mean, it's so—what's the word I'm looking for? Old-fashioned. Boy meets girl. Girl meets wicked step-mother. That kind of stuff." Her fingers stop tapping and grip the arms of the chair. "People nowadays want to read blood-and-guts novels."

"And, if I can speak from an editorial perspective," says Bunny, interrupting, "I'd change line two about the bread and water to read 'She had fled in such haste from her mother that she brought neither bread nor water.'"

"Yes-s-s," hisses Mariah. "That's what I was trying to say but it came out wrong." She strikes through the line and adds Bunny's suggested change, but Bunny isn't finished.

"Also two lines later it's 'lie' not 'lay,' and somewhere in the paragraph that starts with 'Willow felt tears,' you've used 'turned' twice in two successive sentences." She tidies Mariah's pages to indicate that she's finished her critique.

Mariah's head comes up and she addresses Jemima. "Now, regarding your less than charitable comment about my work being old-fashioned and of no interest," Mariah says, while digging into her bag with gusto, "there are people who are more clever than some I could mention who think my work *is* worth publishing." She flourishes a cream-coloured envelope and continues, "I happen to have a letter here that I was saving for the end." From the envelope she slides a folded page of heavy, bonded stock in the same shade of cream. "Just this morning I received word back from The Bodice Ripper, a publishing company, which, unlike you, enjoys what I write. They want to see more. More!"

Mariah thought there would be a lot of excited commotion but instead there's open-mouthed wonder. Bunny holds her hand out to receive the letter, then haltingly reads it aloud.

"It says, 'Thank you for your query letter and the first chapter of your novel-in-progress, *Willow's Cherry*.'"

"Willow's Cherry?" Sari and Jemima echo.

"You people might think my book is old-fashioned, but there's going to be sex in it. I just haven't written it yet. I've been waiting for Sari to fill us in on her romance so I can use it but she's been a real disappointment."

"Sorry to upset your plans," says Sari. "I wouldn't mind a little bit of old-fashioned sex myself but I can't do it alone. Well, I can, I guess, but it's not quite the same."

Bunny continues reading aloud. "'Our editorial board was quite taken by your clean writing style and content and we would appreciate reviewing the first five chapters at your convenience. Sincerely, Angelina Dorchester, Assistant Editor of Lust and Love Division, Bodice Ripper Publishing.'" Bunny releases the letter to an unbelieving Jemima, who scans it twice before passing it to Sari.

"That's wonderful news, Mariah. We're so pleased for you." Bunny rises enough to give Mariah an awkward hug. "You're the first one of us to get a query letter answered. We mustn't forget that Sari got a poem printed in the newsletter the funeral homes put out."

"Not quite the same as having a publisher, though," Sari states.

"No, dear, but it *was* nationally distributed," Bunny assures her.

Jemima finally finds her voice. "You have five chapters written?"

"More than that. Not going to be a problem."

"Have you told your mother?" Bunny asks.

Mariah replaces the letter in her bag. "Unfortunately, yes. Flora has telephoned my brothers, leaving messages on their machines. And she's baking something for when I get home."

"Well, we won't keep you too much longer," Bunny answers. "I don't have much written. Jemima?"

"Please don't rush on my account," Mariah urges. "Flora had the blue food colouring out and those little steel ball-bearing sprinkles. And a can of tuna. She was tying her apron on when I left." Mariah bestows a woeful smile on the group. "If I don't make it through the night, I'd like to take this opportunity to thank you for whatever help I've had with the book."

Jemima sorts through her papers and distributes them to the

others. "As so many of us are advancing in age—the exception in our group being Sari—I thought my column would ponder getting old."

There is a saying that getting old isn't so bad when you consider the alternative.

Being older means taking your time making decisions, making dinner, making love. Yes, dear reader, old people still do that … to the shame and horror of their children. Residents of nursing homes or long term care facilities are starving, not for food, but for affection and the human touch. When you visit at the Home, hold someone's hand, rub their feet, brush their hair. It will do them a world of good. And have a tea party. Bring your best teapot and china cups from home. Ask the staff to add boiling water to your jasmine tea and serve it to the residents with some home-baked goodies. Ask them about the last time they attended a fancy tea. Or ask how they served tea on special occasions. Think how much knowledge and life experience these wonderful people have. Men who were carpenters, farmers, policemen, fathers. Women who ran for office, cooked fourteen thousand meals in their lifetime, raised children who didn't end up in jail.

Bette Davis once said, "Old age is no place for sissies."

Women who live alone once their spouses die can still have a life. Join other single women and travel, go bowling, write your life stories or volunteer. Just get out of the house and enjoy the world around you. Have a roll in the hay with the young guy next door. You have much to give so don't sit around feeling sorry for yourself—live the life you have left to the fullest. Tell off somebody who's been rude to you. Wear all that lingerie your kids sent you over the years. Burn that beautiful candle you've been saving. Eat ginger chocolates.

"When men reach their sixties and retire, they go to pieces," says Gail Sheehy, "but women go right on cooking." And for those women who go right on cooking, here's a recipe for ginger poundcake.

Ingredients:
    8 ounces unsalted butter at room temperature
    2 ⅔ cups flour
    2 ½ teaspoons baking powder
    3 teaspoons ground ginger
    ¾ teaspoon salt
    ¼ teaspoon baking soda
    ¾ cup white sugar
    ¾ cup packed brown sugar
    1 teaspoon pure vanilla extract
    4 large eggs
    ¾ cup buttermilk
    Confectioner's sugar for the top if you wish.

Preheat oven to 375°. Grease a 10-cup fluted pan and dust with flour. Use standard method for making cake. Pour into pan and bake about 55–60 minutes. Cool on wire rack for 15 minutes, then invert the pan. Sift with icing sugar just before serving.

Serve this cake with your special tea at the Care Home.

"I think that last sentence about 'serving this cake with your special tea' gets lost at the end, so why don't you put it just before the recipe?" Mariah critiques. "And are you really putting in all those sexy bits? You're liable to get run out on a rail."

"'Course I am. I mean it. Old ladies can be so ... stodgy. They gotta get out and breathe. What do you think, Bunny?"

"Oh, you're right, Jemima," Bunny says, but her mind is on Jemima's line about having a roll in the hay and she's thinking about herself and Dr. Woolcott.

"It's kind of creepy thinking about old people making out in bed," Sari says, folding the working pages and handing them back to Jemima. "All that loose skin flopping around."

"And do you think you won't ever get old, Sari? That you won't have a wrinkle or two?" Jemima counters.

"It's not going to happen anytime soon," says Sari. "One more little thing, Jemima, I know you believe that everybody can put a cake together, but I'm not all that familiar with baking from scratch. May I suggest you tell us how? If your readers don't need it, then they can gloss over it."

"I don't know whether there's space in the column, but I'll write down the method for mixing and see what kind of adjusting I can do. Thanks, all."

Bunny folds her small pile of papers and, hiding a yawn, says, "That about does it, ladies. Well done."

"Wait a minute," Sari says. "We haven't heard yours."

"I'll pass tonight," Bunny is beginning, when Sari rises, takes the papers from her and distributes them.

Bunny sighs but accepts her fate. "Well, you've been warned. Oh, has someone got two page forty-twos? I'm missing mine." When the pages are sorted out, she explains, "You'll remember that Mr. Smith, Tiara Ballestaire's hired assassin, had made one attempt on her husband's life and failed and Tiara decided to kill him herself, but before she could do that, Smith tried again. Then Lance had come home to tell her that he had nearly been the victim of a drive-by shooting." She begins reading.

Tiara Ballestaire was livid when she slammed into Mr. Smith's office. It was located on the floor above the service bay of an Esso station, a hot little room that reeked of diesel fuel. She knew his being there was a temporary thing and that should anything go wrong, there would be no trace of him and no one answerable for renting him this cramped space.

"Mr. Smith!" She left the door open and strode the three steps it took to reach the table he sat behind. "You had him and you blew it."

Mr. Smith raised his arms, locking his hands behind his head. The pose strained the buttons on his black shirt exposing the mat of dark hair padding his chest.

"Don't look so smug, you—you—weasel," she fumed.

He tongued his dead cigar from one side of his mouth to the other.

"And don't you threaten me, mister." It *was* a threat, showing her what big muscles he had. Those thick hairy forearms and the barrel chest.

His breathing was controlled, which angered her even more.

"How can you sit there so complacent when you botched the job?" She braced her arms on the table and leaned over it.

Mr. Smith unclasped his hands and dug into his pants pocket.

Tiara backed off, her arms limp at her sides. He was going for his gun.

Mr. Smith fingered the lighter from his pocket and struck the wheel repeatedly until it produced a flame. He sucked the heat into his cigar. "Siddown," he said in a haze of smoke.

Tiara fanned her hand in front of her face.

"I said siddown!" Mr. Smith scraped his chair against the oiled wooden floor and stood. He lifted his wingtip shoe to the seat of the chair and propped his elbow on his upraised knee to give Tiara his profile. Turning only enough to use the cigar as a pointer, he directed his comments quietly and firmly. "You come in here, all high and mighty, Miss Blueblood, calling me names when you don't know dick."

She didn't even want to speak to the man but in the gaping silence (she hated a gaping silence) she reluctantly asked, "Who's Dick?" She hoped she wouldn't have to pay somebody else, like a partner he hadn't told her about.

He dropped his head back to look at the ceiling. Tiara also looked. She figured he probably had the place wired and this was his way of checking to see if the thing was running.

"Are you as dumb as you look or is it all a big act?" He sounded tired.

"How can I answer a question like that? Either way I lose." She had planned to have the upper hand on this visit but now she was losing ground. "Mr. Smith," she began reasonably, "what happened? Why," she asked, lowering her voice to just above a whisper and looking back at the ceiling, "didn't my husband meet with an accident as planned?"

Mr. Smith examined the end of his cigar and then laid it in the hubcap he used as an ashtray. "I had him lined up," he said wearily, "in my sights ..." He illustrated with thumb cocked, forefinger aimed directly at her, "... right in front of his girlfriend's apartment when she comes out the door of the building, see, and she's holding a baby."

Tiara's jaw fell. "He didn't tell me about a baby. Or a girlfriend. He said there had been a drive-by shooting in front of his office and that he came close to being killed. He was quite, quite shaken. What happened next?"

Smith dropped his foot to the floor and adjusted his pant leg. "I'm ready to fire, see, my finger squeezing, squeezing. Christ, it was all I could do to deflect at the last second. POW!" His finger jerked back as if it had been fired. "The slug went right between them and lodged in the door frame." He played with the hubcap, spinning it on the desk. The cigar dropped into the accumulation of ashes inside. "You'd think the guy was in a war zone. He grabbed the girlfriend and the kid and slammed inside that building so fast—"

"You think it's his baby?"

"How the hell would I know? I'm just supposed to kill the guy, not find out who he had for lunch a year ago."

"When are you going to try again? Are you up to doing this? Maybe I should get a specialist?"

He held up his large square palm. "I'll do it! Even if I have to blast a goddamn little kid to get him. I'll do it!"

Tiara rose. "There'll be no shooting of children," she said loftily.

He rubbed at the discoloured bags beneath his eyes. "Whatever."

"Perhaps it will be a better day tomorrow, Mr. Smith."

"Perhaps it will, Mrs. B."

They wait for Mariah to start the critique, but instead of charging right in with corrections, she looks at the papers, front and back, and just says, "Hm-m-m-m."

"What does that mean?" Bunny asks suspiciously. She had worked at this piece and knew it wasn't *terrible*.

"When I say hm-m-m-m it means just that: hm-m-m-m."

"Well, Bunny, I think it's very good," Sari offers. "I like your Mr. Smith. I didn't at first, but now that you show him tired and baggy-eyed, he appears to be more filled out. More three-dimensional. I think you're heading in the right direction with these two."

Mariah dips her head to gape over the top of her glasses. Even Jemima can't believe Sari's review—Sari who usually makes only cordial minor changes to the work of the others.

Sari continues, "Your protagonist is quite believable as the naive wife who's not so naive. She's not so stupid. She's deeper than she appears."

Mariah waits to see if Sari has more to say, then jumps right in when she doesn't. "When I said 'hm-m-m-m', it was because I was still thinking. And I was thinking that this is a good piece. Mr. Smith, like Sari said, is rounded. The one quibble I have is with what's-her-name ..." She looks up, expecting Bunny to fill in the blank.

"Tiara."

"Tiara calling Mr. Smith a *weasel*. That might not be a strong enough word, especially when she roars into his office ready to slay dragons. What'd'ya think?"

"She's right," Jemima says. "Wouldn't she at least call him—I don't know—a bastard, perhaps?"

Bunny says, "Sari, what do you think?"

Sari shrugs and shakes her head, offering no answer.

"I think," Bunny explains slowly, "that Tiara is a lady at all costs. No matter what the situation, she must be on her best behaviour, even if she's angry at someone, really angry. She's been living the role of the dutiful wife and clever hostess for years so this role continues throughout whatever challenge she faces. Does that make sense?" She doesn't wait for affirmation but goes on. "She would probably like to call him an expletive, and if goaded far enough at some point, may even want to throw things." Bunny pushes her hair from her face. "But this would never happen, of course. She's under control."

"I don't agree," Mariah begins, "but I get your point. She's a lady when it counts. But isn't trying to murder her husband just the opposite?" She chews on her pen, waiting for Bunny's response.

"It's a controlled anger. She loses it only when Mr. Smith botches the job. She expects things to go as planned. No hitches. She figures if she can arrange a formal sit-down dinner for twenty or thirty people, is it too much to ask for the same dedication to duty from Mr. Smith?" Since no one ventures another comment, Bunny collects her pages, and as the women rise from their chairs, she assures them, "I'll be sure to get more writing done this week. I'm feeling a bit more comfortable with Gerda, knowing she's not made of Dresden."

"What's Dresden again?" Sari inquires, taking her navy wool pea jacket from the pile on Leland's chair.

"It's a china that's rather fragile."

"Oh, I remember," Sari says as she worms into her coat. "James tried explaining about Dresden figurines but I really didn't care then. I still think that old stuff should be in a garage sale." She waits for Jemima, who has made a quick trip to the powder room off the front hall before the drive home.

XIII

LIKE SARI, ACE ALSO WAITS, but he's pacing as he anticipates her arrival. He's decided to tell it to her straight out, and if she raises hell, well, too bad. There's only so much a guy can take. He's rehearsed his part of the discourse and can only imagine what her comments will be. He's going to tell her he's leaving and he's not coming back. The "For Sale" sign will hit the window of his trailer in the morning.

He feels short of breath when he thinks of not seeing Mooney again. So he won't think of him. Maybe just one last look before she gets here. He walks lightly to Mooney's bedroom door and leans in to watch him sleep. He has put him to bed on his back but, being a stomach sleeper, he's flipped himself over and now lies sprawled, the sucked paw of his blue bear near his mouth. And it hits Ace that maybe this has been the last night that he will give Mooney his bath and his story and his now-I-lay-me-down-to-sleep.

"I'm home," Sari calls from the front door. Mudd doesn't even give a warning anymore. He knows it's her and all is right with his world.

"Bye, big guy," Ace whispers, his throat tightening. He closes Mooney's door completely in case there's a commotion later in the living room.

Sari sets aside her bag, removing the evening's poems with the corrections and comments. "How was Mooney? He go to bed okay?"

"See, that's what I mean," Ace begins, all the rehearsed rhetoric forgotten for the moment.

Sari is confused. "Did I miss something?" She unbuttons her pea jacket and shrugs out of it.

Ace snaps off the television. "Yeah, you missed saying, 'Hello there, Ace, and how was your day?'"

Sari blinks and looks amused. "Is that all? Then hello, Ace, and how was your day?"

He calms himself down and takes a deep breath. "It's too late for that now."

"What's with you? You been into the sauce?" She heads for the closet to hang up her jacket.

"Sari," he announces, "I'm leaving in the morning."

She slides the closet door open. "For where?" she asks without turning around.

"I'm heading back to Saskatchewan. My place will be for sale by the end of the day." He is very nervous.

Sari is thunderstruck. "You're leaving because I didn't say hello?"

"More or less," he says, regaining confidence. "What have I been doing for the past seven weeks?"

"Is this like *Jeopardy!*?" she asks, feeling a creeping apprehension.

"It's been seven weeks. Fifty-one days, counting tonight, that I've been looking after Mooney."

Sari's legs weaken and she needs to sit. "You're leaving?" she repeats, unable to comprehend. "Just like that?"

"It's not 'just like that.' For a while I'd been thinking maybe you and I had a future," he says, deciding to resume his pacing, although it means stepping over the dog. "You, me and Mooney. A family. But now I don't see any future beyond me being your convenient baby-sitter." He stops before her to deliver the *coup de grâce*. "I love you, Sari, and I love that little kid in there. Like I was his real dad. But it's a one-way street, isn't it?" He pauses long enough to allow her the chance to jump in and say, "You got it all wrong, Ace." But she doesn't. "Young Mooney thinks the sun rises and sets on me but I need that from you, too, you know?"

She shrugs. "So go."

He staggers back with her slap-in-the-face words. This wasn't how he pictured it at all. He had hoped there would be tears,

what-will-I-do-without-you cries of distress. A little earnest pleading would have gone a long way to changing his mind. He could still
retrieve all the boxes he taxied to the bus depot while she was at work.

She strides to the front door and opens it, hanging on to the
knob. "It's been great, Ace, and I'm truly indebted to you for finding
Mooney and looking after him, but if you feel the need to move on,
then so be it."

Ace picks up his leather jacket and looks around for Mudd.
"Come on, son, time to go." On the porch, his dragging heel clips the
top step and he throws a hand to the railing to maintain his balance.

Sari closes the door before he's halfway across the grass, thinking
she'll make it to her bedroom before crying, but her ragged sobs start
immediately. She slides to the floor and sags onto her side, drawing
her knees to her chest.

She wakes later cold and stiff and stumbles off to bed, falling
into it fully clothed to sleep fitfully for a few hours until hearing the
motorcycle start near the mailboxes. He must have pushed the bike
far enough away so that Mooney wouldn't be disturbed by the noise.
Ever-considerate Ace. The clock reads 6:15: too early to get up, too
late to go back to sleep. Sari switches on the radio and shifts onto
her back to wait. Her mind is empty; her chest, where she feels everything—pain, joy, anger—is cavernous. Scooped out hollow.

It isn't until she hears the automatic coffeepot click on that the
heaviness seeps in to pin her arms to the bed, fill her chest with a pressing coldness. He even made coffee for her. Probably has her lunch in
the fridge. She wills herself to roll over and sit up. Lethargically she
undoes her braid, then finally stands, strips off her clothes from last
night and shuffles to the shower.

"What am I going to do with you today, little man?" she says, as
she lifts Mooney from his crib, setting him on the floor. He crawls
ahead to the living room and hoists himself onto the sofa, where he
snaps open the buttons on his sleepers and works his arms out.

Before changing his diaper she asks, "You want to watch *Barney*?"
She flips on the television for him but as soon as his new diaper is on,

he squirms off the sofa to follow her into the kitchen.

As she pours a coffee, Mooney pulls himself up on her leg. She hands him a thick teething biscuit, then drags his mesh playpen before the sofa. After plunking him in and pushing his toys within reach, she crosses to the door and steps out into the cool fall morning. Mudd's dinner bowl is still at the bottom of Ace's stairs, but Mudd is gone, as is the Harley. The dog would be riding in the side car now, ears flapping, mouthing a grin, happy as hell to be heading anywhere with his human buddy.

Sari has been hoping it isn't true. That he hasn't left after all. But there's no telltale sign of smoke from the chimney and no lights on. She re-enters her trailer, warms her cup with fresh coffee, then sits near Mooney. "It's cold in here, baby. Let's put your PJs on." She picks her son up and lays him on the couch so she can work his wriggling arms and legs back into the sleeper. She does up one of his fasteners. "Mummy did a very silly thing." Snap. "Mummy told Ace to leave and not come back." Snap. "Which means stupid Mummy has no babysitter." Snap. "No neighbour." Snap. "And worst of all, no friend." Snap. Snap. She rises restlessly to peer out the window.

"Aith," Mooney lisps, sitting himself upright, eyes fixed on the TV screen.

Sari leans over the back of the chair, vacantly watching the purple dinosaur like Mooney is. She tends to stall in a crisis. Move at a crawl instead of making decisions.

Finally, a few minutes after eight o'clock, she picks up the phone. After a terse conversation, she sets the receiver back with more force than necessary. "Bitch!" she says under her breath, jamming her hands into her jean pockets. She returns to her bedroom for a thick sweater and sits next to her son. "Mummy just phoned in sick but Mrs. Bahadoorsingh, bless her little pointed head, wasn't impressed."

"Head?" mimics Mooney, applying both hands to his red hair.

"That's right, head," Sari smiles, leaning over to kiss his face. Mrs. Bahadoorsingh did not, in fact, believe a word. She threatened that this was Sari's last sick day and said if she was sick tomorrow, not to bother showing up again, ever. "Mummy is doomed," she says, butting Mooney's shoulder, knocking him sideways. "Doomed," she crows, pinning his hands and burying her forehead into his tummy.

Following lunch, with Mooney down for a nap, Sari decides to take a chance and phone Bunny.

"I have a big problem."

"Oh?"

"Ace abandoned ship this morning. Left for parts unknown."

"Oh, no. What happened?"

"I don't want to go into it now, but the thing is, he's gone and I have no one to look after Mooney while I'm working."

"Uh-huh."

"You're the only person I'd trust to watch him." The silence seems answer enough but she adds, "I'll pay you."

"That's not it, dear. I'm just wondering how I can juggle Mooney and Gerda."

"Yeah, you're right. I forgot about her. It's too much to ask. Thanks anyway."

They hang up but a few moments later Bunny returns Sari's call. "The house is pretty quiet with only Gerda here and God knows she doesn't say much. Maybe the sound of a baby would be sort of neat. So, what the hell! I'm here anyway. I'll give it a try."

"He's a good little boy."

"I'm sure he is. When do you want to start?"

"Tomorrow?" Sari says tentatively. "I phoned in sick today."

"That's fine. Will you bring all his stuff over?"

"In the morning."

"How early?"

"About 8:30, maybe a bit earlier. Thank you, Bunny. I really owe you."

"You sure do, kiddo." Bunny eyes all the things she'll have to move out of range. If she closes off the library, Mooney could use the kitchen and the music room. Gerda will have to share. Struck by a sudden thought, she tightens her sweater around herself and heads out the kitchen door onto the porch, where Gerda's old rubber boots are still moldering. She continues on to the wisteria-covered triple-car garage. Her Beamer is in the first stall and Leland's classic Jag in the next. Beyond them a four-wheel-drive Range Rover takes up the third space. She checks to see if its plates are still valid and returns to the house.

"Hi, Sari. Me again. I have two perfectly good cars sitting here doing nothing. I think you'd be able to get all Mooney's stuff into the wagon if you'd like to borrow it for a while."

Sari is speechless, her mouth hanging slack.

"Did you hear me?"

"I can't believe you're doing this." She has to sit down.

"Well, they're just cars and I know Leland would be glad to press them into service." Leland will have a fit but what the hell. "You take good care of the car and I'll take good care of the baby. No dints or scrapes on either one."

"I'm getting the best of this deal," Sari says, sniffing back tears.

⁓

"YOU DID WHA-AT?" MARIAH BARKS. Another week has gone by and they are once again seated in Bunny's library.

"You heard me. And all in all, I feel pretty good about it," Sari says, shifting Mooney to a more comfortable position on her lap.

"What's the matter with you, girl? He liked you. He liked your kid. What more do you want? Now the kid is stuck with Bunny."

"I'm not *that* bad," says Bunny, scowling at Mariah.

"You know what I mean."

"What happened, anyway?" Jemima asks.

"Let me put Mooney down for the night and I'll try to explain, if I can."

"Miss Rosella's in there putting Gerda to bed. She should be finished in a few minutes. There's a bottle in the fridge for Mooney." Bunny has taken over Mooney's care quite capably. She is even toying with the idea of inviting Sari to move into the house for awhile. No use in her driving back and forth with the baby when he could stay and not be disturbed morning and night.

When Sari returns from settling Mooney into the music room, she tucks her hands between her knees. "You see, all my life I've knuckled under. To my parents, to the guy who got me pregnant at seventeen, to Mrs. Bahadoorsingh, to James. I don't like to admit this, and it goes no further," she says, jabbing a warning finger, "but I did sleep with Ace once. One time only. Right after James left. It was sort of an accident. Just one of those crazy things you do that you may or may not regret later. I could have blown it off as a one-night stand but the next morning he practically crowed. He had this look. You know that kind of look? Like I was some sort of moth already pinned to his wall. I saw the future in that look. I felt if I didn't gain control, I was going to drown. I know," she says, throwing up her hands, "mixed metaphor. But he would have taken over. Become Daddy. Become husband-like. I'd just been through that. I thought James and I were happy and look what happened. He left." She reaches for her cup and sips enough tea to moisten her dry mouth. After accepting a cookie from the plate Jemima offers, she leaves it balanced on her knee. "So when push came to shove, I shoved back."

"He pushed you?" Bunny asks.

"No, not physically, but what he did was a threat. If I didn't do what he wanted, he would leave."

"What did he want?" Jemima asks. "Was it so awful?"

"He wanted us to be together. Like a family."

"The dirty bastard," Mariah hoots, slamming the arms of her chair.

Sari looks up, suppressing the beginnings of a smile. "He isn't as perfect as you think, either. He leaves the seat up on the toilet and he always overcooks the vegetables."

"Well then, you did the right thing," Jemima chimes in. "Kick him to the curb."

"This isn't funny, you guys," Sari says, laughing despite herself. "Mooney keeps looking for him and I actually do miss him."

"It's been almost a week and you're still sort of dragging around. Are you going to do anything about it?" Bunny asks. "Like try to get him back?"

Sari shrugs and bites her cookie in half.

"Do you trust us? Our judgment, I mean?" Jemima folds her arms awaiting an answer.

"It depends."

"Let's take a vote, then. Who thinks Sari has lost her mind?"

Three arms rise like lamp standards.

"Who thinks Sari should go after this not-quite-perfect human being?"

Three arms remain aloft.

"Who can guarantee Sari will live happily ever after?" Sari asks. "What, no hands? Look, you three, I'm not chasing after him. What I did was right for me. He's a good guy but my only regret is hurting his feelings."

"But you sent him away," Bunny counters.

"I didn't send him. He left, remember?"

Bunny wonders how long it will be before the girl finds someone and settles down. As much as she likes her and her son, she doesn't plan on babysitting forever.

"So what about the other one, James?" asks Jemima.

Sari is puzzled.

"Would you take him back?"

Sari shakes her head. "No, that's very over. Done."

Jemima pulls hairpins out of her untidy French roll and lays them on the arm of the chair. "You going to divorce him?"

"Hadn't given it much thought," Sari says, genuinely surprised at the question.

"Well, when you do," says Jemima, weaving the last of the pins back into her hair, "go and see this lady lawyer." She rifles through her handbag and comes up with a dog-eared business card. "She's very good. A bit like a pit bull." At the raised eyebrows, she explains, "She's updating our wills."

Sari takes the card and reads the name aloud. "MacKenzie Teo, barrister and solicitor." But she drops the card onto the nearby end table. Lawyers, especially pit bull lawyers, are not in her budget.

Miss Rosella pops her head through the doorway to announce

that both Gerda and Mooney are sleeping and says to keep the noise down to a dull roar. She slams the front door on her way out.

Bunny presides. "I think we'd better get on with our readings. Who's first?"

Sari digs around in the green leather chair for her handwritten pages. "If I still have the floor," she says, handing around her work, "I wrote this on my lunch break today."

> The experts tell me not to worry,
> things will come to pass.
> Eight hours of sleep, three meals a day,
> four fruits, five greens, seven grains.
> Or is it three hours of sleep? Eight meals a day?
> One fruit, no greens, two grains?
> No matter.
> The experts tell me not to worry,
> Love will come my way.
> Get thin. Look good, be co-o-o-l!
> Designer dress, new hair, new face,
> New attitude that says, Look out, world, here I come!
> Can I find all this at Zeller's? And get double Zed points?
> The experts tell me not to ... not to ... not to ...
> So I won't.

Sari chuckles. "See, I'm back to my usual cheerful self." She pops the last half of her cookie into her mouth, then hauls her ankles up to sit cross-legged in the chair.

"Do you want us to critique it?" Bunny inquires.

"Aw, no," she says. "That was just for fun. Only took me a moment to do it. Once things have settled I'll get back to serious writing."

Jemima fondles the excesses beneath her chin. "You know, Sari, now that I've had a moment to think about it, I have to agree you're probably doing the right thing. You gotta live for yourself, not exclusively for Mooney, and certainly not for any of us who don't reside in your skin twenty-four hours a day. Don't you rush into anything that doesn't feel right."

"Thanks, Jemima, I appreciate that."

The moment floods Bunny with emotion. "Do you realize," she says, her voice catching, "you three are my best friends?" The silence sobers her quickly.

"You gotta get out more," Mariah says, plunging her hand down the front of her blouse to scratch.

"What I mean is—"

"We know what you mean," says Jemima, patting Bunny's thigh. "And you're bang on. You three, other than Joe and my boys, are pretty well my only friends. The people at the newspaper are just somebodies I nod to when I drop off my column."

"And I can't imagine what kind of shape I'd be in if I didn't have this group to fall back on," Sari confesses. "I guess I'd be a basket case."

They look to Mariah.

"If you think for one minute I'm going to go all mushy, you've got another think coming." Cleaning the lenses of her black-framed glasses on her shirt, she peers at them weakly. "Enough said."

Jemima leans toward Sari to stage-whisper, "Inside, she's a marshmallow."

Sari grins behind her hand.

"I'm going to make another pot of tea," Bunny says. "It may be a long night."

She's glad to be away from them for just a moment. A breather in the kitchen. She refills the electric kettle and plugs it in. From the sizable window above the sink she watches the swollen clouds dissolving the crescent moon. Her orchard stands in dark relief against the killing frost. She's comfortable here. The house fits her nicely. She realizes she hasn't had a drink yet today. "Too much to do," she says aloud and dumps the old tea to make fresh. A coyote yips and from a distance a siren answers.

They are talking about Joe when Bunny returns.

"He's getting out of hand," Jemima is saying. "Very hard to live with. I told you about him being in the middle of the road that night. Well, I have to get him to bed before I leave on Tuesdays and then stick his chair on the back porch so he can't get it. He's a worry."

"Is it time for Joe to go into a home?" Bunny asks gently.

"Not without me," Jemima says, ending the discussion.

Bunny indicates the tea and changes the subject. "It's going to be slippery going home tonight. There's a heavy frost and it looks like it could snow. Be very careful. I already heard sirens when I was in the kitchen. Sari, maybe you should stay over? You're no sooner going to get home than you'll have to turn around and come back."

"We'll be just fine."

"Seems a shame to uproot Mooney, but it's up to you," Bunny replies, giving her a moment to change her mind. But she doesn't. "Jemima, what do you have for us?"

Elbows on the chair, laced fingers beneath her chin, Jemima ponders. "I know the taste of my mother's bread," she says, before picking up and distributing her story. "I know the taste of my mother's bread," she reads, emphasizing the word *know*.

> When the families got together, my mother and her sister and all us kids, when it came time to eat, I could distinguish my mother's bread from her sister's even though they both made the same recipe. It had … something. A taste, a colour, a smell that was Mother. Maybe it's because she kept the flour in the bin next to the potatoes. Her bread was earthy. Or maybe because she kneaded it at the table where everything happened. The new babies were bathed on that table, vegetables scraped and cut up, rum-soaked fruit chopped for the leaden Christmas cakes, letters written, candles burned. Her bread absorbed all this history. Absorbed the hand soap she washed with before plunging her fists into the buttered belly of the first rising. Absorbed the zest of metal from the

curlicued metal cooling racks. The taste of the pitted loaf pans themselves, stacked one within the other in the cupboard next to the stove. Every three days the pans were liberally greased and fitted with a fat log of smooth dough. Or maybe its essence came from the warming oven above the wood-burning stove redolent with the cinnamon and nutmeg she'd sprinkle in there to make the house smell nice. We'd beg for Mother's bread fried in bacon fat or slabbed and spread with plum jam.

Jemima closes her eyes and inhales the aroma.

If we cut across the fields to the farmer next door, he'd sell us buttermilk for fifty cents a bucket. Then we'd eat our bread and jam on the back stoop and wash it down with mugs of cold buttermilk. The chickens would gather for the crusts.

Jemima absently folds her page. "I know the taste of my mother's bread. And how I miss it."

"That's an evocative column, Jemima," Bunny says from behind the page she is rereading. "Makes me want to throw together a batch of sourdough tomorrow."

Using Jemima's page to cool the hot flash scorching her face, Mariah complains about the heat in the room. She's flushed and a bit breathless. "Your mother's cooking must have made an impression because you've mentioned it in your columns before. That can either work for or against. Your reader might say, there she goes again, writing about her mother. Or on the contrary, it could evoke a feeling of nostalgia." She quickly scans the page with her finger. "You have a misplaced modifier in the line about sitting on the back stoop eating your bread and jam and washing it down with a glass of buttermilk. Sounds like you're washing down the stoop with the buttermilk."

"Oh, right. Missed that," Jemima says, finding the offending paragraph, striking through the line and adding directional arrows.

"I don't think I make anything that could be pegged to me," Sari states.

"Joe wouldn't have any problem singling out the dreaded lima bean casserole I damn near killed him with. Total recall on that."

"You're dwelling on it," Mariah barks. "Lima beans did not do him in."

Jemima ignores the comment. "He could always tell my baking from say, his sister-in-law's. His brother's a smoker and no matter what she makes it tastes like second-hand smoke."

Mariah crosses her ankles and leans back in the chair, stretching her arms above her head. "Ah, you guys had golden childhoods. When I was young—"

"You walked to school in your bare feet with lard sandwiches," Jemima baits.

"Not quite, but close. Flora couldn't cook. I couldn't cook. Nobody cooked, but my brothers and I managed to get a lunch every day. Cheese and jam, cheese and onion, mashed potatoes. Have you ever had a cold mashed potato sandwich? Even now Flora makes the most—I was going to say disgusting—unidentifiable food. Weird combinations. Like her blue cheese and honey on toast." She shakes her head at the thought. "Oh, and pickled pig's feet. She'd unwrap them fresh from the butcher and whap them on our plates with a chunk of bread and butter and a mound of vegetables boiled to within an inch of their lives."

Bunny grimaces. "See, you could identify your mother's cooking from all others."

Mariah ends her stretch and collapses into a lump. "I guess I could," she admits.

"I suppose it's now my turn," Bunny says, "but the stuff I wrote is so skimpy and unimaginative that I'm not going to saddle you with it. And I might not have anything for next week the way things are going."

Sari jumps in hastily. "It's looking after Mooney and Gerda, isn't it?"

"It doesn't leave me much time."

"I'm really sorry about that. I'll advertise for a babysitter this week. Get him out of your hair."

"Sari, dear, I'm really just using them as an excuse. If I were more organized, I could do it. Write while he's sleeping, same as you. Get up earlier, go to bed later. A real writer would be that devoted, but I'm not a real writer. I haven't even been rejected."

"In order to be rejected you have to send stuff out," Mariah says stiffly.

"I know. I know. Some day I will."

"Speaking of rejection, have you heard anything from the publisher that wanted more of *Derek of Dunston-Greene*, Mariah?" Jemima says.

She shakes her head. "Not yet. These things take time."

"Maybe the newspaper will run it as a serial. Women's page stuff."

"I'll wait. There's no rush. I'm not going anywhere."

ONCE THE RANGE ROVER IS warmed, Sari returns to the house to carry Mooney out. The others have gone, their tire tracks leading away through the newly fallen skiff of snow.

"You're sure about not staying?" Bunny repeats, standing next to the open car door, hugging her arms around her middle, while Sari belts Mooney in.

"I don't sleep well in someone else's house. Don't worry," she says, smiling. "I have this fancy set of wheels. We'll get home just fine. See you in the morning."

Bunny closes the car door and waves through the glass, then turns and heads for the house, treading carefully up the slick stone stairs.

After locking the door, she goes directly to the library liquor cabinet. As she tips the elegant bottle over the glass, she wonders why she pours just two fingers' worth when she knows she'll be back for another. She carries the drink to the music room and Gerda turns her head slightly at Bunny's approach.

"You still awake?" Bunny asks, pulling a chair toward the bedside. She sits, holding the glass of scotch to her chest. "It's been quite a day, hasn't it?" She lovingly rolls the first sip over her tongue. Gerda stares into the distance above Bunny's head. "Are you giving me the evil eye for having one little drink? Well, my dear Gerda, this is my first today. I promised you I wouldn't touch the stuff while I was on duty and now," she says, trying to read the hands on her watch in the dim light, "I'm officially on my own time. No more babies, no more writers." She drains the rest of the scotch. "I'm tired." She tucks her hair behind her ear. "I'm just going to get a touch more and I'll be back."

This time she returns with three fingers of scotch and three ice cubes. "Tomorrow Miss Rosella and I are going to try you in the wheelchair. Dr. Woolcott says there's no reason you can't be up." Bunny walks to the window and pull the drapes aside to peer into the darkness. She puts her forehead against the cold glass. Gone are the sharp outlines of bare trees in her yard; instead cottony snow has caught there, mounding on the branches. "I wonder where Leland is tonight? Do you ever wonder where he gets to, Gerda? Your bright and shining star? Your Mister? You do know he has his female travelling companions, don't you?" She turns her back on the winter landscape and approaches the bed, leaning over the rails carefully so as not to spill her drink. The buttons on her sweater tink against the shiny metal. She is surprised to see that her glass is empty. "You think he's such a good guy and I am the wicked witch of the west, never travelling with him." Gerda's gaze brushes across Bunny's face and drops to throat level. "But he's never wanted me to go with him. Says it would be boring. Too hot or too cold. Or wives aren't welcome." Bunny studies the melting ice cubes as she tips them round in the glass. "You know the thing that bothers me the most? It's the lying." She lowers her voice in an imitation of Leland. "'Where the hell d'ya get that screwball idea? Miss Spring-Dunning is only my secretary. That's all!'"

She pulls the blankets over Gerda's shoulders and bunches the pillow on either side of her head. "Sometimes I get so lonely here I could curl up and die. Just wither away and no one would even notice." She smoothes her patient's hair from her forehead. "I haven't had sex for five years." She sags onto the chair. "And Dr. Woolcott is starting to look pretty damned good. Like a four-course meal." Bunny rubs at the back of her hand. "Oh, I forgot to tell you—although it probably wasn't so much forgetting as setting up a mental block—Leland's mother will be over for lunch tomorrow to see for herself how you're doing. She thinks you're at death's door, but we'll prove her wrong yet again and have you bright-eyed and bushy-tailed by the time she gets here." She dumps the rest of the ice water from her glass into the potted chrysanthemum Leland had ordered for Gerda. "A little lunch, a little visit and poof! she'll be gone again." She adds that she'll be down to say goodnight after she gets ready for bed and dims the lights. On her way to the stairs she detours to the kitchen and places her glass in the dishwasher.

MARIAH SETS OFF AT HER usual breakneck speed and discovers the road is as slippery as Bunny warned. It's only when she cuts her pace to suit the conditions that the wipers are able to clear the snow from the windshield. Finally, she turns into her driveway, thinking it looks like an old-fashioned Christmas card with the snow blanketing its defects and a welcoming rosy glow issuing from the kitchen windows. She sits for an admiring moment then stiffens. *What the hell?* She fumbles with the car door handle and steps ankle-deep into winter then gallops for the front of the house and slams open the door. Smoke pads the ceiling.

"Flora?" she bellows. "Mother?"

There is a muffled reply from the bathroom. "Wha-a-t?"

Mariah shoulders the door open to find her mother semi-submerged in a tub of bubbles. The rim of the tub is aglow with candles.

"Shut the door, will you?" Flora says. "You're letting smoke in."

"Get out of there! The house is on fire!" Mariah hauls Flora up and out of the bath, wrapping a towel around her. Then, realizing this will not be enough cover, she reaches back into the linen cupboard and grabs the first thing that comes to hand—a daffodil-coloured bedskirt. She flips it open and surrounds her mother with it. "Put your slippers on," she says, kicking them closer to Flora's feet. "We gotta get out of here." At the last moment she sweeps all the candles into the water.

Crouching low, they scurry through the heavy smoke in the living room and head out the open door, but Flora stops dead on the front porch. "Get the bird!" she shrieks, before she doubles over in a coughing spasm.

But Mariah is not going back for some goddamn stupid bird. She tries pushing Flora down the front stairs, but Flora pushes back. "I have to get Axel."

"Get in the goddamn car!" Mariah orders and returns to the flaming ruins of her house. She scuttles on hands and knees below the level of the smoke in the living room, moving toward Flora's bedroom where the bird should be. The bloody thing is probably a goner anyway, she thinks, like the doomed canary in the mine. The bedroom door is ajar and she slides inside and kicks it shut just as there is a sudden *whoosh* behind her: the living room windows have blown outward and the flames, fuelled by the fresh air, lust across the ceiling.

"Where the hell you been?" squawks the bird beneath his cover. "Where the hell ..."

So much for the canary in the mine, she thinks. Groping toward Axel's voice in the complete darkness, she finds the base of his stand and rises to her feet to release the cage from its hook.

"It's party time!" cries Axel. Mariah sets the cage down while she muscles open the window, then throws a leg over the sill and grabs the birdcage before dropping to the ground. The air is cold and crisp and it takes a moment for her to catch her breath. She is heading for the car when she sees her mother in the middle of the front yard, softly illuminated in the snow. "Come on! I've got him."

"Brass monkeys," the bird complains. "BRASS MONKEYS!"

Flora approaches, draped dramatically in the bedskirt, yellow ruffles kicking out with every slippered step, wet hair steaming in the cold.

When they get to the car, Mariah starts the engine and turns on the heat. She reaches into her purse for her cell phone and calls for an ambulance and a fire truck. She backs the car up until she can lodge it behind the tool shed, giving the driveway up to the emergency vehicles, which should arrive long after the house is consumed by the flames. Flora hacks into her bedskirt and when the coughing spasm is over, mother and daughter watch in silence as their house burns. The scene no longer resembles Currier and Ives.

"Amen," says Axel. "A-men."

XIV

BUNNY IS IN HER DRESSING gown coming down the stairs when the phone rings and she hastens to answer it in Leland's study, thinking it's probably him. But before she can even say hello, there's a woman on the line cannonading words into her ear at gunfire speed and Bunny holds the receiver away until there's a break in the excitement. "Who is this?"

"It's Mariah, for Chrissake. Don't you listen?"

If it weren't for the panic in Mariah's voice, Bunny would hang up on her rudeness. "Slow down. I can't understand a word you're saying."

"She burned down the goddamn house! Flora burned down the goddamn house!"

"No!" Bunny exclaims, collapsing into Leland's office chair.

"It's gone. Every fucking thing I own is up in smoke."

"What happened?" Bunny asks, feeling a knot in her stomach. There's a brief silence and all Bunny hears is the sound of heavy equipment on the other end. "Mariah?"

"Wait a sec," Mariah orders as she flicks the butt end of her cigarette into the dirty snow before slamming the doors of the phone booth again. When the snowplow finally rounds the corner, she sounds a little less agitated. "You still there? I'm in a phone booth. My cell phone died."

"Yes. Are you all right?"

"Am I all right?" she mocks, stomping her feet to regain feeling. "Not really." She lights another cigarette. "I'm chain-smoking and I have to pee but I no longer have a bathroom."

"And your mother?" Bunny finally asks, afraid of the answer.

"I dragged her out of the house and they took her away in the ambulance," Mariah states wearily.

"Poor Flora," Bunny commiserates.

"There's no visible signs of damage, but she's coughing up a lung and now I've gotta find a place to stash the bird."

"You rescued the bird *and* your mother?"

"Unfortunately. She insisted on saving the goddamn thing so I had to go back in."

"Well, good for you," Bunny says.

"Can't you grasp the situation? I have nothing but the clothes on my back and a storage shed that may or may not be there when I get back. It's a good thing my memory sticks were in my purse or I'd really be up the creek. All that writing—" Her voice catches and she presses the receiver to her chest while she recovers.

"I'm so pissed about her burning down the house that I'm not thinking straight. I can't even remember why I'm phoning you." She rubs a porthole in the steamy glass to make sure her car, parked next to the phone booth, is still running and spots the cage in the rear seat. "Ah, right! I need a place to stash the damn bird until I can find somewhere to live."

Mariah rests the back of her head against the glass and wipes her cold nose on the sleeve of the only jacket she now owns. "Once I left your place, I should have kept going. Somewhere nice. Instead, I drive home and find the place already burning and I thought she was dead. But she was in the bath and had no friggin' clue that she'd soon be soup. I got her out, gift-wrapped her, and she stood there in the cold while I went out her bedroom window with the bird. I ended up tromping through the snow holding the cage out in front of me like—like—what's the name of the guy that went out looking for a truthful man?"

"Diogenes," Bunny replies.

"Doesn't matter," says Mariah. "And Flora's saying, 'Shoot me. Just shoot me.' If I'd been armed, I would have done it. Put us both out of our misery." She pauses to exhale smoke at the roof of the phone booth. "Anyway, can you keep the bird for a while? There's really nobody else on such short notice."

"Sure. Bring it over. Do you want to stay here, too?" Bunny asks, hoping it will be for only one night.

"Thanks, but I've already phoned my friend Chloe. I can hole up with her for a week or so if I have to. But she's got dogs and cats so I can't take the damn bird there."

"Is your mother going to Chloe's when she gets out of the hospital?"

"Hell, no. I'm going to put her on a bus and send her to my brother Clive. She insists she's going back to the Briar Rose Home for Pioneers. I'll figure something out in the morning. I'm too tired now." After saying an abrupt goodbye, Mariah slogs to the car in her street shoes, her winter boots now a smoldering lump of black plastic back there where her house used to be.

∽

"YOU GOT ANYTHING TO DRINK?" Mariah asks, by way of a greeting, when Bunny comes to the door in her dressing gown and slippers. She didn't think this visit required a change of clothes.

"Yes, of course. Come in." She stands aside so Mariah can manoeuvre the birdcage through the door.

"Where do you want him?" Mariah asks, starting for the music room.

"Gerda is sleeping. Set him on the island in the kitchen for now." Bunny leads the way, turning on the necessary lights. "He'll be okay in here." When Mariah plunks the African Grey on the counter, Bunny lifts the cover to peek inside. "He's okay, isn't he? Not singed?"

"Seems to be fine, although he hasn't said a word since Flora was hauled away."

Bunny lowers the cloth and gives the top of the cage a pat. "Now, you said something about a drink? Tea, or something stronger?"

"Stronger and I don't care what."

Mariah's wet footprints lead them back down the hall and the two women veer off into the library. Bunny heads straight for the liquor cabinet while Mariah paces restlessly from the window to the unlit fireplace.

"Rum and Coke? Vodka? Sherry?"

"Sure," Mariah answers.

Bunny pours a sherry and takes one for herself. "Are you hungry?"

"I don't think so," Mariah says as she takes the glass in hand. "Chloe will probably have something ready when I get there."

"Where does she live? Fairly close?"

"You know the dairy out on the perimeter road? Well, she's about a mile further still." Mariah finishes her sherry in two quick swallows and hands Bunny the glass.

Bunny is satisfied with her decision not to offer Mariah the good scotch. "More?" she asks charitably.

"Gotta go. Thanks for watching the bird. He shouldn't be too much trouble. There's enough food in his dishes for at least two days. I'll scrounge some in town and drop it off."

"If you give it to Sari, it'll save you a trip. She's here twice a day with Mooney. And don't worry about the bird. He'll be good company for Gerda."

After cautioning Mariah to drive carefully, Bunny calls goodnight from the doorway and heads for bed again. Mariah still has a forty-five minute drive ahead of her.

∽

NEXT DAY, AS PROMISED, MOTHER deLore arrives and, after giving instructions to her driver to wait in the car, allows herself to be guided into the music room. Bunny returns to the kitchen to finish preparing lunch. A little while later, as she nears the music room to check on her visitor, she hears a dry, rusty gasping noise and, fearing that Gerda is choking, rushes in. But Gerda seems to be laughing, not choking. Mother deLore, sitting next to the bed on a straight-backed chair, has a stricken look on her face and is clutching the neck of her blouse. Bunny is puzzled. "What happened?"

All Mother deLore can do is point an accusing finger at the bird-cage. Bunny checks to see if Axel is okay, that he hasn't unlocked his door. "What happened?" she repeats.

"I was telling Gerda about the highlights of the hospital auxiliary AGM and my re-election as vice-president when this—this fowl said something entirely inappropriate."

Of course! This is the bird that was responsible for getting Flora thrown out of the seniors' home. "Now what could a bird possibly say that would be inappropriate?" Bunny asks innocently.

Mother deLore gathers up her entire five-foot height and says haughtily, "I'm certainly not going to repeat it."

Bunny examines Gerda's composed face. "Was she laughing when I came in?"

"It was involuntary." Mother deLore clips the words. "I'll not stay another minute with that bird in the room."

"I have nowhere to put him for the moment. I'm making lunch in the kitchen and Mooney is sleeping upstairs and the bird scares him."

"I don't wonder at that! That creature has a nasty look about him."

Axel certainly doesn't seem all that bad as he sits fluffing his plumage. In fact, his attitude is quite cheerful as he delicately picks at his head with one talon. "I'll just put his cover on and that should keep him quiet." Bunny flaps the cloth over the cage. Before leaving, she gives Gerda a guarded glance. She swears she sees a hint of a smile. "Mother deLore, do you want your lunch in here or in the kitchen?"

"The kitchen?" her mother-in-law says as if it's a dirty word. "Well, Delores, as I came all this way to see Gerda, I'll dine in here." She leans over the rails and raises her voice for Gerda's benefit. "You're enjoying our little visit, aren't you, Gerda? I must tell you the news from Mrs. Penny and Mrs. Nickel. You remember them, dear? From my bridge club? You thought I didn't know, but you used to call them the Money Bags." As she pours half a glass of water from the bedside jug, she notices Bunny is still in the room. "What is it?"

"Nothing. I'm just checking to see that Gerda's not getting too tired."

"Surely I can be the judge of that, Delores. My visits perk people up, not put them to sleep."

Bunny thinks if she doesn't leave the room and head for the kitchen, she may say something spiteful. She has lunch almost assembled and only has to lay a clean napkin on the tray and arrange the shrimp croissant, small salad (no dressing), and the chocolate eclair. Her mother-in-law will have tea with milk and two sugars. Tomato is the soup du jour for Gerda. Bunny herself will eat when it's quiet, after the Black Widow has gone back to her web and before Mooney gets up. When she returns to the music room carrying the loaded tray, she squeezes past the straight-backed chair to elbow aside the clutter on the bedside table and set the tray down. "Mother," says Bunny pleasantly, handing her the croissant on a clear glass plate. "You can get started while I feed Gerda."

The elder Mrs. deLore pries the top from the sandwich to appraise the contents. "It's seafood!" she squeaks. "You know very well I can't eat seafood with my gout."

"That's a misplaced modifier," Bunny says under her breath as she cranks the handle to raise the head end of the bed.

"I'll be up all night if I eat seafood."

Bunny sighs. "I'll make you something else then."

"No need. I'll just make do with my little salad."

When the bed's at the right height, Bunny unfolds a clean hand towel over Gerda's bony chest. She then carries the soup cup around to the other side of the bed. "Here's your soup," she says, showing Gerda the spill-proof drinking cup. "It's tomato."

But Gerda chokes on the first mouthful. Then she tips away from Bunny, until her body is leaning over the railing and spews what she can't swallow across Mother deLore's pearl grey suede walking pumps.

"My Guccis!" Mother deLore bawls, the hard g discharging bits of romaine onto the skirt of her classic fifteen-year-old Chanel suit. "Jeezus H. Christ!" she fumes. She propels her plate onto the tray as if she's throwing a Frisbee and on her way out of the room she flicks bits of salad from her suit.

Bunny, still holding the soup cup, stares open-mouthed at the empty doorway. Grasping Gerda's sleeve, she rights her with little effort. Gerda serenely settles her splinted wrists into her lap while Bunny looks for signs of distress on her face. There are none. "Did you hear what she said? I've never heard words like that coming from her mouth before. And in front of the parrot, too." She offers the cup again, but beneath the sheet Gerda's chest is fluttering like a butterfly. For a moment Bunny thinks it's a heart attack but then realizes that Gerda is silently chortling. "Did you do that on purpose?" Bunny asks in awe. Gerda's toothless grin is reminiscent of an apple doll, withered and aged into sepia lines and wrinkles.

"You did, didn't you?"

Her mother-in-law stands in the doorway. "Delores!" she says crisply, "I'm leaving."

"You and I are going to have a little talk when I come back," Bunny whispers, aiming a finger at Gerda's face, though not too closely. She sets the soup cup on the tray and leaves the room to speed Mother deLore's departure.

"You got the soup off your shoes," Bunny says with some admiration.

"I rinsed them in the bidet." That would explain the squishing sound and the watery outlines as she tramps toward the closet to reclaim her sheared beaver coat. "I've had a most—" she struggles to be polite, "—interesting day. Please give my regrets to Gerda but I must be heading home. I'm liable to catch my death with these wet shoes." Her mouth sets in a grim line. "Shall I inform Leland or will you?"

"About what?" Bunny asks, folding her arms over her middle.

"My ruined Guccis," she says, turning her generous collar up. "And who will pay for the blocking and restoration."

Bunny's cheeks flush. She makes for the door and flings it open. "I thought perhaps you wanted to tell him how well Gerda is doing. How good she looks under my care. How cheerful. How her hair is cut and shaped and her nails polished."

"Well, don't you think you're something special in your pseudo-nursing costume?"

"Please, don't let me keep you," Bunny says, grasping Mother deLore's furry elbow to escort her out the door and down the stone steps. Her driver is asleep in the car but is rudely awoken by Mother deLore's sharp rap on the window. Bunny leaves her standing in the driveway and re-enters the house, locking the door behind her. "I hope her shoes freeze to the gravel," she mutters on her way back to the music room. "And yes, dammit, I am something special." Her head goes up and her shoulders square.

Gerda stirs as Bunny enters. "She's gone. Sorry to subject you to that but she insisted." Gerda's eyes close. "After all, you two were together for a long time, weren't you?" Bunny smoothes the covers. "She probably feels it's all my fault you fell, but you and I know it was an accident." Gerda's eyes snap open and her head turns. The look she gives Bunny is so chilling that Bunny clutches her throat.

But Bunny perseveres. "You know bloody well that I didn't push you down the stairs, Gerda. Yes, I threw my coffee cup, but you fell on your own in those stupid slippers."

Upstairs Mooney suddenly wakes up screaming. "I've got to go," Bunny says, relieved to be out of the room.

∽

JEMIMA IS IN TEARS. FOR the second time today Joe has pulled all the sheets and blankets off the bed and is in the process of dumping out his dresser drawers, looking for the keys to the tractor that was sold and hauled away long ago because he couldn't stand to look at it after being pinned beneath it. They'd never had another. Their boys hadn't wanted to carry on with the grunt work of plowing, seeding, fertilizing and watching the bills grow higher than the crops. Jemima turns from the mess and plods to the kitchen. Does she call the boys again or the doctor? She pulls a handful of paper towels from the roll, yanks out a chair and with elbows on the table buries her face in them, angry at the injustice of it all. His episodes are a warning of things to come. The confusion. The headaches. His slurred speech. She wipes her nose, then fires the wad of paper toward the sink. Joe. Joe. Joe. Maybe she'll feel better after phoning the doctor.

∽

"MARIAH, IT'S YOUR MOTHER," CHLOE calls from the kitchen door. She waves the phone at her.

Mariah slams the trunk of the car with her free hand and lumbers toward the house carrying a large cardboard carton. She's been back to her cottage to see the destruction and was surprised to find some salvageable things—dishes, woolen blankets stacked so tightly in the cupboard they had not burned, and other smoky-smelling odds and ends. Her biggest delight was what she found in the tool shed. Set amidst the rusting garden tools, Flora's bicycle and plastic pots was the merry-go-round Clive gave her as a birthday present. The firemen must have saved it.

"Be nice," Chloe counsels as she holds the door for her. Mariah slops across the floor in her rubber boots to transfer the box to the kitchen table. Chloe rolls her eyes and clicks her tongue.

"Don't fuss," Mariah tells her. "I'll take my boots off in a minute." She picks up the receiver and Chloe returns to the cooking show on television. Mariah shifts from foot to foot as her mother spends all the words she's been banking. "I know you're sorry, Flora, but sorry isn't going to get us another house now, is it?" Mariah moves the receiver to her other ear and leans against the counter. "Thanks much, but giving me your pension cheque won't do much more than buy groceries." Mariah briefly covers the receiver to stage-whisper, "She's bawling." She waits a moment until the tears have subsided. "Flora? It's okay. Maybe burning the house down was for the better." Chloe looks over her shoulder in astonishment. Mariah shrugs. She'd like a coffee right now but is too far from her cup and the carafe. She covers the receiver again. "Chloe, would you get me a coffee?" She points to her cup in the sink. "Flora? Flora? Listen. I have some good news. I found your purse underneath your pillow. It stinks but that's fixable. And your bicycle is safe and sound." Chloe slaps down the half-full mug near the phone and stomps back into the living room. Mariah holds the receiver against her bosom and forces a smile. "Thank you, sweetheart." She returns her attention to her mother. "Things will look up, Flora. We'll find another place. How are you and Clive making out?" She slurps the hot coffee, burning her tongue. "Well, why didn't he take you with him?" Mariah gazes out the window at the dirty melting snow. "So, if he's off to New Orleans, who's looking after you?" Earlier Chloe had scraped the sidewalk that leads to the kennels, and now the packed snow bank is melting in muddy rivulets, forming puddles on the pitted concrete. "Who is this neighbour?" Her heavy eyebrows rise and disappear beneath her bangs.

The dogs are playing in the muck in their runs, and Mariah sees a big job coming up later today when they have to be groomed. "Well, that's nice you have a neighbour coming in to visit, but you can never tell about strangers. Keep your door locked, okay? You'll be fine until I find a new place for us." She reaches for the newspaper she folded earlier to the For Rent section. One listing is circled. "I have one to see this evening when the owner gets home." Changing the subject abruptly she asks, "Did you get your hair cut yet? All the singed bits gone?"

Chloe prowls the kitchen during the television commercial, pointedly stepping over Mariah's boot prints.

"Uh-huh," Mariah continues into the phone. "What colour did you choose?" Mariah looks toward the ceiling in exasperation but bites back the caustic response she would normally deliver. "I'm sure it looks very nice, Flora. Gotta go now," she says, cutting her off in mid-sentence. "Talk to you later. Bye." Mariah stoops to remove her boots, carrying them to the back door where she throws them on the rubber mat. Chloe is again in front of the television. "She's always felt cheated she wasn't born a redhead." Mariah directs her remarks to Chloe's back, knowing she's been listening to her phone conversation. "Unfortunately, Clive has left her to her own devices. She's been having little tête-à- têtes with a neighbour. An older gentleman, as she puts it. Wears a red bow tie and wingtip shoes."

Chloe snorts and changes the channel.

*

BECAUSE SARI HAS THE RARE pleasure of a Saturday afternoon off, she also has the newspaper under her elbows. She runs her finger down the Businesses for Sale column. It's no more than half a page long and contains a dozen or so ads for mom-and-pop corner stores, transmission repair shops and pizza take-outs. She almost misses the two lines that read "Must sell due to ill health. Three-chair beauty salon.

Good location. $85,000." Sari forgets to breathe as she rereads the advertisement. She reaches for the phone and calls the listed number. A woman answers with such gusto that Sari is caught off-guard. She doesn't sound like she's suffering ill health.

"I—I'm calling about your ad. The shop with three chairs?"

"Yeah? Whatcha' wanna know?"

"Um, where's it located?"

"You know the Bevanda Veranda restaurant? And the new fitness place that's going in? Well, it's between the two."

"The grey building with the blue shutters?"

"That's the very one, honey. She's a nice little shop with three chairs as advertised and two sinks, three dryers and a storeroom that could be turned into, I dunno, a massage parlour or a tanning bed or somethin'. Ya wanna come have a look?"

Sari knows the place. She even left a résumé there once when she was looking for a job. They never called back. "I think I would, yes." As Bunny's loaner is low on gas, she'll put Mooney in the stroller and walk over. Shouldn't take her more than thirty minutes. "Say in an hour?"

"Well," she booms, "if there are others interested, I'll have to deal on a first-come-first-served basis. This is a hot property. Gonna go fast."

The woman's plump voice echoes in Sari's head as she wakes a truculent Mooney from his nap, but he manages to fall back to sleep while he's being pushed the mile to Perle's Parlour. There's a red and white plastic *For Sale* sign stuck to the window. She butts the door open with her backside and pulls the stroller in behind her. The interior smacks of inexpensive hairspray. When the brass bell above the door sounds at her entry, an enormous woman in daffodil-yellow tights, a daisy-print smock, and leopard-print bedroom slippers eases her bulk through the arched doorway at the rear. She pauses partway to throw her hand against the wall and catch her breath.

"Whoo-oo. Got up too fast. Dizzy," says the woman, fanning her face with a magazine she picks up from the loaded table between the dryers. "You're the person who called?"

"I'm Sari Button," Sari extends her fingers to be enveloped in the bread-dough consistency of the woman's hand.

"That your kid?" the woman asks, wiping her face on the sleeve of her daisy-print smock.

"This is Mooney." Sari adjusts his blankets as she points him in the woman's direction.

"Uh-huh," she says, lumbering toward the low counter facing the door. "So whadd'ya think?" she asks, throwing wide her jiggling arms to encompass the room. "Pretty classy, eh?"

Sari appraises the room. The curling grey and white lino tiles will need replacing as will the black-measled mirrors. The splayed hairbrushes have seen better days as well, but the dusty flower arrangements will be the first to go. "It has possibilities," she answers cautiously, spying hairy combs soaking in glass tubes of turquoise goo.

"Hey, honey, this place is a gold mine. My daughter has to turn customers away, she's so busy."

"Your daughter?"

"She owns the place. I do the books and the ordering. I have these bad legs, you see." As if to demonstrate, she groans and drops her weight into the beat-up swivel chair behind the counter.

"Is that why she's selling? Your bad legs?"

The woman turns the chair around to face the counter and flips through the appointment book. "You can see here that my Bethie had seven clients today. Seven times twenty bucks is a hundred and forty. Not bad, huh?"

"Can I talk to Bethie? Or is she the one who's sick?" Mooney is beginning to stir in his stroller.

The woman swings around to heft a pole that's long enough to reach the ceiling of the shop. She bangs three times and Sari can see the circular indentations from previous summons. "That's our way of signalling. Beats screaming at the top of our lungs." She points upward. "We have the suite upstairs and believe me it's no picnic to climb those damn stairs anymore than I have to." She jerks the pole upward to give the ceiling three more shots. "She's probably in the can. Likes having her baths."

"Well, maybe I'll just come back," Sari blurts. "She's probably busy. Maybe she can give me a call later." But she hears the closing of a door and the rhythm of feet descending the stairs.

Seconds later a small, very pregnant girl in a terrycloth robe bursts through the doorway. She is about to lambaste her mother but sees Sari and stops dead.

"Bethie, this lady—sorry, honey, I forgot your name."

"Sari Button," says Sari, extending her hand to Bethie.

"She's here to see about the shop," the woman says with exaggerated sweetness.

"I'm Beth Ann Perle." The girl takes Sari's hand in hers and pumps twice. "What can I do for you?"

Leaving Mother Perle breathing heavily in her chair, Bethie, not waiting for Sari's answer, leads the way to the dryers. "Have a seat, Sara Button. How old's the baby? I'm due in five weeks," she says, running both hands over her belly. "Time to get out of the hairdressing biz. I keep bumping up against the clients. The guys don't mind but some of the women ... well," she says, pulling a face, "they get a little spooked about it. Strange but true." Bethie digs into the pocket of the robe and, much to Sari's disgust, hauls out a battered cigarette package. "Now you just wipe that look off your face," Bethie says with good humour. "I don't smoke it. I just stick it in and pretend." She taps out a smoke that shows all the signs of having been used before and holds it delicately between her fingers. "See? I'm going to be a very good mama despite what some people think." She flashes her mother a look before returning her gaze to Sari. "I tell you honestly, Sara—"

"Sari," she corrects.

"I'm about ready to just walk away from this place and head for Vancouver. It's been on the market for three months." Her mother emphatically clears her throat. "I'm asking eighty-five thousand dollars but make me an offer I can't refuse."

"Does that include the suite upstairs?"

"Calling it a suite is a bit optimistic, but yes. It's the whole building."

"That doesn't seem like very much for a whole building." Mooney's eyes open and fix on Mother Perle. She sticks her tongue out. He lets out a howl and Sari picks him up and settles him on her knee.

"What's his name?" Bethie asks, running her fingers over his head. "Where'd he get the beautiful red hair?"

"On my hus—on his father's side of the family."

"You're a single mom then?" Bethie asks, tapping the non-existent ash from her cigarette onto the floor. "Me, too." The audible gasp from her mother causes her to sigh dramatically. "My mother is having problems with me being what she calls an unwed mother, but this is the new millennium and we're a more understanding society, aren't we?"

Avoiding that trap, Sari inquires about how soon the closing date could be.

"As soon as you make me that offer I can't refuse, we'll talk." Bethie rises from the chair, replaces the cigarette in the pack and tightens the belt around her bulging middle. "I know you'd like to see the upstairs but it's a mess and I gotta date. I'm already late so if you could come back tomorrow? You do know how to do hair, don't you?" Bethie asks. "Great," she says when Sari nods. "When you come back tomorrow, I'll show you around. As far as I'm concerned it's yours. We'll do some creative financing, okay?"

Sari fairly bounces along the sidewalk on her way home.

After feeding Mooney—she is too excited to eat—she takes a few big breaths and picks up the phone. Mariah beats Chloe to it, answering on the second ring.

"Have you got thirty thousand dollars?" Sari asks all in a rush.

"Excuse me?"

"Have you got thirty thousand dollars?"

"Just like that you want to borrow thirty grand? Are you nuts?"

"I have a very good deal for you," Sari begins, slowing down to carefully sell her idea. "I have this perfectly good—" she hesitates at calling it a trailer "—uh, mobile home. It could be moved to your property and you could live in it, you know?" She closes her eyes to await the reaction.

"Doesn't what's-his-face have a claim on it?"

"It's actually in my name," she replies, sitting upright. "I don't think James wanted his name on the sale in case we couldn't pay for it down the road. But anyway, I'm the one who has made all the payments."

"How much you still owe on it?" Mariah inquires.

"About seven thousand. Seven thousand two hundred, to be exact." She wasn't about to reveal to Mariah that she and James had bought the thing for $15,000 with her $1,500 in savings as the down payment. It had taken them ten days to haul away the litter and debris left by the previous owners. "Does this mean you're interested?" Sari's heart pounds against the palm of her hand.

Only the distant television can be heard on the line, then Mariah answers. "I'm always receptive to new ideas ... as you well know."

Yes-s-s! "Come and have a look. I'll tell you what I have in mind."

When Mariah agrees to drive over, Sari flies into a whirlwind of tidying up, much to Mooney's amusement.

Chloe and Mariah gabble and cluck as they shuffle from Sari's bedroom through the living room and down the hallway to Mooney's room. Sari worries that the place appears shabby. That it could use newer furniture, fresh paint. She's feeling queasy and restless. She crosses her fingers. In the living room Mooney stares open-mouthed from his playpen as the women retreat down the hall to enter his room. "Chloe says it seems like a good deal," Mariah begrudges after they return. "But I'm not so sure." She plods to the kitchen and peers into the cupboard beneath the sink. Leaning over the sink on tiptoes, she gawps out the window. "Who's your neighbours?"

"I dunno. Quiet people who mind their own business. Ace lived on the other side."

Mariah squints down the length of countertop. "Not much room for stuff."

"It's only until you get your new house built, isn't it? Then you can resell it. Probably for more than you paid," Sari prompts.

"So what do you have in mind that you're trying to get me to buy it?"

"Come sit down and I'll tell you." Sari says, lifting Mooney onto her lap. "I saw this wonderful little hairdressing shop over on Duckworthy Street. Maybe you know it—Perle's Parlour?"

Not being familiar with such establishments, as she cuts her own hair, Mariah admits to never having heard of it.

"I'm not surprised. It's a narrow grey building," Sari says, slipping her hands either side of Mooney to mimic the shape of the building, "wedged between two bigger ones, and," she quickly adds, "it's got potential." The excitement animates her face. "I haven't seen the upstairs where the owner lives, but whatever it looks like, I can make it into something better. Mooney can be with me while I work." She feels herself running on but can't slow down. "There's three chairs and three dryers and a big picture window. I'd have plants everywhere. And new mirrors. And if I need to, I can expand because there's another room beyond that one. If I get too busy, I can rent out a chair."

"How much?" Mariah manages to squeeze in.

"Eighty-five thousand. Only eighty-five thousand dollars. Can you believe it?" She rocks back with Mooney and nuzzles his ear.

"So you want thirty for this place?" Mariah draws out the last two words, and Sari's mood sobers.

"I'm asking thirty, yes." She holds pat, quaking inside, ready to knuckle under.

"Thirty?" Mariah echoes.

Chloe begins to fuss with her hair, embarrassed at Mariah's gall.

"Thirty."

Mariah drums her fingers on her knees, staring at Mooney's playpen. She stops drumming long enough to push her glasses back into position. "Think we can cut a deal at the bank, Chlo?" The tension eases as Chloe nods and Sari breathes again. "Our insurance money will arrive sometime in the near future," Mariah continues, "and I really have to get Flora back to reality."

"Not to mention giving me back my own space," Chloe remarks.

Mariah is aghast. "I thought you liked my company."

"Oh, I do, dear," Chloe smiles, leaning to kiss Mariah's cheek.

"But there are limits."

"Well, I'll be go to hell," Mariah says, wiping the kiss off with the back of her hand.

Sari jumps to her feet, slinging Mooney to her hip. "Do you want tea?"

"Yes, please."

"You want me to leave in the morning?" Mariah says, bracing herself for the answer.

"God, you're such a—a—goose. You take everything so-o-o seriously."

Sari doesn't want their fist fight in her house. "Mariah, take Mooney," she says, thrusting him at her before heading for the kitchen to plug in the kettle.

Mooney looks startled at suddenly being in the care and control of this owlish-looking woman and opens his wet mouth to howl. Chloe digs her elbow into Mariah's puffy behind as she bends to put Mooney onto the floor. When Mariah straightens, Chloe also gives her the eye, which should quell any more argument.

The message is received. Mariah shifts away from Chloe. "This place is portable, isn't it?" she says, indicating the trailer. "There's wheels and stuff underneath?"

Sari charges back into the room enthusiastically. "No, no, these things don't have wheels anymore," she states, as Mooney stands unsteadily with the aid of her leg. "They're blocked up and the man who runs the trailer park has a flatbed truck for moving them." She elaborates with wide-spread arms. "He checks it all out. Costs about $300 the last I heard." Seeing Mariah's mouth working, Sari adds, "We'll go halfers on it. Whatever it costs, fifty-fifty, okay?"

Behind Mariah's back Chloe gives Sari a thumbs-up.

"I think we've done enough damage for one day," Mariah says, slapping her palms over her knees. "C'mon, Chloe, I need some air." The two women struggle to their feet and as they reach the door, Mariah casts a last look around. "I'll talk to the bank and get back to you."

"And she'll do it ASAP," Chloe chimes. "First thing Monday morning."

XV

JUST BEFORE LUNCH THE NEXT day Bethie calls to say the suite is now fit for human habitation. With the weather still holding, Sari and Mooney wheel over to visit Bethie and Mrs. Perle at the salon.

Mrs. Perle, reclining in a tweedy overstuffed chair, mottled legs thrust before her, makes the place look cramped and cluttered. The bosom of her Hawaiian muumuu rises and falls with wheezy regularity as her gaze follows Sari carrying Mooney from room to room. There's a spacious bedroom overlooking the alley in back of the building, a cavernous bathroom with a window that allows a tea-spoon of light to enter, and a storage space that now houses suitcases and unopened cardboard boxes. It's all transformed in Sari's mind into her bedroom, their bathroom, and Mooney's room. Maybe she'll paint carousel horses on the walls.

In the doorway of the dim airless kitchen, Sari ducks the hanging birdcage. On the swing within it, a faux canary gives her a glassy stare. The kitchen's two-burner stove heats an old-fashioned perco-lating coffee pot. Pink sunlight filters through the red velvet drapes, which barely conceal the dusty bow window over the sink. *It will work!* Sari decides.

"Well, Sara, what'cha think? A little piece of paradise, right?" Bethie gleefully notes the unconcealed delight on Sari's face. "All this could be yours a week after the cheque clears the bank."

"I'll get back to you," Sari says firmly, trying to play hardball.

"Don't leave it too long, dearie," Mother Perle interjects from the other room.

Sari returns to the living room to reply. "My friend is going to buy my place but she has to see the bank first thing Monday morning. So if I say I'll take the shop today, it's conditional. No deposit or anything."

"I understand," Bethie nods. "Sit down and we'll talk, okay?" Casually she indicates the table and three chairs pushed beneath the window. At least outside this window there's a living thing—a tree with thick inviting branches. "You want coffee?"

When the coffee is poured and Mooney is hanging onto her knee forcing a cookie into his mouth, Bethie whips out an official-looking agreement for sale form, smoothing it on the tabletop. She writes, "Conditionally Sold to Sara Button ..."

"Sari. S-A-R-I."

"Yes, yes," she says, correcting the mistake and starting again. "Conditionally Sold to Sari Button—the house, contents and business known as Perle's Parlour located at 88 Duckworthy Street, Grievous, BC, subject to the sale of ... Where's your house?"

"Number twelve Golden Maples Mobile Home Park."

"A trailer," Bethie says, cocking an eyebrow at Sari.

"Yes." Sari gives her a what-of-it look.

Bethie drops her gaze. "And the agreed-upon price," she says, her pen poised above the paper. "Of this place," she clarifies.

"Eighty-two five," Sari states, trying not to disclose her fright.

Mother Perle expels a windy "Pfa-a-a-w!"

"Eighty-three," Bethie says, rubbing circles on her bulging tummy. "Don't forget, all this furniture goes with it."

"Not my velvet Elvis," her mother reminds her. A young Elvis, lip curled, hangs squarely above the queen-sized bed.

"Eighty-three," Sari echoes, trying not to dwell on how sorry she's feeling for Bethie who is not only pregnant but has to share a bed with her mother. "But that floor downstairs all has to be replaced and—"

"Those boxes in the room behind the shop are floor tiles. We just never got around to laying them. They're green and purple plaid, aren't they, Ma?" She laughs at the look crossing Sari's face. "Just kidding. They're navy and white."

"Let's talk money," Sari says, fingering the edge of the paper, nervously folding the corner. "Say that my friend gets her loan to buy my place and I give it all to you, all thirty thousand, are you willing to hold the mortgage for the rest? With reasonable interest, of course."

Bethie flips open her calculator. "Let's see, eighty-five minus—"

"Eighty-three," Sari corrects.

"Ah, right. Eighty-three minus thirty is fifty-three thousand. Say over a ten-year period, that's about four hundred fifty a month. Can you do it?"

"What's your shop bring in a week?"

"Between five and eight hundred tops."

"Then I shouldn't have a problem."

"Ma, is that okay with you? Can we live off your disability pension and the thirty grand?"

"Don't forget I'll be paying you another four-fifty a month if this goes through," Sari offers.

"Do what you want," Bethie's mother says. "My opinion doesn't count for much around here."

The papers are duly filled out and signed. "I'll get back to you just as soon as I hear from my friend," Sari says. "Probably by about noon Monday." Sari is so happy her throat feels constricted. She wants to spin and sing out Hallelujah! but she doesn't. Instead she sweeps Mooney from under the table where he has crawled, buries her face in his hair and tickles his ribs. His squeals of delight are hers as well.

MONDAY MORNING, AS SHE STRIPS Mooney of his jacket, Sari fills Bunny in about the impending deal. Sari is so ebullient that Bunny hopes she's not going to be disappointed. "How much did you put down on this place?" she asks, as she hangs the jacket over the newel post at the bottom of the stairs.

"Nothing! Isn't that great? Mariah and Chloe are going to the bank this morning. At least that's what they promised." Sari hands over Mooney's backpack full of his favourite toys and bends to give him a kiss. He never fusses about staying with Bunny. He likes having the run of such a big house. Bunny closes off the living room and library, which gives him the whole hallway to scoot up and down. Lately he's even begun to climb the stairs to the upper floor but Bunny quickly distracts him from that pursuit. He is persistent but so is she. There aren't going to be two invalids in this house. Preoccupied as she is with Mooney, it is a minute before Bunny notices that Sari isn't leaving the house in her usual hurry.

"What's up?" Bunny asks.

Sari releases her breath in a whoosh and plops onto the third step up. "This place is going to be a money-maker. I can do so much better than Mrs. Bahadoorsingh, and she's making a killing. My clients will follow me, I'm pretty sure."

"So what's the problem?" Bunny shifts Mooney to her other hip.

"I still owe seventy-two hundred on the mobile. I have no savings to speak of what with James not paying for anything. What I want to know is—gawd, I hate asking this—can I borrow seventy-two hundred from you and pay you back monthly?"

"We'll talk about it when you come for Mooney—but it's a possibility."

"Oh, Bunny, thank you!" Sari says, jumping up to give Bunny a quick hug before heading for the door.

"Wave bye-bye to Mummy," Bunny instructs, standing him up, but Mooney drops to all fours and crawls away toward the music room. "Gotta go, he's looking for Gerda. Good luck with the bank," Bunny calls as she trails Sari's son. "You get back here," she growls, and he doubles his efforts.

Gerda hears him coming and turns her head toward the sound. Her hand rises from her chest and stretches toward him.

"See," Bunny says, lifting him onto the hospital bed, "here's our Gerda." Mooney sticks his thumb in his mouth and snuggles briefly, popping up before Gerda's arm clamps down on him. At first, when she had dropped her arm across him, he could push it off, but now there is resistance. She is growing stronger and more alert. Miss Rosella still comes daily to give Gerda baths and make sure her skin is staying healthy, but the span between the good doctor's visits has now become several days and Bunny misses him.

When Mooney is lowered to the floor, he crawls toward the fireplace, looking over his shoulder as he goes. "You aren't going to cooperate today, are you?" Bunny scoops him up and returns to Gerda's bedside. "I'll be right back," she informs her. "I'll just get him into his walker." His fists grip her index fingers as he marches before her, stepping high in his belled shoes. The bird in his cage bangs on his nameplate in response.

Later that afternoon Sari phones to tell her the bank deal has gone through and Mariah will be buying her trailer, so she is now the new owner of a three-chair salon. "I'm so excited I'm having trouble keeping down my lunch. God, Bunny, my own shop! Can you believe it?"

"I can believe it. You are a resourceful woman and you'll do well. How about instead of loaning you the seventy-two hundred dollars, I invest ten thousand? You'll need start-up money and enough to pay your wages for the first month or so. I'll be a silent partner."

There's a hush on the other end while Sari tries to stop herself from sobbing like a fool into the phone. Once she has herself under control she says, "Bunny, I couldn't ask for a better business partner. Thank you."

When the call is over, Bunny tiptoes into the darkened library to check on Mooney, asleep in his playpen. He has kicked off his blanket and is spread-eagled over the mound of it. "What am I going to do without you?" Bunny whispers. He stirs and she quickly backs out of the room. With Gerda and Mooney both sleeping, Bunny opens a container of yogurt and makes a pot of jasmine tea. She enjoys the brief quiet but is always happy to lift a drowsy Mooney from his playpen and set him on the floor in the hallway. Today she'll try to get a little maintenance cleaning done while he's playing. Dust lies thinly on the piano and the tables that are not in daily use. Mooney doesn't like the sound of the vacuum so she waits until he's gone home with

Sari before cranking up the beast. She's been putting in full days since taking them both in. They are the perfect counterbalance—Gerda silent and immobile and Mooney ebullient and colourful—but she is having a problem finding the time to build on her novel. In the past she would think about how the plot should evolve, then sit down at her computer to put her thoughts in order. Not the way a real novelist would do it, she knows, but then real novelists probably have to hold down a job and find time to write. But now, when Bunny does write, she finds herself staring at the screen, hands gripping the arms of the chair, yearning for something else. Something she can't put a name to.

Tonight she gets up from the computer and wanders to the kitchen, throwing open the refrigerator door only to discover it's not food she wants. She opens the back door and stands on the porch inhaling the winter night but the longing still weighs on her. She turns from the night sounds and re-enters the stillness of the house, somnambulistically walking to the hall closet where gloves, scarves and hats have been folded away until winter calls them forth again. She brings down a sweat-stained baseball cap, once red but now faded to brick. Ron's hat.

In the morning she strips off her nightgown on her way to the shower. As she works the lather through her hair she fantasizes about Ron Woolcott being in the shower with her. About washing his back with the bar of Tiffany soap Leland sent her from Hong Kong. She can't see him turned around yet. She will just luxuriate in doing his back. His broad, flawless, delicious back. "Where is my mind?" She rinses the shampoo, letting the water beat against her upturned face.

∽

MISS ROSELLA IS BRUSHING GERDA'S thin hair and securing it to the top of her head with a clip.

"How's our patient this morning?" Bunny inquires, speaking to Miss Rosella but peering around her into Gerda's face. Gerda is propped up, looking clean and fresh.

"Pretty good," says the nurse, gathering up the nightclothes and wet diaper she has removed. "She's looking better all the time. Won't be long now and we'll have her dancing a jig. I am going to get her a commode and by next week there'll be no more diapers."

"That will make us all happy, eh, Gerda? I think Dr. Woolcott should come and have a look at her before we try that, though." Bunny winks at Gerda.

"What kind of music do you like?" she asks him when he arrives later that evening. She has left him a voice mail message to say that Gerda is looking a bit peaky and perhaps should have her blood tested.

"Music?" he echoes, distracted by her question. He is trying to listen to Gerda's heartbeat. "Anything," he says, dropping his stethoscope into his bag. "Anything that's not hip-hop or rap or," he hesitates, looking skyward, "heavy-metal rock and roll."

"You like classical?" she asks, fingers playing down the knife-edge pleat in her linen pants. Should he give her an enthusiastic yes, she will spring up and press play. She just has to know which composer to select. "Brahms, Mozart, Handel?"

"*Carmina Burana*," he replies.

"*Carmina Burana*?" She delights in his choice. "It's one of my favourites." She crosses to where he is leaning casually against Gerda's bed, looking very elegant in his black slacks and tan shirt. She warms under his gaze and fusses with her hair, hooking it behind her ear. "Would you like me to put it on in the library?"

"No, thanks," he says, "but if you're thinking of getting Mrs. Von Hauffman a commode, what I'd like is to see you transfer her to a chair."

"Now?" Bunny asks, surprised at the request.

"As good a time as any."

Bunny cranks down the bed then drags an armchair across the floor to a spot next to the bed. She adjusts the positioning of the chair before lowering the bed railing. "Okay, Gerda, I'm going to sit you up and then transfer you to the chair. You understand?" Bunny gets Gerda to a sitting position and senses that Ron is on standby should something untoward happen. She braces her feet on either side of Gerda's legs and, after securely hugging Gerda to her, transfers the woman neatly to the chair. She straightens and looks the doctor in the eye. "How's that?"

"Impressive," he says. "Now put her back."

Bunny returns Gerda to the bed and then tucks the blankets around her. "Looks like we passed the test," she says.

"Yup, you passed. She will get a commode tomorrow. Now I'll be on my way."

"Would you like a coffee or something?" Bunny asks, turning down the lights.

"Not tonight—even though the offer is tempting."

"Tempting?" She grabs his remark like a lifeline. "Anything else I can offer?" The words float like dandelion down and she wonders who said them. But they are her words and they have escaped.

He sports a lopsided grin and scrubs his hand over his chin. "What do you have in mind?"

Gerda turns her head on her pillow and sucks in her bottom lip.

Bunny's feet sweat inside her shoes. "I ... uh ... I ..."

"It's okay," he says, retrieving his bag from the foot of Gerda's bed. "I'm just teasing."

Bunny gives a fleeting smile and ducks her head, her hair swinging forward to obscure her face.

But he reaches to brush it back. "Sorry if I embarrassed you. I can be a real jerk sometimes."

She feels the heat from his hand and smells the soap he's used to wash it. She has a flashback to her shower this morning. Now she forgets how to breathe. There's a constriction in her chest and she hopes she will faint dead away so he will perform mouth-to-mouth, his square clean fingers expertly sliding between her breasts to find her heart.

He shifts his bag, using it to indicate Gerda. "She's looking pretty good, considering where she started from. You're doing an outstanding job."

"I am?" She chokes on the words. Tears feel very close but she wills them away. "You're surprised?" she asks, finding her voice.

"A little." He heads out of the room, Bunny trailing behind him. "I thought it would be too much for you and we'd have to find a place for her. I even put her on a waiting list for The Oaks. Probably won't be necessary as long as she keeps improving at this rate."

She walks him to the door and now stands ready to open it. "Thanks for coming."

He bestows a brief smile and says, "I'll be calling on her regularly if that's not an imposition."

"Hardly an imposition. We'll both look forward to it." She realizes how stilted that sounds and wants to call it back, but he's gone. She returns to Gerda and finds her bright-eyed. "Dr. Woolcott says he's going to drop in regularly to see how you're doing. Lucky you," she says. When the phone rings they both jump. Bunny answers it in the music room to keep Gerda company. "Oh, Leland, it's you," she says, relieved it's not another Mariah-crisis-in-the-making. She puts it on the speaker phone and continues preparing Gerda for the night.

"I finally heard from my lawyer today," he says without preamble, "and we're not liable for Gerda's fall."

Bunny's eyes widen, but as she turns to take the phone off the speaker, Gerda grasps her wrist.

"Seeing as she won't be working for us anymore," he says, "see if you can't get her into some place that's clean and cheap."

"Leland, shut up. She can hear everything you're saying." Bunny works her wrist free and hurries to pick up the receiver. "What the hell are you talking about—some place that's clean and cheap? This place is clean and cheap and it's her home." Bunny dares to look at Gerda but she's turned her head away. "She's not going anywhere."

"You going to pay for all the stuff she needs with your household money?"

"That's what I've been doing all along."

"Suit yourself. But if you think I'm coming home to an invalid stinking up the house, you're sadly mistaken."

"You said she was family," Bunny hisses, turning her back to Gerda.

"She was while she could work for a living." And he hangs up.

Bunny approaches Gerda's bedside. "Gerda, you're not going

anywhere, you hear?" She holds the old woman's hand. "This is your home for as long as you want to stay."

Gerda squeezes back with determination, rolling her head to look directly at Bunny. "Ya!" she says. "Ya!"

Bunny feels eerily calm as she dims the light and leaves the room. She heads for Leland's office and leans against the door frame, taking in the whole of it. The Stickley desk will go for a couple thousand. The hand-knotted silk rug about the same. She'll sell the Range Rover to Sari for a dollar down and a dollar a week. With what she's squirrelled away from her household money, she'll have enough. "This will work," she tells herself. "This is good."

If she feels so damn good about it why is she crying?

"You son of a bitch! You lying, cheating son of a bitch."

She proceeds to the liquor cabinet and, after viewing the bottles, adds "Order another case of scotch" to her list of things to do in the morning. She tips some of the amber liquid into a glass, carries it to the computer and turns it on. While she waits for the screen's inviting glow, she builds on the germ of an idea. Before her is a blank page and she sets down her drink to begin typing.

> For twenty-five years I have been comatose but today
> I start the brilliant period of my life. I am a dancer,
> a singer, an artist, a gardener, a whirlwind, a crème
> brûlée, a butterfly pupa, a pugilist, and a writer. I'm
> going to slug it out with the best of them and I will win.

Once Miss Rosella has departed next morning, Bunny stands looking out the window of the music room for a long time. She is fingering a card in her pocket, the card that Sari left behind a couple of weeks ago. Finally she turns on her heel and heads for the phone, punching in the numbers printed on the business card. "I'd like an appointment with Miss Teo, please. It's regarding divorce proceedings." Her throat is so dry that the words stick. While she waits for the receptionist to slot her in, she paces, stopping to uncover the bird.

"Morning, Axel," she says in answer to his squawk. "Today is Tuesday and it's going to be monumental." She turns her attention back to the phone. "Yes, I'm still here … Thursday at four? I'll be there."

After she puts down the phone, she turns to see Gerda has untangled her hand from the covers and is giving her a thumb's up.

~

"IS JEMIMA COMING TONIGHT?" SARI asks when the group meets in the library. She shifts Mooney into the crook of her left arm. She's letting him stay up an extra half-hour so the ladies can admire him before they begin their session.

"Yes," Bunny says as she puts the tea tray down. "Apparently she's contacted a service club in town and some of Joe's old cronies are willing to sit with him one evening a week." She lingers behind Sari's big green chair wanting to tell the group about her Thursday appointment but instead returns to the kitchen for the teapot.

"Well, I hope she got some work done," Mariah says, settling into her favourite chair. "We've all been slacking off lately."

"It's not as if we haven't had things to do, Mariah," Sari says. "You with the fire and trying to get your mother to come home, Bunny slaving after Mooney and Gerda, although she does look pretty perky this evening. And it's going to be even more hectic what with you and me both moving. At least we don't have to pack up the furniture, eh?" Sari lifts a finger to stall Mariah's reply. "That sounds like Jemima's car now." She rises from her chair to walk to the window with Mooney on her hip. "Yup, it's her." She brushes Mooney's hair from his face but it springs back to hang over his forehead. "You need a haircut in the worst way. Hard to believe your mummy's a stylist."

Jemima is coming through the front door as Sari and Mooney cross down the hall to the music room. He's quite happy to be sleeping there. He turns his face toward Gerda, puts his bottle in his mouth and settles right down. *This is how it will be at the shop*, Sari predicts. *He'll sleep when I have customers and be awake when I have time to play. It'll be perfect.*

She joins the group in the library in time to see Jemima hand Bunny a covered platter.

"You'll have to heat it up," says Jemima. "It's my new and improved recipe for spotted dick."

The weight of the pudding is substantial and Bunny grins. Stacked on the table next to her chair are ten paper-clipped pages for each of them. She looks around at her remarkable writing group and clears her throat to get their attention.

"Help yourself to the sherry, ladies, because I have an announcement!"

Acknowledgements

I WOULD LIKE TO ACKNOWLEDGE the publisher at Caitlin Press, Vici Johnstone, and Kathleen Fraser for her keen editorial eye. It's been a pleasure working with them both.

MAUREEN FOSS's first novel, *The Cadillac Kind*, was published by Polestar in 1996. The zany masterpiece was serialized on CBC's "Between the Covers." Her second novel, *The Rat Trap Murders*, was published by Nightwood Editions. Maureen was born in New Westminster, BC, and now lives in Lac La Hache in the Cariboo.